Lawless
In
Brazil

Also available from Rosstrum Publishing

Fast Track for Caregivers

366 Tips for a Successful Job Search

Coming Soon

Timberline

Visit www.rosstrumpublishing.com for details

Lawless
In
Brazil

By

Mike Johnson

To: Paula –
Hope you enjoy! 7-6-09
Best wishes –
Mike Johnson

Rosstrum Publishing
Nashua, NH

Rosstrum Publishing books are available at discounts when purchased in bulk for premiums and sales promotions as well as for fundraising or educational use. Based on quantities, special editions can be created to specification. For details, contact the publisher by mail or by e-mail.

Lawless in Brazil is a work of fiction. Names, characters, places and incidents are products of the author's imagination or are used fictitiously, and any resemblance to actual persons, living or dead, business establishments, events or locales is entirely coincidental.

 ™ Rosstrum Publishing
8 Strawberry Bank Road
Suite 20
Nashua, NH 03062-2763
RosstrumPublishing@gmail.com
www.rosstrumpublishing.com

Library of Congress Control Number: 2009927091

Manufactured in the United States of America
First printing April 2009
1 3 5 7 9 10 8 6 4 2

Acknowledgements

I owe a tremendous debt of gratitude to many people for their help on this book. Thanks to my wife, Maureen Keefe Johnson for patience, understanding and guidance. Thanks to my sister Karen Johnson, who co-founded the Tyngsboro Writer's group with me, for getting me back into the writing life, and to my sister, Linda Perigny, for faith in this project. Thanks to the members of the Tyngsboro Writer's Group: Champa Bilwakesh, Rick Cooper, Ruth Duddy, Peter Ewing, Patricia Gagnon, Brian Hammar, Matt Lewin, Maureen Mullin, Dale Phillips, Ted Pottel, Joe Ross, Todd Savelle, Peter Spring, Pam Thresher, Cindy Young and Bernie Zeigner, for friendship and red ink. Thanks also to Jamie Boudreau, Chrissy Caezza, Cheryl Cummings, Emile Destroismaison, Lisa Doherty, Tami Dristiliaris, Denis Ducharme --parachutist extraordinaire, Pat King, Ted and Kathleen Lutter, Sarah Jane Paquette, Pam Parkinson, Michelle Pinkston, Cathy Stamp, and Wania Vasconcelos, for reading, technical assistance and advice. Thanks to Randy Robertshaw, Connie Spickler and the staff at the Tyngsboro Library. Special thanks to Dave Daniels for reading the manuscript and for your kind words; to Joe Ross at Rosstrum Publishing for editing and all the other things that publishers do, and to Bernie Z for graphics help.
My apologies to anyone I may have left out.
All errors are mine.   ---Mike Johnson

To my parents, Alta D. and Melvin C. L. Johnson
whose love of words inspire me.

Chapter 1

"There's a kid over there looking for you," Shelly, the bottle-blonde waitress whose bra size was larger than her IQ said, pointing toward a booth near the entrance to the White Stallion Pub. "Is he yours?"

"No, smartass. He isn't," I answered. "I hope," I muttered so that she could barely hear me as I walked in the direction of the booth and the kid. He was a gangly looking boy, about 14. His head was shaved except for the very top that sported a Friar Tuck outcropping without the bald spot. It reminded me of the Chinese-restaurant-type fungi that my first wife, Witch Number One, used to call pecker mushrooms. He looked out of place framed by the green vinyl booth with the "Make-Mine-a-Bud" sign flickering over his head.

"You looking for me?" I asked. "Kids aren't supposed to be in here unless they're with a parent."

"Are you the detective? Brewster J. Lawless?" He was fidgeting in his seat looking everywhere but at me. "I have an appointment."

"Well, my friends call me Jake. I run Lawless Investigations during the day. Tend bar here part-time nights. But I don't remember having an appointment with you."

"Mr. Baxter? From this morning? About the divorce?" He was trying to make eye contact.

"Is that your father?" I asked. I remembered a groggy 8:00 a.m. phone call from a man by that name, something about tailing a cheating wife. I had asked Mr. Baxter to meet me at the White Stallion as the Lawless Investigation's main office was being redecorated. Actually, the L.I. office was 144 square feet of my condo with a beat up roll top desk and an answering machine.

"My friend, Morton, called for me. He sounds just like his dad on the phone. We ... kinda lied. I didn't think you'd see me if I told you the truth ... that I'm just a kid." He paused. Then he reached into his pocket and pulled out a crinkled bill. "I can pay you." He began unfolding the bill. "I want you to find my mother." He was staring at the bill, snuffling, and rubbing his nose, and I saw tears forming in the corners of his eyes.

"I don't understand, kid. Find your mother?"

"She's missing. I don't know if she's alive ... or ..." Tears began running down his cheeks and he rubbed his eyes with his knuckles.

"Take it easy, kid. Want a Coke?" I didn't wait for an answer. I went to the bar and poured two Cokes. It was 4:30 and Larry, the day bartender was getting off a little early.

"I'll just be a couple minutes, Larry," I said. His tips were counted, and he was ready to go. And I did owe him plenty of time because I was late more than I was early. "Big investigation, Larry. I'll make it up to ya." He nodded without smiling and I went back to the kid. I put the Cokes down and gave him a handful of bar napkins. He took them, wiped his eyes and blew his nose.

"Thanks," he mumbled and took a gulp of his soda. "Can you help me?" For the first time, his eyes met mine. They were blue-gray and hazy with tears and reminded me of an early-morning Boston sky. I looked down at my Coke, tried to avoid his sad, pleading face.

"If your mother's missing, you should be talking to the police. What's your name, anyway? I don't wanna keep calling you 'kid'," I said.

"Tommy. Tommy Baxter. And my father *is* a cop. He told me she ran off with a guy from where she works. But I don't believe it. She wouldn't just leave without saying good-bye...without leaving a note. Something. She loved me too much." Tears were welling in his eyes again and he poked at them with the soggy napkins. "Please." He pushed the crinkled bill, a fifty, across the table.

I didn't know what to say to him. How could I tell him that grownups sometimes do things like that? Maybe tell him about my boy, Rob, about two years his junior, and how Witch Number One hauled him off to Utah? Or how Witch Number Two left with Mandy, then three, after cleaning out our savings account, maxing the Sears, Visa and Discover cards and scribbling "Goodbye, Asshole" on my pillow in lipstick? How could I tell him that life wasn't fair?

"Look Tommy, I'd really like to help you," I said, still avoiding his eyes. "Really. But this isn't my kind of job. I could get into all kinds of trouble. Lose my license even, messing around in a cop's private affairs."

I guess he could tell by the tone of my voice that argument was useless. I knew he was looking at me. I continued staring at my Coke. A minute passed before he took his money and quietly got up and walked out the door. It was time to go to work. All I could think about were his sad eyes and the words on the pillow. Maybe she was right.

Chapter 2

The White Stallion Pub is in the oldest building still standing in New Stratley, Massachusetts. Built as a public house in 1847, it had served as a railroad station, numerous inns, boarding houses and restaurants until 1971 when Gus and Brenda Ferguson, armed with lots of bucks and an ancient rendition of a horse at full gallop hammered onto a copper placard, got it listed on a national registry of historical buildings and re-opened it as the White Stallion Ale House. From its cupola, where Witch Number two and I spent some of our happiest moments five stories above Jefferson Street, you can see the hazy spires of Boston reaching toward the heavens and a small part of the Charles River as it wends its way from the Blue Hills to meld with the Atlantic Ocean.

When Gus died, his son, Willy, took over. He changed "Alehouse" to "Pub" and the rustic-tavern atmosphere to that of a sports bar in hopes of attracting students from New Stratley University, which it did. I met Willy when I was working for Intimate Investigations. He wanted to find out why the Pub was always busy and he wasn't making any money. I had done some bartending during my paid-for-by-Uncle-Sam two years at Northeastern, Criminal Justice major, English Lit. minor, and I went undercover two days and three nights a week. My investigation resulted in the firing of just about everybody who worked there. I was amazed at how blatantly and callously they stole from Willy who, I thought, was a pretty decent guy as bar owners go. He was understanding about things like using the cupola for romantic interludes or having a frosty or two, but never three, while on duty. He'd been in the business his whole life and he considered stealing and serving minors the two greatest sins.

Unknown to Intimate, a very happy Willy Ferguson gave me ten crisp Franklins and offered me a job as night bartender and head of security. I'd been there ever since. I quit Intimate and opened Brewster J. Lawless Investigations, partly so that Willy would have a company name to put on my security paycheck, and partly because I had the dream of owning the largest detective agency in Massachusetts. Like horse players chasing the hundred-to-one shots and authors dreaming of the best-seller list, detectives, at least all I'd met, are waiting for the "big score," the billionaire generously grateful for the return of a loved one, or the random uncovering of a fortune in jewels or old coins that belonged to no one. As with the gamblers and the authors, the "big score" seldom comes. Most weeks my tip jar is more full than my PI account.

It was a late May Thursday when Tommy had come trying to hire me, country-western night at the Pub. It was a short while ago that CW lived mostly in the west. That year, with Reba and Garth getting more air time than Janet and Elton, and with Hank Jr. firmly en-sconced in the Monday Night Football gig, CW had taken the coun-try by storm. The ever-entrepreneurial Willie Ferguson, hoping to cash in on it before it went the way of disco, deemed Fridays and Sundays as "Country Western Nights at the Stallion." *Back on the ranch right here in New Stratley!* Willie bought cowboy hats, ker-chiefs and holsters with cap guns for all the employees. I agreed to wear the hat and kerchief but drew the line at the cap gun, which Sherry immediately confiscated. One for each hip.

I was too busy that night to think much about Tommy Baxter. It was loud, smoky and I ate enough salsa and chips to feed the Mexican army. I got home about 3:00 a.m., drank two big swigs of pink stuff and crawled into bed. I wasn't sure if my stomach or my head hurt worse. Miraculously, I fell asleep almost immediately.

I dreamed that I was in the woods with my son, Rob, and my dog, Chester, named that because he walked like Marshall Dillon's sidekick. We were looking for bottle caps for some unknown reason. Then Chester ran off and we searched for him for what seemed like days. We were both yelling his name and crying when my dad drove up in his old Buick station wagon. Chester's body was in the back. My dad said he'd been hit by a car. Somehow, we had three shovels and all dug a hole to bury him. I woke up in a soaking bed with sweat pouring down into my eyes. It had seemed so real. My dad had been gone for several years and Chester was killed when I was twelve.

As I lay there in the crackly dimness that's not quite asleep and not quite awake, I realized that I had to do something to help the kid, to get him some closure like I got when we buried Chester. Common sense and a basic knowledge of human conduct told me that it would be fruitless, that in fact Tommy's mother *had* run off with her co-worker. Nevertheless, he had to know and I'd try to find out for him. For myself and for Rob also.

***

At 7:15 that morning, I was parked on Beacon Street by New Stratley High School. Tiny raindrops peppered the windshield of my ancient Chevy van as I watched the waves of mushroom-headed boys and bouncing, chattering girls converging on the school. Hot oil dripping from my gonna-get-it-fixed-any-day-now leaking valve cover gasket and the steam from my egg and muffin sandwich mixed to create a sickly-sweet aroma. My black coffee wouldn't be cool enough to drink until long after the sandwich was gone, one of my pet peeves. Tommy was a good head taller than most of his peers and I picked him out almost instantly. I got out of the van and motioned him to come over, and he did after brief words to his two pals.

"Hey, Tommy," I said. "I really don't know why, but I'm gonna see if I can locate your mother." His eyes widened and his face opened up into a toothy grin. "Now, I don't want you to get your hopes up," I continued, "because I'm pretty sure I'll find out that

~ 6 ~

what your father said is true, that she ran off with that guy from her work."

"I just have to know what happened to her."

"I'll need you to get some things, a picture or two of her, her information -- date of birth, social security and driver's license numbers and so forth." He was nodding as I spoke. "Also I'll need names, numbers and addresses for her friends -- anybody who might know where she went. And Tommy, real important, this is just between you and me. Okay? I especially don't want your dad to find out. I don't need any trouble with the police."

"He's a jerk!" Tommy spat, the grin gone from his face. "He doesn't even care that she's gone. Don't worry. I won't tell him anything. I'll get as much stuff together as I can and I'll bring the money I have. Should I meet you here?"

"No I really don't like hanging around the high school."

Tommy told me that he raced slot cars at "Richie's Raceway" on Sunday afternoons and I agreed to meet him there at two. I also told him to hang onto his money until we knew what was going to be involved.

Chapter 3

"Richie's Raceway and Hobby Emporium" had been a fixture on Decatur Street since my teenage days. I walked in just after 1:30. The air was rife with wonderful, memory-jogging smells of plastic treasures, 3-In-1 Oil and the unmistakable tang of small induction motors. I was a half hour early so I thought I'd take a few laps around the track, give the kids a driving lesson. Richie was there behind the counter looking just like I remembered him. An unlit pipe drooped from his mouth and his shirt pocket was jammed with pencils, pens, pipe cleaners and a small ruler. He had two cars for rent, a bright red Ferrari and a '57 Chevy Nomad. I opted for the *Testa Rossa,* ten bucks for an hour.

"Watch out for that young lady," Richie said. "She's been track champ two years in a row now."

"I'll go easy on her," I said. Richie smiled.

I took a place in the "pits" with the pubescent A. J. Foyt wannabes, four boys and the girl. Her jacket proclaimed that she was Laurie, track champion and driver of car #7. *Just don't get in my way, little sister,* I thought as I lowered the Ferrari into the groove of lane 6.

I plugged in the controller and it felt good in my hand, sleek almost sensual, as if it had been designed by Enzo himself. A blue Corvette came tearing out of the last turn. *Watch this kid!* I thought, as I floored the button and raced into the first turn. I was beating him, too, when I spun the Ferrari right into the Corvette's side. *Damn cold tires.* The blue car came out of its groove and flipped end over end off the track.

"Watch out, Mister!" said the pimple-faced Corvette driver. He retrieved his car, checked it for damage and then put it back on the track. Somebody put my errant Ferrari back into its groove and I was going again. I made it through the next three turns fine but spun out on the hairpin just before the back straight, stopping the action. *Nice and Easy*, I thought as I pushed the controller button more cautiously this time. I'd take a few laps and then open it up. And they went flying by me, one after another. Zip, zip, zip. And the track champion was something, power sliding #7 through the turns twice as fast as her male counterparts. I unplugged the controller and brought the Ferrari back to Richie.

"There's something wrong with this one," I told him.

"Wanna try the Nomad?" he asked.

"No. I think I'll watch awhile," I said. Richie smiled.

I got a Diet Coke from a machine, sat at a small table next to a line of video games and watched a ten–year-old punk race my Ferrari around the track. Shortly after, Tommy came in.

"What the hell happened to you?" I asked.

"Got into a fight." The left side of his face was a red welt and his left eye was black, puffy and shut tight.

"That's *one* ugly bruise," I said. "Who hit you?"

"I don't wanna talk about it," he replied, and I knew at that moment who had done it.

"It was your old man, wasn't it?" I asked. He didn't answer. He pushed a beat up sneaker box across the table. "Look, Tommy, if you want my help, you're gonna have to level with me. If your father did this to you because of this investigation, I *have* to know."

He snuffled and I could see tears welling in his open eye.

"He did it, OK? He caught me snooping around for some of this stuff." He pointed to the box. "He told me that as far as we're

~ 9 ~

concerned, Ma is dead. He was drinking and I think he'd been fighting with his girlfriend. He doesn't know about you."

This whole business was beginning to stink. His bruised eye was a lot more than a father exercising parental discipline. But what could I do? I couldn't go to the cops, and if I dropped a dime to the Department of Social Services, Tommy would never tell them the truth. Maybe if I could find his mother, I could convince her to take Tommy back into her life, whatever that was now.

"Do you have any other family, grandparents or somebody you can stay with?" I asked. "He shouldn't be hitting you like that. I'll get us some Cokes." I got him a Coke and me a Diet Sprite from the machine. I would have rather had a beer, and Tommy probably would, too.

"Thanks," he said, and took a drink from the can. "I'm alright. Really. It doesn't hurt much now. It's just me and my sister, Jessica. She's nine. He doesn't hit her too much. After I find out where my mother is, I'm splitting and I hope I never see that jerk again."

I told Tommy to call my office Thursday and gave him one of my cards. He said he would and told me he was going to race his car for a little while.

"See that little kid with the Patriots' hat, the one racing that red Ferrari?" I asked. He nodded. "Run him off the track for me, wouldya?"

I brought the sneaker box back to Lawless Investigations Corporate Headquarters: my condo. The real estate lady called it a garden-style home, but I pay condo fees, and belong to the condo association and get in trouble with the condo manager when my old Chevy spits oil on the hot top. There are two twelve-by-twelve bedrooms a large living room and a modern kitchen with a slider leading to a deck with a nice view of a man-made pond. After I bought the place, I very quietly had the bathroom enlarged and installed a huge Jacuzzi. Condo managers aren't fond of projects like that. I would have just used the money to buy a new car, but I was pretty attached to the old Chevy. And oil is cheap. The second bedroom is what I use as my office, which I think is also against the condo rules, but so far no one had bothered me. I got a Red Stripe beer, which I needed for energy, and went to my desk with the sneaker box and dumped out its contents.

I was pleasantly surprised at how well Tommy had done. Her name was Heather Baxter and she was 37 years old. There was a pay stub with the address of the company from where she had supposedly run off. IotaTek. There were several family-type pictures and a posed five by eight with *Glamour Girl Studios* embossed in gold across the bottom. She looked nice in the family pictures, but the posed shot was spectacular.

After what I'd seen of Baxter's handiwork on Tommy's face, I couldn't blame her for running away. But I agreed with Tommy that she wouldn't leave him and his sister with that bastard. I looked through the shoebox and jotted a few things in my notebook. I was sipping my beer and listening to some Reggae while I worked. It sure beat the hoedown at the Stallion. When I'd finished going through the box, I put it away and turned on the TV. I was looking for something funny to take my mind off Tommy and his bruised face.

***

It was Wednesday night, six days since I'd first met Tommy Baxter. I was sitting on my postage-stamp sized deck enjoying my last Red Stripe and an unusually-mild late-spring breeze that whispered across Hunt's Pond, when the phone rang.

"Jake. It's Bart. I need to talk to you." My friend's voice was soft, almost muffled.

"Sure. Wanna come over? Or meet me at the Stallion?"

"No. How about Jaxie's place? Forty-five minutes?"

"OK Bart --" The phone clicked off before I could finish. Mysterious. I put on a light jacket and headed for the van.

Bartrellious C. Schell had been my friend since grammar school. We played together on the New Stratley High football and baseball teams, and joined the army together. We spent two years as MPs in Germany, and applied to the New Stratley Police Department when we got out. Bart was hired, the first black officer on the New Stratley force. A background check showed an indiscretion I'd had when I was seventeen involving alcohol, my father's station wagon and

~ 11 ~

Reverend Petrie's daughter, which kept me from being hired. Check out the movie "Footloose."

I drove down Route 9 into Brookline and parked around the corner from Jaxie's. It was dark and smoky inside and a bearded guy was playing a guitar and singing about Viet Nam and being blue. Sometimes, Bart sat in on drums with a jazz trio and jammed to a mixed audience of music lovers and drunks. I sat at the bar, ordered a beer and listened to the bearded guy. About ten minutes later, Bart came in and took the stool next to me.

"What's up, Bart? I asked. "You sounded strange on the phone."

"Sometimes you amaze me, Homie. You got a death wish or something?" He was wearing his uniform under his jacket. I didn't answer. Just looked at him and waited for him to continue. "You been messin' with Syd Baxter's kid? The word's out he's gonna rearrange your face. He's a mean son of a bitch. Why are you doing this?" He took a long drink of the beer that the bartender had brought him.

"His kid found me somehow and asked me to find his mother." I went on to tell him the rest of the story.

"His mother took off with a guy who she worked with. End of story. If you knew Syd the way I do, you'd know why."

"I know him," I said. "He's been drunk at the Stallion a few times. Wanted to screw most of the women and fight most of the guys."

"That's him and that's why she left him."

"But why wouldn't she let the kid know? Even take him and his sister with her?"

"No idea, Homes," Bart said, but it's none of your concern. I don't think anything good'll come of you sticking your nose into it. 'Cept maybe getting it busted."

***

I had stayed at Jaxie's until closing time, and when the alarm went off at 7:00 a.m., it seemed like a giant church bell ringing in my head. Too much fun with Bart drinking draft beers and listening to his comic tales of the New Stratley Police Department's misadventures. I took three aspirins with a glass of orange juice, put on my sweats and headed for a three-mile jog.

I knew my head would hurt, but I tried to run at least four times a week and I was way behind schedule. It was a beautiful morning, and I enjoyed the aroma of the Charles that was teeming with new spring life.

The insurance job I'd been on Monday and Tuesday was over. I'd snapped a couple rolls of film of Mr. Adelbert Szyminski loading large grocery bags and four cases of beer into his car and then, ten minutes later, into his house. He drank one of the beers on the way and threw the can into the street. This was hardly the appropriate activity for a man who claimed serious back injury. Metoxi Life and Casualty would pay well for these pictures, well enough that I could devote a day or two to the Baxter case.

After talking to Bart, it was obvious that Tommy's father knew about me and that I was working on his wife's disappearance. Tommy had promised me he wouldn't tell him, but maybe his old man beat it out of him. That might explain the bruises on the kid's face. I couldn't blame Heather Baxter for leaving an abusive relationship, but I was more and more convinced that Tommy was right, that she would have left a note, or called, or something. Maybe she did leave a note and Pa Baxter threw it away. Next stop would be the company where Heather worked.

Chapter 4

At 10:30 a.m., I pulled into the parking lot at IotaTek Industries in Waltham. The building is one of many glass and chrome monoliths along Route 128, or 95, or 295 depending on which sign or map you were reading. Massachusetts's highway system.

"IotaTek—Leading the World into the 21st Century" was chiseled into a large chunk of granite in front of the building. *World Leaders*, I thought. Impressive.

I went through the main entrance, from Waltham into an Arizona desert, or so it seemed. The walls were murals, bright blue sky, purple mountains and an endless sea of sand with painted cacti. The lobby had a half dozen ten foot high plastic Joshua trees shading as many chrome and plastic chairs. I half expected a plastic Gila monster to emerge from somewhere and latch onto my leg. The receptionist's name was stamped on a gold plaque on the counter. Ms. Adelle Karnes was beautiful in an artificial way and she fit right into the plastic desert. She asked if she could help me.

"I'm Jake Rammstein," I said and handed her a business card that I'd swiped from Metoxi Life. No reason to use my real name. "I'm investigating a claim from one of your past employees."

"Have a seat, please," she pointed to a chair in the corner. "I'll see if Mr. Judkins can see you."

I was there over twenty minutes when a man came into the lobby through a door that was part of the desert mural. I stood up and held out my right hand for him to shake. "Mr. Judkins?" I asked. He didn't shake my hand, just nodded.

"What can I do for you." He was well over six feet tall and I could tell he was muscularly built beneath his dark blue jacket. He wore a red tie, what I guessed they called a power tie. *Unfriendly* was my first impression.

"I'm Jake Rammstein, and I work for Metoxi—"

"I saw your card," he said. "Your name isn't on it. What do you want?" *Hostile.*

My company is investigating a claim by a Mr. Syd Baxter that his wife received an injury two years ago. She was working here at the time and has since disappeared, and--"

"Mr. Rammstein," he cut me off again, "if that's really your name, all our employee's records are strictly confidential. If Metoxi needs something they must follow proper procedures and the information will be mailed to them."

"All I needed was—"

"Perhaps you didn't understand me—"

"I understood you." My turn to cut him off. "What does this company do anyway, make personality pills?"

"Good day," he said. I could see his muscles flexing under his jacket. He turned and walked to the door imbedded in the purple mountains.

I sat in the van for a while looking at the façade of IotaTek Industries and wondering why Mr. Judkins had been so rude. I guess he thought I was an imposter. I'd gotten plenty of information in the past using the insurance-investigator scam. Maybe someone saw me get out of the old van. Or maybe the name *Baxter* shut things down immediately. If they were hiding something, I would have thought Judkins would've told me a lie or two to throw me off track.

I drove to a nearby fast-food place and ordered two burgers and a Coke. The order person suggested french fries. Why not? Something from each food group. I got my meal and headed back to the IotaTek lot. I parked so that I could see the entrance and about half of the hundred cars there. IotaTek had the first two floors but there were other companies above them and I wasn't sure which cars belonged where. I took my field glasses from their case, began eating my lunch and waited. Just after noon a silver Mercedes sports job circled the lot. The plate was a Massachusetts vanity, JUD-KIN. I wrote it in my notebook.

My pal, Jud, didn't pull right out of the lot. He circled behind me, then drove in front of me, gave me the evil eye and chirped his tires as he left. And I was gonna share a burger with him. Shortly after, the plastic receptionist came out and got into a red Escort. I jotted down the plate number. She had nice legs.

I stayed for another half hour. I wanted to leave before Judkins got back and called the cops on me. I did a little shopping, took a quick shower and got to the Stallion at 3:30 so Larry could get to a doctor's appointment. Or so he said.

Thursday was a bad day. I'd stayed late at the bar, doing my security gig while a cleaning company did the floors. I made sure they didn't steal anything. Of course I had a couple cold brewskis while I waited. I got home at 4:00 a.m. and slept 'til noon. I was off that night, so I was in no particular hurry to do anything. Later in the afternoon, I went to the Speedy Mart and found they had lost the surveillance pictures I was waiting for. The teenage clerk assured me it was a mix up at the developers and they would find them within three days or cheerfully give me three rolls of film. I explained how important these pictures were and she flashed me a smile which said, only-morons-trust-important-pictures-to-Speedy-Mart. I bought some gum and left. I ran a few errands and got home around six.

There was a cryptic message waiting on my machine. It was from Bart and it sounded like he was whispering: "Pick up the phone, idiot. You better not know where he is. Call me ASAP." I dialed his number but there was no answer. What could he be talking about? I wondered, as I popped a Hearty Man in the microwave. My question was answered a minute later. The doorbell rang. Two New

Stratley police officers were standing on my steps. I recognized them as Jablonski and Sweeney. Bart called them Tooty and Muldoon.

"What's up fellas?" I asked. "Looking for directions to the donut shop?"

"Cut the crap, wise guy," said Sweeney. "We're looking for Tommy Baxter."

"Don't know him," I said, but I could tell they didn't believe me. So that was what Bart was trying to tell me.

"Tommy's dad found your business card in the kid's room, and he thinks you know where he is. Maybe you're even hiding him. Mind if we look around?" Sweeney asked.

"Sure you can ... if you got a warrant," I said. "You guys are barking up the wrong tree. I know the kid and I know his father's a mean bastard. If he took off I wouldn't blame him, but I don't know where he is. Now if you don't mind, I've got a gourmet dinner cooking."

Jablonsky spoke. "You think you're pretty smart. Well, kidnapping's a big rap. We'll be watching you real close. Maybe we will get a warrant and let Tommy's dad serve it."

"See ya later, boys." I said and slammed the door. This wasn't what I had been bargaining for. I tried Bart's number again and this time it was busy. I was sorting through some bills when the microwave beeped. I opened the door and was met by a torrent of smoke. I took the box out of the trash and read the instructions. Seven minutes, not seventeen, dummy. My turkey medallions were now charcoal medallions. I threw them away and as I was opening the window, the phone rang.

"Hi, Mr. Lawless. It's Tommy."

"Tommy! Where are you?" I asked.

"I ran away." I could hear traffic in the background. Pay phone.

"I know that. Where are you? The cops have been here already looking for you. You just can't run away like that."

"I had to run away. He was gonna hit me again. Can you hide me for awhile?"

"Are you crazy?" I asked. "I told you the cops were just here." There was silence on the other end. "Look, kid, I'll see what I can do. Where are you, and do you have any money?"

"I'm at the Mall, at a pay phone. I have some money but not a lot. And what I've been saving to find my mother."

"There's a Pizza Alley at the Mall. You go in there, get yourself a couple slices, and eat slow. I'll be there as soon as I can figure something out."

"Great!" he said. "And ... thanks." We hung up.

A little voice in the back of my head was telling me to grab a one-way flight to Florida. Hang out there for a week or two. Tommy was warm and safe eating pizza. Sooner or later, the cops would find him and bring him back home. But then he'd be back with his father and maybe not that safe. I had to think of something. I made a mental note to look up his old man some day, no guns, no uniforms, and see how he'd make out against somebody his own size.

What was I going to do with Tommy? I couldn't keep him. The cops would surely be watching me. I couldn't bring him to the social services people. They might investigate, but I was pretty sure they'd return him to his old man. There was only one thing I could think of. Shelly. She and I had the same night off. It was a long shot. I thumbed open my phone book and dialed. She answered.

"Hi Shelly, it's Jake."

"What do you want. I'm not coming in to work."

"No, not work. I thought maybe you were lonely, maybe like a little male company."

"You're kidding," she said and I could tell she was laughing. "I don't mess around with guys I work with. Call somebody else."

"Not *me* Shel. Look, I really need a huge favor. There's this fourteen year old kid I'm kinda looking after and he--"

"You are soft!" she interrupted. "Soft like puppy shit. I'm not baby-sitting some fourteen year old kid."

"He won't be any trouble. His old man beats him and his mother is missing. I'm trying to find her. Just give him a place to sleep tonight and I'll figure something out by tomorrow morning. Promise."

"I don't know, Lawless. I'm not much good with kids. Why should I do you any favors? You're always picking on me."

"This is real important, Shelly. I'll owe you huge."

"I must be crazy. OK, bring him over. But if he gets fresh with me, I'm gonna kill him ... and then kill you."

"You're a doll. I'll be there in about a half hour." I hung up and headed for the van. No sign of any cruisers or unmarked cop cars in the lot. I'd go for a little ride just to make sure they weren't following me. I didn't think they would be, not for a runaway kid. I started the van and then I noticed a small piece of paper under my wiper blade. I got out and unfolded it. There was one quickly scrawled sentence with a local phone number: call Iris at 8 p.m. exactly.

I drove to the Mall, watching my mirrors to make sure nobody followed me. If they did they were real good. There was no sign of any unfriendlys at the Pizza Alley.

Tommy was sitting in a booth in the middle of the place. He saw me and started to get up. I motioned for him to stay seated and slid into the booth across from him.

He'd done in all but two pieces of pizza.

"Mind if I have one, Pal?" I asked.

"Have 'em both," he said.

"Thanks. I burned my supper and I'm starved."

"What are you gonna do with me?" he asked.

"There's a friend of mine, a lady I work with, who said she'll put you up for tonight. Tomorrow . . . I don't know."

"I don't want to go home again," Tommy said. "Never. Not unless my mother is there."

"Don't worry about that tonight. Take your drink and let's get going." He stood clutching his cup which had "Super Swallow" boldly emblazoned in bright red on it. It looked like it held enough to fill three healthy bladders.

Tommy was silent on the ride to Shelly's. I told him he could adjust the radio, and he did. He found an abominable mixture of screaming voices and screeching guitars accompanied by a satanic drum beat. We jousted with the volume control a few times until I gave up.

"You'll have to turn Shelly on to this music," I said, "after I leave.

***

Shelly met us at the door and I introduced Tommy to her.

~ 19 ~

"He's a great kid," I said. "You won't even know he's here. He loves music."

"And I'm not gonna get in any trouble?" Shelly asked.

"Nah. His mother will be grateful, maybe even pay you something. When I find her." I neglected to tell her about every cop in the city looking for the boy. No sense worrying her. And I made a mental note to stop teasing her about her IQ.

"I'm sure we'll be fine," Shelly said as she led Tommy into her small living room. "Lucky for you guys I didn't have any plans tonight." She gave Tommy the remote and turned on the TV for him. I followed her into her kitchenette. "You sure you didn't kidnap him, Lawless?"

"No way, Shelly," I said. "Have you got an extra beer?"

She opened her refrigerator and handed me a can of Bud. I drank about half of it in one gulp. She was staring at me.

"Just washing down some pizza," I said. "You saw the bruises on that kid's face? His old man is a total idiot and he beats the kid. You don't have anything to worry about. I'll pick him up first thing in the morning and get him some help." I noticed her clock. It was just eight. I asked her if I could use her phone to make a quick call."

"Lawless, if I'm watching this kid so you can go on a date--"

"Strictly business." I cut her off. "All work and no play for this private eye."

"Private eye, my ass," she said but pointed to the wall phone and then went to join Tommy. I dialed the number on the paper and, after two rings, heard it picked up.

"Hello." A woman's voice, almost a whisper.

"Hi. Jake Lawless calling. Is this Iris?"

"That's not my real name," she whispered. "I have to talk to you."

"About what? Who are you?" Standard detective questions.

"It's about IotaTek. Can you meet me? I don't want to talk on the phone."

I agreed to meet her in a half hour at the lounge in the New Stratley Hotel. I asked her how I'd know her and she said she knew me. I finished the Bud, said goodbye to Tommy and Shelly and headed to meet Iris. Or whatever her name was.

~ 20 ~

Chapter 5

The lounge was dark and about half full. Soft Jazz was playing from hidden speakers. I took a stool at the bar near the TV and ordered a beer. There were open stools on both sides of me. I'd been there about ten minutes when a woman sat in the stool on my right. She was wearing sunglasses and I wondered how she could see in the darkened room. She had shoulder length auburn hair that bounced when she moved. I figured she was about thirty.

"Should I call you Iris?" I asked. "Would you like a drink?"

"My name is really Trudy, Trudy James, and yes I'd like a Dewars on the rocks, water on the side. I motioned to the bartender, and when he came over, ordered her drink and another beer. She was trying to light a long filtered cigarette but her fingers were trembling.

I took the matches and lit it for her. I figured I'd get right down to business. "How do you know me?" I asked. "And how do you know I'm interested in IotaTek?"

She took a long drag on her cigarette and drank half the glass of Scotch. She didn't chase it with the water. She was staring at me through her dark glasses and the haze of cigarette smoke. Sizing me up, I guessed.

"I work there," she began, almost a whisper. "I'm a secretary. I saw you when you came in yesterday, and I, well I listened to some of your talk with Mr. Judkins. I recognized you. We live in the same condo group. I'm in the 700s. By the pool."

"Small world," I said. She ignored that.

"I know you're a detective and I was surprised when you told Mr. Judkins you were an insurance man."

"I don't think he bought it either."

"He's not a nice man." One more swallow and her Scotch was gone. I motioned the bartender for another.

"Yeah," I said. "I kinda got that impression. I'm still wondering why you contacted me. I mean, can't you get in trouble with the company?"

"That's putting it mildly," she said. She took off her glasses and her eyes scanned the room, darting back and forth like a small scared animal. She lit another cigarette from her first, took a gulp of her Scotch and then told me her story.

She'd begun working at IotaTek Industries six years ago, shortly after it moved to Waltham. She worked in shipping and receiving at the start and within a year had been promoted to the office.

For the first two years everything was fine, good benefits, frequent raises. She was dating an attorney then, and they had planned to get married. One day things changed dramatically - the day new owners bought the company. Since then many strange things had happened, including the disappearance of Heather Baxter.

"What does IotaTek do?" I asked. She had finished the Scotch and was on her third cigarette. She squirmed in her seat and I could see small drops of sweat forming on her forehead. "Maybe you should lay off the hard stuff awhile. How about a Coke?"

"I'm not a child," she snapped. "I really need another drink to get through this. Don't worry. I'm not driving. I took a cab. Actually I took two cabs to make sure I wasn't followed."

She took off her sunglasses and laid them on the bar. "I can tell you don't believe me. You think I'm paranoid, but I have plenty of reasons to be. When I heard you mention Heather's name to

Judkins, I got excited. Nobody's done anything about her..." She stopped to sip from the new drink.

"About her 'running off'," she made quote marks with her fingers. "I don't think she left with Bruce like everybody says. I thought maybe if I helped you, you could help me."

"Protect and serve. That's me," I said. I saw my second beer was gone. The tension this lady was emanating was apparently catchy. "You seem quite upset with the company. Why don't you just leave?"

She got up to go to the ladies room. "You don't just *leave* IotaTek," she said.

While Iris/Trudy was gone, I took out my small notebook and began jotting down what she had told me. I ordered myself another beer and got her another Scotch. She came back, took her stool and immediately lit a cigarette.

"Those things are bad for you," I said.

"That's the least of my problems," she said, and she was right.

"What's Bruce's last name?" I asked.

"Anderson. A really nice guy. Nice wife. I met her a couple times. Margot's her name. They were trying to adopt a baby. He was very excited about that. It was all he talked about." She stopped for a gulp of her drink. "There's no way he ran off with Heather Baxter. No way."

"What did Bruce do for IotaTek?"

"He was an engineer. He'd been with the company from the start. But he wasn't happy, either, with the new owners. He went to South America on business--somewhere in the rain forest--Brazil I think--we got all kinds of mail from Bella something or other. He was really different when he came back."

"Different how?" I asked. "Maybe he was having an affair and his wife found out?"

"No. Nothing like that. It was like he was scared. He asked me if I'd type up his resume for him, on the sly, you know, and I said I would. He was gone before he gave me the information."

"Why doesn't everybody just leave that crazy company?"

"Money. Fear. Judkins's an intimidating bastard. He's one of the new owners. They pay real well. Almost double any other company for the same job. You get used to a lifestyle, you know?" She looked at me, I guess, like I'd understand how great our condos were.

"There's a lot of things. You'll need a book a lot bigger than that," she pointed at my note pad, "to write them all down. The big thing IotaTek tries to do is keep down employee turnover."

"What is this some kind of *The Firm?*" I asked. "You know John Grisham's book about an evil empire of bad lawyers?"

"Oh, yeah. I saw the movie. I just love Tom Cruise. I'm not sure what IotaTek is up to, but I'm sure it is evil. And I'm sure that it caused Heather and Bruce to go away. I'm afraid they're . . . dead."

"There really has to be a better--," I was cut short by a noise.

Phhht!

Iris's body jerked. Her hand flew forward sending her glass smashing across the bar. Her eyes were wide, startled. A female patron screamed.

Phht! Phht!

There was more screaming. Iris fell against me. I looked in her eyes and knew she was dead. I heard the bartender frantically dialing the phone.

Phht! Phht!

I lowered Iris to the floor. There was something wrong. My arm was burning. Something definitely wrong. I was hit in the left arm. I couldn't tell how badly, but my fingers were tingling and it hurt like hell. The bartender had dialed 9-1-1 and then left the phone dangling before he crawled out of the room. All the patrons had bailed out, too, or were hiding under tables. That left just dead Iris, the shooter and me, and the shooter was coming toward me. He was a good six feet tall, medium build and was wearing a Red Sox sweatshirt. He had surgical gloves on his hands and a blue knitted ski mask covering his face.

The shooter looked down at Iris. He fired once more at her. His mistake. I grabbed a bar stool and hit him with it as hard as I could. The gun flew from his hand and clattered onto the floor. He lunged for it but I caught him with a right that knocked him backwards. I heard sirens in the distance. I grabbed the gun and turned towards him. He gave me a shove and ran for the exit. I fired once but didn't hit him. A second later he was out the door.

I went to go after him but was met by a man coming into the room. He was a small man with a neat navy-blue suit and a pencil-thin mustache. The hotel manager, his name tag announced.

What's going on here?" He was looking at me. Then he saw the gun and then Iris. "Oh my God! You killed her! Please don't shoot me," he screamed and then ran from the room.

The sirens were getting closer. I figured I'd better run, too. I could feel wet trickling down my left arm. Blood. I was holding a murder weapon in my right hand, one I'd just fired.

There was nothing I could do for Iris. I headed for the red "EXIT" sign in the back of the lounge. I pushed on the door. It had a placard warning an alarm would sound, and it did. I went outside into the night. A very fine rain was falling and it felt nice in a surreal way.

I was in the lot behind the hotel. There were dumpsters there and a small dock for deliveries. My van was parked in the front, no way I could get to it without running right into the arms of the approaching police. I wanted to run but I was getting drowsy. I was losing blood and I had to take care of my arm real soon. More sirens coming. I wondered if it was Tooty and Muldoon. Or maybe Tommy's father. I hoped it wasn't Bart.

I walked down Wardley Street and went left onto Beasley. Beasley Park was about an eighth of a mile down on the right. I got to the park and started down an old path that I remembered from my childhood. There was a playground with benches near the William P. Beasley Elementary School. Night lights shining from the school were enough for me to see the damage to my arm.

Chapter 6

The night was full of sirens. I took off my shirt and inspected my left arm. The bullet had taken a pretty good chunk about three inches above my watch. I wrapped my shirt around it and tied it as tight as I could using my right hand and my teeth. I sat on the bench, taking deep breaths and wondering what my next move would be. Why did I run? I didn't shoot Iris. Of course I was hiding a cop's runaway kid. I had fired the murder weapon which was now in my pocket. The hotel manager was convinced that I was the killer. I was pretty sure the bartender knew I hadn't done it, but I was also positive that the cops would arrest me without asking too many questions.

I had a lot of questions of my own that I couldn't get answered in jail. Shelly's apartment was about six blocks away. That seemed like the best place to go. She'd be mad, but I'd make it up to her. The bandage was working, I wasn't dripping blood any more.

I wondered if the cops would try to follow me, maybe get a dog to follow the blood trail. Rain began falling a little heavier, and that would help. I wanted to keep off the main roads. It would take a little longer, but I figured it would be worth it. I must have been a spooky sight hobbling to Shelly's in my tee shirt, soaking wet and covered with blood.

***

It took me about a half hour to get to Shelly's. I took several detours along the way, one down a slimy alley between a Chinese Restaurant and a pizza place, which was rife with the smells of rotting meat and vegetative substances. I almost gagged a couple times. Rats and mangy cats hissed at me and scratched away as I stumbled along. This should throw any pursuing hounds off the trail. I was getting paranoid. Surely by then the bartender would have told the cops the real story and I'd be in the clear.

I knocked on the door to Shelly's apartment as quietly as I could. I was beat. I felt like I was going to pass out.

"Who's there?" Shelly whispered.

"It's me, Shel, Jake. Let me in please. Hurry."

"What the hell happened to you?" she asked after she unchained the door and opened it to let me in. Tommy joined her in the small hall. Apparently they had been watching TV. I could see it flickering in the living room. I smelled popcorn.

"It's nothing," I said. "Just a scratch. Caught a stray bullet."

"A G.S.W.," Tommy said. "That's cool." He looked at Shelly.

"G.S.W. Gun shot wound. Who shot you?"

"I'm not sure, but I plan to find out."

"You better go in the bathroom and wash up," Shelly said. "There are towels on the shelf and I have a huge old bathrobe that'll fit you." She looked at my clothes. "I'll get you a trash bag for those things."

I put my clothes in the bag she brought me and took a shower, as hot as I could stand it. She had a lot more water pressure than I did and it felt good. I made a mental note to complain to my condo association manager. I dried off and looked at my wound. All cleaned up it looked pretty ugly. It was still bleeding some. Shelly had left a box of 4 x 4 gauze pads and a roll of bandage. I ripped open two pads, loaded them up with first-aid cream and pressed them to the wound. I wrapped the bandage around them until the roll ran out. Good as new.

~ 27 ~

"Jake," Shelly said, and I didn't like the way she said it. "Come see this. Hurry."

I threw on the bathrobe and went into the living room. Shelly and Tommy were staring at the screen. I was familiar with the newscaster, had seen him on the ten o'clock news for many years.

"...live in New Stratley," he said. The scene shifted to a female reporter standing in front of the New Stratley Police Station. "Jennifer Logan" flashed across the bottom of the screen and "Live via Satellite-Cam."

"Thank you, Chaz," Jennifer said. She had perfect teeth. "The New Stratley police are being quite tight lipped at this time. We do know that a veteran Stratley Police officer, Syd Baxter and an un-named woman believed to be his girlfriend were shot as they sat in Baxter's car in the driveway of his home, just three blocks from here. Officer Baxter was pronounced dead shortly after 9 p.m. The woman has been airlifted to Mass General. Her condition is not known. Also, Chaz, and this is really bizarre, an unknown woman was shot and killed at the New Stratley Hotel some twenty minutes after the officer's shooting."

Jennifer Logan paused as a large truck rumbled past. A man handed her a piece of paper, and she scanned it quickly. "Just breaking," she said, white teeth flashing, "the New Stratley Police Chief, Everett Wannamaker, has just announced that they have a suspect in the murder of Officer Baxter. The man is also wanted for questioning in the shooting at the hotel."

The camera panned to show a form with fingerprints on the bottom and photo on the top. "Chief Wannamaker warns that the man is considered armed and extremely dangerous. If anyone sees him, don't approach him, but dial 9-1-1 or call the New Stratley Police or the Massachusetts State Police." Phone numbers flashed on the screen. "The suspect is a private investigator from New Stratley named Brewster J. Lawless, A.K.A., Jake Lawless."

The TV station switched to a commercial. Tommy sat on the couch staring at the screen. Shelly looked back and forth between us. She looked like she had a million questions but didn't know where to begin.

"Did you shoot him?" Tommy asked.

"No," I said, "I didn't."

"I'm gonna be sick," Tommy said and then ran into the bathroom. He wretched loudly. Shelly looked at me.

"That's his father," I said. "The cop who was shot."

Shelly's face went white. She staggered to the couch and sat "Oh my God, Jake, what kind of shit are you involved in? Are *we* involved in?" She began crying.

I put my hand on her shoulder but she shrugged it off. I didn't blame her. I wanted to apologize to her, but words wouldn't come out. I went into the kitchen and filled two glasses with brandy. She clutched the glass with two hands and took a big drink.

In the bathroom, Tommy was scooping cold water onto his face. I handed him a towel.

"Do you think my dad's dead because of me?" His words were slow and trembling.

"Definitely not," I said, trying to reassure us both. "I don't know what's going on, Tommy, but I plan to find out."

"If my mother is . . . " he began. He wiped his face with the towel. "I mean, am I an orphan now? What will they do with me? And my sister?" He took the glass of brandy from my hand. I took his arm to stop him from drinking. "Don't sweat it. I've been snitching my father's for years. He took a sip and started coughing. I took the glass back.

The realization of the whole mess was starting to hit me. The police wanted me for murder, probably kidnapping as well. My left arm was throbbing and needed medical attention pretty soon. How was I going to keep poor Shelly from getting more involved? What was I going to do with Tommy? Somehow I had to get to the bottom of this mystery. That was the only way I could see to clear myself. I had to find out who killed Tommy's father. And what happened to his mother.

***

Shelly was tending to Tommy in the bathroom and I was in the kitchen. I was weak and hungry. I made a ham sandwich and took a big bite. I washed it down with the brandy. I thought it was comical that I was so hungry "at a time like this." I was debating about getting one more of my friends in the shit. I had to let Bart know

~ 29 ~

that I was innocent. I dialed his number, and he answered after three rings.

"Bart," I said "it's me, Jake."

"Where the hell are you man?" he screamed into the phone.

"I'm still in town. I had to call you to tell you I didn't kill anybody."

"Station called a few minutes ago. I just got ordered in. The old man called in everybody. Everybody, Jake! To find *you*! Shit man. What's going on?"

I told him the story. He paused me a few times with an interjected profanity. When I was through, I drank the rest of the brandy in my glass. Bart was silent for a minute, as was I.

Finally I spoke. "I don't want to get you involved. I just wanted you to know I didn't kill anybody."

"I never had any doubt that you'd kill anyone unless they deserved killing. I'm trying to think of how I can help you."

"Thanks, buddy," I said, "But, I'll be all right. I don't want to get you mixed up in this."

"Bullshit, Man. You'd be there for me. You never told me where you are. Can you get to McBain's Deli by one a.m.?" I told him I could. "Okay. I'm going to the station now to see what I can find out. You wait behind the store, and if I'm a little late just hang in there." We said terse goodbyes and then hung up.

***

Shelly came into the kitchen as I was finishing the ham sandwich. "What are you gonna do, Jake?" she asked.

"For starters I'm getting out of here. I don't know what to do with the boy."

"Leave him here."

"This is no time to get maternal," I said and was immediately sorry I said it. She sat at the table and put her fingers to her eyes. "I'm sorry, Shelly. I really appreciate your helping us out but I don't know what's going to happen next. People are turning up dead."

"He's a good kid, Jake. He's scared and confused. I talked to him in there," she pointed to the bathroom, "He doesn't want to answer a million questions right now. He wants to be alone, you know, to get his thoughts straightened out. We both know what the cops will

~ 30 ~

do to him, and when they're done they'll turn him over to D.S.S. He'll have to go to the funeral and then I'll just do what I can for him."

I went to say something but she stopped me. She pulled a crinkled bill from her pocket. "He gave me this fifty. Kind of a down payment on his room and board. Naturally I'm not gonna keep it."

I looked at the bill. It was the same one he had offered me to find his mother. "He can stay, I guess. For a little while. Remember, Shelly, real important, you never saw me after I dropped him off. I'll tell him the same thing. I'm going to see what I can find out. If it gets real bad and they catch me I don't want them to know that you helped me."

She acknowledged me with a broad smile and went to the other room to tell Tommy.

"Hey, I need my clothes, I can't go out in this bathrobe."

"You cant wear them. They're in the trash. Have another sandwich and I'll be back in a couple minutes and see what I can do."

I didn't want another sandwich, but I did help myself to another beer. Shelly came back in about ten minutes with a handful of clothes. She put them on the table and looked at me. A small smile was forming at the corner of her mouth. "I don't have much that will fit you," she said, "but I thought, since they're looking for a guy, a disguise might be called for." She pulled a platinum blonde wig from the pile of clothes. "I bought this for my mother when she was doing the chemo thing, but she wouldn't wear it."

"And neither will I," I said. "This isn't Halloween, Shelly."

"You don't have much choice. Your face has been all over the TV and every cop in town is looking for you. Not to mention that most of them don't like you. Here, put on this skirt. It wraps around, and then I'll pin it for you."

It felt silly, but I knew she was right. I'd have to walk about six blocks to McBain's Deli and this was probably my best chance. I wrapped the skirt around and she pinned it and then she gave me a pink sweater that was way too big for her. She told me her great aunt had given it to her and that the old lady thought everyone was the same size as she was. Shelly put the wig on and adjusted it. She seemed to be having fun. She clipped on some huge gaudy earrings and then went at me with a tube of lipstick.

I protested, but she pushed my arms down and painted me. "We want you as authentic as possible," she said. "Don't we, girlfriend?" She started laughing.

"This is all very cute, Shelly. I hope some day I get to return the favor."

She finally stopped laughing and handed me a pair of sandals. "That's the best I could do to cover those feet," she said. "You'd look pretty silly with those sneakers of yours."

"Like I don't look silly, now," I said. I crammed the sandals on my feet. They were about three sizes too small but the straps were very adjustable. They'd do for six blocks. I hoped. She gave me a gold colored purse that she said matched the earrings. I put my wallet, keys and the confiscated 9mm inside the purse.

"I guess I'm ready. Say goodbye to Tommy for me, would ya? I don't want him to see me dressed up like this. And tell him what I said about the cops." She said she would and walked me to the door.

"Good luck, Jake." She got close and for a second I thought she was going to kiss me. Instead she squirted me in the face with some awful smelling perfume. I slammed the door and I could hear her laughing on the other side. I couldn't help myself, and I began laughing too.

***

The rain had stopped but the streets were still soaked. I breathed in the aroma of the wet asphalt, a city smell that I had always loved. I heard distant sirens reminding me of the serious problem I was facing. Two people murdered and me the prime suspect. I was sure that after everything had been investigated, I'd be cleared. Pretty sure. I was hoping that Bart would be able to help me with the police end.

I was about half way to the Deli when I heard a car approaching from behind me. I didn't turn around, just kept walking. The car slowed and pulled next to me. It was a police cruiser with two uniforms in it. The passenger spoke to me. "'Scuse me, ma'am."

"Yes," I squeaked. "Just going home."

~ 32 ~

"Sure you are." he said and mumbled something to his partner.

My heart was pounding. There was no way I could outrun them in Shelly's sandals.

I heard their radio squawk and the driver started talking on the mike. His partner spoke to me. "We gotta run. I'd get off the street if I was you. There's a killer out here somewhere." I put my hand to my mouth feigning terror. The blue lights came on and the car screeched away. The last thing I heard the cop say as they were driving off was something about "uglier all the time."

Chapter 7

It seemed like it took hours to get to the deli. My feet were killing me. It felt like they were locked in two vices that got tighter with every step. I went into the alley behind the deli to wait. I had to get out of Shelly's sandals. The ground was slimy and covered with small shards of broken glass that twinkled in the moonlight. No place to go barefoot. I found a cardboard box inside the dumpster that looked clean and relatively dry. I took off the sandals and stood in the box. Relief. I quietly cursed Shelly and tossed her sandals into the dumpster. Occasional tires hissed by the alley but none stopped. I'd been there almost an hour when I heard a car slow. Bare feet or not, I was ready to make a run for it.

The car pulled slowly behind the deli. I recognized the white fender and blue stripe of a New Stratley police cruiser. Just before the headlights blinded me, I saw Bart looking at me with a huge smile on his face. "Well aren't you a cute one, Sugar," he said as he got out of the car. "Does your pimp know you're goofin' off?"

I said, "You're a real comedian. Any chance you brought some fresh clothes with you?"

"But you're so cute," he said and pinched my cheek. I pushed his hand away and then winced in pain. I had forgotten my bullet wound. "Lets get that little scratch taken care of." Bart took a case from the cruiser and then unlocked the back door to the deli. "Come on in. Don't worry, I know the owner."

We went into the deli, and Bart had me sit at a small table. He took the bandage off and inspected my wound. "That looks like it hurts," he said.

"Brilliant. They should make you a detective. So, what's the talk at the cop shop?"

"The place was a zoo when I got there. Chief was a raving lunatic. He wants this case solved NOW." Bart spoke as he was rubbing some foul-smelling stuff on my arm. "You're pretty lucky. The bullet took off a good chunk of skin. You probably should have a doctor look at it."

"Say I go to a hospital and get this taken care of, then what? What are my chances with the police?"

Bart was shaking his head as he began wrapping a new bandage around my arm. "Right now I don't like your chances. There are a lot of cops who would like to bring you in zipped up in a body bag. You know, ask questions later. Speaking of questions, I have a few myself. Like how the hell did you get involved in this?"

"I'm not really sure, Bart. Ouch! easy on the bandage. One minute I was talking to a lady about IotaTek, and the next minute she gets blown away."

"You think she was the target or maybe they were after you?"

"Something doesn't make sense. The shooter could have got both of us. I never saw it coming. And then the gun. He seemed to give it up too easy." I took the gun from my "purse" and popped the clip. There were four rounds left in it. They were all blanks. Bart and I looked at each other.

"Come on cutie," he said. "Let's get you some clothes."

I rode to Bart's apartment lying on the back floor of the cruiser. All I could smell was the bleach that had been used to clean up after horrible prisoners had vomited there. And worse. "Hurry up, Bart! It stinks back here," I said.

"Almost there. You should've smelled it before they washed it down. Just pray I don't get a call before I can get you out of there." He started laughing. I felt the car slow, turn and then pull to a stop. "Hang on a little longer. I'll make sure the coast is clear."

~ 35 ~

He was back a minute later "Let's go," he said. I ran through the door that Bart held open. He lived on the top floor of an old three-decker that had been renovated in an urban redevelopment project and it was pretty clean. He led up the stairs and I followed. He got me a pair of sweats and a tee shirt and I changed out of Shelly's duds as quickly as I could. I washed the gunk off my face and met Bart in the kitchenette. He had opened a Diet Coke for him and handed me a beer. The two-way radio on his belt was squawking. Lots of cop chatter in a small city after a double homicide.

"You can stay here tonight," he said. "Any plans for tomorrow?"

"This whole crazy mess seems to be tied to the disappearance of Tommy Baxter's mother. Iris, or whatever her name was, gave me something to go on. The name of the guy that supposedly ran off with her is Bruce Anderson. I'm gonna try to find his wife and see what she has to say." I finished the beer and Bart got me another one.

"You also better talk to an attorney because I think pretty soon you're gonna need one. He will advise you to turn yourself in and let us professionals handle this."

I gave him a funny look but didn't say anything. He was really sticking his neck way out for me and I appreciated it.

Bart told me he usually left a couple lights on and the radio so I'd be OK as long as I stayed away from the window. "There's beer and some food in the fridge. I'll be back in the morning." He left and I heard the key turn in the deadbolt, and I was alone.

I found Bart's phone book and opened it to A, and found Anderson. There were Seven: an Andrew, a Martin, a Thomas, three Williams and an M. No Bruce. Maybe the phone number was unlisted. Or maybe in the wife's name. M. Hadn't Iris said her name was Margot? I'd try some phone tag in the morning. I had two more beers and then fell asleep on Bart's couch listening to a jazz station on his radio.

***

I was awakened by footsteps and then the snicking sound of a key in the deadbolt. I got up and got ready to run. The door opened and it was Bart.

~ 36 ~

"Get some sleep?" he asked, and I nodded. "They're starting to piece things together. The manager swears you were the one who killed the woman at the hotel, but several patrons came forward and said that it was another guy with a stocking mask. They have even less on who shot Baxter and his girlfriend. The captain had me in his office for an hour this morning. He knows we're friends."

"I've been thinking about turning myself in."

"You better talk to a lawyer first. You're still suspect number one. Here." He handed me a white bag. Golden Arches on the front and a delicious aroma coming from it. "Breakfast." Bart had a coffee while I ate and then he left again, four more OT hours to go.

When he had gone, I took my notebook from Shelly's purse. I dialed the number for M. Anderson. It was 7:50 a.m. Maybe I'd catch someone.

"Hello." A pleasant man's voice on the answering machine. "This is Bruce. Margot and I are busy. Please leave your name after . . ." I hung up. Bingo!

I was drinking my second cup of coffee, thinking about a possible disguise I could use to get around town when the phone rang, startling me and causing me to spill half the cup on Bart's table.

"Shit," I mumbled to myself. "It's just the phone." I let it ring and finally the machine picked it up.

After Bart's message and beep there was a brief silence and then a woman's soft voice. "This is Margot Anderson. I just got a call from this number and--"

I picked up the receiver and cut her off. "Mrs. Anderson, I'm very sorry to bother you." I'd forgotten about damn caller ID and now she had Bart's phone number. "I'm calling about your husband--"

"Who is this?" she demanded. "What do you want with me?"

"Please, just listen to me for a second. I'm a private investigator and I'd like to find out what really happened to your husband." She tried to interrupt me but I kept talking. "I think everybody's been lying to you, and I'm just trying to get to the truth. I don't think your husband ran away with another woman."

There was a minute of silence and then she spoke. "Why are you interested in my husband?"

"I was hired to find the woman he supposedly ran away with. I'm not sure what's going on. I'd like to talk to you. You might know something that will help me get to the bottom of this."

She was silent again for over a minute, and I can't say I blamed her. She was probably struggling to get her life back together and here was a stranger on the phone trying to scramble it up again.

"Why?" she said and then began to cry.

"Just answer one question for me, Mrs. Anderson. Please. If the answer is *yes* I'll hang up and never bother you again." I took a breath. "Do you really believe that Bruce left you for another woman?"

"Yes...I...I...No! No, in my heart I don't. It's what everybody says... and the notes... and the police."

"Can I meet you then?" I said. She didn't respond. "I may be the only hope for finding out the truth. No one else seems to care."

This seemed to weaken her. I knew she was afraid and that she wasn't sure about me or my story, but I was probably a last ray of hope in her own search for what really happened.

"One question," she said, "before I agree. "Who hired you? I spoke with the woman's husband--the policeman--and he seemed almost happy that his wife was gone."

"Tommy Baxter. Her son," I said. I probably shouldn't give my client's name, but I really had to talk to this woman.

After a brief pause she gave me her address and asked me to be there by nine.

***

It was rainy and raw for so late in May as I walked to Margot Anderson's house. She lived on Eastern Avenue, about a mile and a half from Bart's place. I was wearing Bart's long trench-coat and his funny looking leather cap with earmuffs that pulled down, like a World War I pilot would wear. It smelled like it had been in his closet since the Great War with the Kaiser, too. He only used it on the coldest traffic details. His sneakers were two sizes too big but they were a lot better than Shelly's sandals. All-in-all not much of a disguise but I didn't think I looked out of place considering the weather.

I had put the 9mm and the shells in a brown paper bag marked "GIVE TO POLICE" with a note inside that explained what had happened. I wrote that I would be turning myself in shortly, after they calmed down a little and got me cleared. I didn't want them shooting me as a cop killer. I dropped the bag in a mailbox on Harvard Street. I stayed off the main roads and got to the Anderson house just about at nine.

Her house was a small yellow two-story with "ANDERSON" and "78" neatly painted on the mailbox. A gray Toyota four-door, about three years old, sat in the driveway, and I noticed the inspection sticker had expired two months ago. That was probably something that Bruce took care of. I'd mention it to her. I walked up the three steps and rang the bell. She opened the door as far as the safety chain would allow and looked out at me. I've never really understood safety chains on doors. One good shove and the bad guy would be in. But I guess it made her feel a little more comfortable while she sized me up.

"Hi," I said. "I'm the guy from the phone. Jake Lawless."

"Come in," she finally said and opened the door for me. She led me into the kitchen just off the main entrance and asked me to sit. She offered me coffee or tea and I told her a coffee would be great. She poured two cups from a small coffee brewer on the counter and put them on the table. I declined milk and sugar and she sat down. She was maybe 5'-2" and in her early thirties. There were deep circles under her eyes which were red and puffy. Her hair was light brown and hung in wisps around her forehead. I thought she'd be quite attractive if she was fixed up, but it was obvious that she hadn't been for some time. She noticed me looking at her fingernails which were bitten short.

"Bruce and I both quit smoking when I was pregnant," she said and put her hands in her lap. "Sometimes I really wish for a cigarette, but I don't want to start again." She took a sip of her coffee.

"You have a child?" I asked.

"I had a miscarriage. We were trying to adopt. I left his voice on the answering machine, I guess you heard. Sometimes I play it just to hear him. My mother thinks I'm crazy. I keep telling her I'll erase it, but...you know, it's hard for me." She pushed a half-full box of white powdery donuts towards me. "You said on the phone you think Bruce might not be with...if not where would he be?"

"That I don't know." I took one of the donuts. "I really want to find out though. Right now I'm leaning towards the company, Iota-Tek, having something to do with it. That's a strange place. I was hoping you could fill me in on some of the goings-on there. And you said something about notes. Can you tell me about them?"

"I can show you them." She pushed herself up from the table. "I'll be right back."

She returned in a couple minutes with a manila folder clutched to her "Pluto" sweatshirt. She put the file on the table and opened it. "These are letters the company brought me. Mr. Judkins. Have you met him?" I nodded. "They say these are e-mails from Bruce's computer to the woman's."

I looked at the first one.

"Let's meet for lunch. Same place. Love Bruce."

She handed me several more about the same. The last one was more detailed it was about them leaving together, heading for New Mexico and an art colony. "Then there's this." She handed me another sheet. I read it while she refilled our coffees.

> Dear Margot,
>
> This is very hard for me. I'm in love with another woman and I want to live with her. This is not your fault, all mine. Please try to get on with your life.
>
> Bruce

I finished reading and looked up at her. There was a definite sheen in her eyes.

"I don't believe he wrote these," she said. "For two reasons. He wasn't a coward. If he really was leaving he would have told me face to face. And he had this *thing* about starting a letter with 'Dear.' He was almost anal about it, you know. Ever since college, he'd send me notes with 'Hi Hon' or just Marg but never 'Dear.'"

"And nobody at work would know that, right?" I asked.

"I don't think so. At least whoever really typed this letter didn't."

"How about the signature." It was a scribbled, 'Bruce.'

"That's how he signed things. Almost a scribble, you know. But I think it would be easy to copy. I can't tell for sure."

"What about the police? You mentioned them."

"They came to the house. I told them I wanted to file a missing person's report. They told me that, unless there was some evidence Bruce was kidnapped or crazy, he could leave if he wanted to. Free country, you know. They bought the story that Bruce ran away with that cop's wife." She stood up and leaned on the back of her chair. "He came over to talk to me. The cop, Baxter. He told me we, that's him and me, were both victims in this. I gave him coffee and talked for a while. Then he suggested we go to bed together. Some kind of 'grudge' thing since our spouses were doing it." Her knuckles were white digging into the chair. "I threw my coffee in his face and told him to get out. Can you imagine the nerve of the guy? That's why I couldn't believe that he hired you."

I was starting to feel like a crumb. I was there using her for information and she didn't even know about the killings. It was time for some truth telling on my part, but I checked her coffee cup and it was almost empty. I wouldn't get too wet. "Mrs. Anderson," I began.

"Call me Margot, please."

"OK. Margot. There's some stuff I have to tell you. I guess you haven't been listening to the news. Maybe you should sit down." She sat. I told her about Baxter and his girlfriend, about Iris and that I was the prime suspect. I sat there waiting for her to react, to throw me out or to run for the phone.

She just sat there thinking. Finally she spoke. "I guess I haven't been entirely honest with you, either, Jake." Her eyes were focused on me as she spoke. "I heard about the killings. I was amazed when you called me, you know. I had to take a chance; do anything to find out about what really happened to my husband. My father was an FBI agent--killed in the line of duty two years before he would have retired--and he had a favorite saying. 'sometimes you have to dance with the devil to earn a divine dinner.' I think he made it up."

"And so I'm the devil?" I asked.

"I wasn't sure. That's why I wanted to meet you."

"And if I was the devil?"

"Then,"--she reached behind a cookbook on a shelf next to her and produced a stainless-steel revolver which she pointed directly at my sternum--"the dance would be over."

All kinds of crazy thoughts ran through my mind as I looked over the barrel into Pluto's eager puppy eyes. Was this the killer? Had she killed Iris? Baxter? Maybe even Heather and her husband? It didn't seem possible. But if she had, and she killed me next, she'd be able to blame everything on me.

"Margot," I could feel my voice quivering--had to stay calm-- "there's no need for the gun. I'm not the devil." She was too far away to lunge for. Had to talk my way out of it somehow. "If I *was* the killer, why would I be here talking to you at all? Don't you think I'd be as far away from here as possible?"

"Yes," she finally said, "I believe you." She lowered the gun to her lap, and I exhaled a large amount of what a few seconds ago I thought might have been my last breath. "I'm sorry I scared you. I wanted to let you know that I could protect myself. I guess I also wanted to watch your reaction. Wow, you're really sweating! I thought all you private eye types laughed in the face of danger." She curled her lips in a little smile.

"I don't know what's going on, Lady," I said getting up. "I don't have a clue about any of this. All I know is this is twice I've had a gun pointed at me in less than twenty-four hours. Every cop in the state is looking for me and half of them will shoot me on sight. And, if I can't get some answers pretty soon I'm looking at an awful lot of time behind bars. And all because I agreed to help a kid look for his mother. I'm getting real pissed off at this whole thing and everybody involved with it!" I pushed my chair in and turned toward the door. I had made up my mind if I heard the click of the hammer I was jumping head-first through her kitchen window.

"Wait." she yelled. "Don't leave. I'm sorry." She opened the revolver's cylinder and ejected the shells into her hand. Then she put the gun on the table and dropped the shells into her pocket.

"Did your Dad teach you how to handle a gun?"

"Yeah." She was smiling again but I could see that two big tears had streaked down her cheeks. "That was his. It's a Ruger .357, but I think Dad made more parts for it than the Ruger people. Look...I know you've been through a lot. We both have. I couldn't sleep at all last night after I heard the news. I was gonna lay down for a while when I saw the caller ID number flashing. I almost fainted when I found out who it was. I'm sorry about the gun. Really. That wasn't what I was trying to do. How about a drink? A beer?"

"It's 9:30 in the morning," I said.

"So. This is a special circumstance. I could sure use one."

"OK, I'll have a beer. Might as well drink all I can before they put me in the big house." She took two beers from the refrigerator and pried the caps off. It was some kind of micro-brew with pictures of mountains on the bottle. I took a drink. It was heavy, but cold and tasted pretty good.

We drank the beer in silence for a few minutes. I was reflecting, as I assumed she was, about the events of the past day and about our strange meeting.

"You're a little bit of an actress?" I finally asked. "First, the grieving wife, distraught over your husband's disappearance, and then the tough-as-nails FBI agent's daughter ready to blow my brains out."

"Guilty of both," she said with a smile. "And I did study acting a little in college."

"A couple things bother me," I said. "Why did you let me come to your house? What if things had gone bad? Your neighbors would hear that cannon for sure if you shot me. And how would you explain my dead body?"

"You caught me by surprise." She got two more mountain-view beers from the fridge. "You had my number, so I knew you had or could easily get my address. I thought about calling the police and having them here waiting for you, but I had to know what you knew about Bruce. I've been doing a lot of studying on his disappearance, as you call it, and I think the puzzle might be getting a little clearer. I thought you might have a missing piece or two."

As she spoke, I imagined what she would look like fixed up. Pretty good, I was sure. Her eyes, I've always had a thing for eyes, were lush chocolate brown, so dark it was hard to discern where the pupil stopped and the iris began. The light glinted off them in a magical way that reminded me of champagne glasses and a roaring

~ 43 ~

fireplace. I had to get thoughts like that out of my head and get down to the business at hand. After the second beer was gone we decided to return to coffee. She had a little grinder that made short work of some great-smelling beans.

After the coffee maker began to drip, she went to get the information she'd been gathering. She opened a large loose-leaf notebook and laid it on the table in front of me. There was a scent to her now, lilacs, which she didn't have before she went to get the book. I was going to comment on it but thought better.

"You really have been busy," I said as I thumbed through the crowded book. She had neatly labeled index tabs separating the different sections. The first was *IotaTek,* then *Memos, Baxter, South America, Newspapers* and finally, *Bruce and Me.* The last section had been stapled shut so I couldn't open it. I looked at her.

"That's personal stuff," she said. "I made lists of everything I could think about—problems, fights, disappointments, things we'd said to each other. You know, anything that might make him leave the way he did."

Her file was in a three-inch binder, and a good two inches was devoted to IotaTek. There were memos her husband had received and sent, pay stubs, employee notices about benefits and company policies, a copy of a secrecy agreement Bruce had signed, and at the end, in a gentle cursive that I assumed was hers, three pages with the heading *IotaTek History.* Margot filled our coffee cups and then busied herself loading the dishwasher, while I read about the strange company that apparently was shaking a lot of people's worlds, including mine. Interesting reading.

Bennet Scientific was founded in Cambridge in 1982 by a mathematician, Claude Maurais, and a businessman, P. William Bennet. They supplied technical support to small and start-up companies, very successfully. In 1990, they moved to the first two floors of the monolith in Waltham where they employed over a hundred people. Bruce Anderson was hired five years ago as a chemical engineer in their biological division. A year after Bruce was hired, P. William killed himself by driving his Lamborghini off Route 128 at over 150 miles per hour and embedding it into two large trees. Claude, distraught at his partner's death, and after a month in seclusion, decided to semi-retire and promoted Elvin Judkins to CEO. The first couple years under Judkins seemed fine. Salaries went up almost thirty percent. Then, for no apparent reason, Judkins's personality seemed to change. Against the wishes of P. William's widow and Claude Maurais, he changed the company name to IotaTek. They threatened to sue, but much to their and their attorneys' surprise, they learned that Judkins had manipulated himself 52% of the company's stock. They figured he used some friends and completed the transactions so they couldn't be traced. Within a year, Judkins had bought them out completely.

These corporate maneuverings went relatively unnoticed by Bruce Anderson who was engrossed in the fledgling stages of a pharmaceutical company in Brighton. The Brighton job went well. Bruce received a five-thousand dollar bonus for his efforts. Except for Margot's miscarriage, things were looking pretty good. They planned to adopt and there was still a chance a baby of their own would come along. In late November, Bruce went to South America for a week. When he came back, just as Iris had noted, he seemed different, troubled.

Margot finally got him to confide in her. He was unhappy about the South American job. It was a huge pharmaceutical plant planned for *La Paz*, Bolivia. At least that was what Bruce thought. When he got back from his trip, Bruce was re-assigned to a different account. Judkins was handling the South American job himself, with the assistance of Dr. Meacham, the company's chief biochemist.

Bruce had tried to log his computer into the South American job, but his access was denied. He asked Judkins why he was taken off the project and reminded him about his success with the Brighton company and his experience with pharmaceuticals. Judkins told him in no uncertain terms that the CEO alone was in charge of assigning personnel and that he had his own reasons for picking the people for the South American job. And they were confidential.

Margot told her husband they were doing quite well and he should forget about that particular job. And she thought for the most part he had. They had a great Christmas, spent New Year's week in Vail visiting Bruce's sister and learning how to ski. In January, they began the adoption process. In February, they talked about buying a new car and a small boat. And in March, Bruce was gone.

Margot stood by the sink watching me. The dishwasher was gurgling and the lemon scent of the soap made a strange mix with her lilac perfume.

"Are you sure it was the job that was bothering him?" I asked.

"I'm sure. He really put a lot into that Brighton place. He learned so much, and he couldn't believe he was being shut out of the biggest job in the company's history." She started walking towards me and seemed to be staring at something.

"The South American part is empty," I said. I felt her hand on my shoulder. "You don't have any—"

Her fingernails dug into my shoulder. "The police," she whispered. "The police are here."

Chapter 8

"In there." Margot said. "Quickly." She opened a door into a pantry room. I got to my feet and headed to the open doorway but apparently not fast enough for her. She gave me a shove that sent me reeling into a stack of brooms and mops and then slammed the door. Seconds later, she opened the door and almost threw the Ruger at me. It was pitch black in the little pantry closet. I felt my heart pound in my neck. I took a couple deep breaths of musty air. There was a knock at the kitchen door. I was holding an empty revolver and that was a very bad idea.

"Hi, officer." I heard her say. "Is something wrong?"

I felt around and found a shelf with cans on it. As quietly as I could I moved the cans forward and put the revolver behind them.

"Morning, Ma'am." It was a young voice. Probably just out of the police academy. "Nothing's wrong. Are you Mrs. Bruce Anderson?" I didn't hear her response. Maybe she nodded.

An awful thought ran through my head. If she had set me up, I'd be a sitting duck. "The killer's in the closet and he has a gun." I'd be dead and the newbie cop would have some bragging rights or a stress-related trip to early retirement. My whole body seemed to tremble. I tried to get my ear as close to the door as possible.

"Don't want to alarm you, Mrs. Anderson. The captain wanted you to be aware of the situation, just in case. We're looking for this man." There was a faint shuffling of papers. "Do you know him?"

"No," she answered. "Should I?"

"He's a suspect in three shootings last night. One of them a police officer."

"What has that got to do with me?" Margot asked. "I don't know him. Would you like a cup of coffee?"

No! my mind screamed. *Get rid of him.* It was getting hot in that tiny closet. Sweat rolled off my forehead and stung my eyes. I moved my hand slowly to wipe them, but somehow caught one of the long-handled cleaning tools and knocked it into the door. It made a thud. Not much of one probably, but in my temporary prison it sounded like a rifle shot. I held my breath.

"Damn cat." I heard her say. "Snowball, what are you into now?"

I wasn't sure if I should meow but decided against it.

"I know you're busy, Ma'am," the young cop said. "Maybe some other time for coffee." Perhaps he thought the older woman was trying to seduce him. *Mrs. Robinson.* "The captain's a very thorough man. He wanted you to know that this suspect -- Brewster J. Lawless is his name, but he's known as Jake -- has been looking for a Mrs. Baxter, the wife of the officer who was murdered. Captain said that she worked with your husband and that you--"

"She ran away with my husband. The captain didn't tell you that?"

There was an awkward silence and then: "No. He didn't."

"Not very thorough then, is he?" She was good.

"I'm very sorry, Ma'am. I'll just leave this picture with you. I think the creep is long gone, but if you should see him, please dial 9-1-1. He's a psycho and he's armed to the teeth."

"I'm sure you're right," she said. I feel well protected with a man as thorough as your captain in charge." The parting volley.

"Yes, Ma'am. Thank you, Ma'am." I heard him say and then the door shut. I waited in the darkness listening to her move around the kitchen. It was probably only two minutes, but it felt a lot longer before she opened the closet door. She was smiling at me when I emerged.

"You've been a bad kitty, Snowball," she said and then started to laugh. I did too. Not so much because it was funny but as a release for the tension of the past several minutes. "You're soaked," she finally said.

"Yeah. It was like a sauna in there. That was another fine piece of acting."

"That was easy. He was just a baby. You should have seen the look on his face when I told him about my husband."

"Baby or not," I said, "he's still very dangerous. I can't believe that 'armed-to-the-teeth' stuff. And did he call me a creep?"

Silently we watched the spot in the driveway where the cruiser had been parked, lost in our private thoughts about what might have happened. Finally she looked at me. "Are you hungry?" she asked. "Have to keep up your strength, you know."

"Yeah, I am." It seemed like an eternity since I had a McMuffin at Bart's even though it had been less than three hours ago.

"I'll make some bacon and eggs." She said. "Is that OK?"

"I love them, but aren't they supposed to be bad for you?"

"They were. Now they're supposed to be good for you and carbohydrates are supposed to be bad. Did you read *The Zone*?"

"Nope," I said. "The only food stuff I read is menus. Guess I'm not up on modern dietary theories."

"It all has to do with insulin, you know. I don't understand it either, but I read the recipes."

I sat at the table and went back to the IotaTek file. Margot busied herself cooking. We didn't talk. She was humming quietly. A Disney thing, I think. I watched her at the stove. Her hair bounced gently on her shoulders as she moved. I was thinking how lucky Bruce had been. I pictured him sitting at the table reading his paper and her cooking something deliciously healthy on the stove. On the back of her shirt, Pluto's orange butt wiggling happily as she worked. And I looked at her butt, and hers was a lot cuter than Pluto's. I forced my eyes back to the file. Can't be looking at her, I thought. But it was too late. Memories flooded back to the forefront of my brain. Two perfect romances. Two great weddings. Two perfect babies. Two horrendous divorces. I hadn't seen Rob for two years. I'd been putting money away to fly him out this summer. Take him deep-sea fishing and to the Constitution. He really wanted to see "Old Ironsides." A hundred bucks a week in support got me two weeks in the summer, plane fare on me, and every other weekend if I moved to New Mexico or if I could afford to commute. And Amy - I hadn't seen her for almost a year. She probably wouldn't even recognize me. Witch number two had struck gold with the dentist. Dentist's appointments two, three times a week? Are you sure he's filling just your teeth? Dentists can hire much more expensive lawyers than bartenders can. And I was the asshole.

"Are you all right?" Margot asked, as she put a plate in front of me. "You looked like you were a million miles away."

"I guess I was. Thinking about my kids."

"Oh," she said. "For some reason, I didn't think you had kids. No ring, you know."

"No ring. No wives anymore. My son lives in Santa Fe, first marriage. My daughter is three and lives in Alaska with the second biggest mistake of my life and her dentist."

"Sorry, I--"

"It's okay," I said. "My support payments are up to date and I hope to see them both this summer. Right now, the most important thing is to find out what's going on with IotaTek. There's no way either of my exes will bring the kids to visit me in jail."

We ate the bacon and eggs. Delicious. She put the plates in the sink and then sat down to go over the files with me.

"I don't see anything under the *South America* heading," I said.

"I don't have anything to put there. Bruce didn't have any information on that project. He knew it was a pharmaceutical plant, but didn't even know what kind of drug or drugs they were going to make."

"Maybe something illegal?" I asked. "Cocaine or heroin or something? That might be why all the secrecy."

"I don't think so. There were some really big American companies involved in the financing. I'm not sure which ones. That was a secret, too, but I don't think they would be putting up huge money for illegal drugs."

"Then why the big secret?" I asked. I knew she couldn't answer. She just looked at me, shaking her head. "And this is everything he had?"

"Yes. Everything I could find. They brought me the things from his desk. Everything to do with the company is in the file."

"How about a computer? You must have a computer?"

"He had one at work. He did have an old laptop that he played solitaire and kept the checkbook on. I don't even know how to turn it on."

"Can you get it? Just in case."

"OK. I'll be right back." She got up and left the kitchen.

The laptop was a long shot, but it was all I could think of. She was back in a couple of minutes with a beat-up leather case. She opened it and took a gray plastic laptop from it and handed it to me. I got it open and hit the power button. Nothing.

"I think the battery's dead," I said. "Is there an adapter?"

"I'll check," she said, and dug her hands into the leather bag. "He hasn't used it for a long time." She found a power adapter at the bottom of the case and I plugged it in. This time when I pressed the power button green lights flashed and the screen flickered to life. It did all the things computers do when they turn on and rewarded us, finally, with a green marbled screen with icons at the top and bottom. I didn't know a lot about computers either but I had bought one a year ago for my private-eye business. Bart had promised to hook me up to the Internet, but I was still waiting.

She was watching me intently, maybe amazed that I could get it running. There was a little icon at the bottom of the page named *program manager* that I wanted to click on but there was no mouse. I remembered my first experience with the plastic rodent and how much trouble it gave me to learn it. Bart roared, watching me until I finally got pissed and made him show me how to use it.

But now there was none. The pointer was in the middle of the page, but I couldn't move it. I tried the *up* and *down* arrows, but nothing. Margot leaned over me. "How about this thing?" She put her finger on a small black half ball next to the space bar. She gave it a little push and the cursor moved.

"I was just gonna do that," I said.

"You men are just so smart when it comes to hi-tech things."

I had no snappy comeback so I ignored her remark. But I couldn't ignore that her breast was resting on my shoulder. I tried to focus all my concentration on the computer moving the cursor and clicking on different programs (I found the clicker without any help). I found the games program and several files with exotic x-dash-something names that I was able to open but had no clue what they were. She didn't move as I explored the laptop's innards. It felt awkward with her so close. I had the odd desire to shift my position and make her move, but it was tempered by the fear that she would. We stayed like that for quite a while. I was about ready to call it quits when I came upon a file name which looked like it might be something:

CALIUBA-SA.

"Look at this one," I said. "SA. Maybe South America." I clicked and it opened. The first page looked like it was copied from a chemistry text. I read it but it was mostly techno-babble that I didn't understand. I did pick out a few things like *leaves, rain forest* and *carcinoma.* At the bottom of the page was a diagram made of several hexagons hooked together and connected at one end to a home-plate shaped structure. There were *C*s and *H*s and *O*s and a couple other letters attached to the thing with little lines. The diagram was labeled *Cali-Plus,* and then a Chemical Name: 8 Chloro something 16.25 methyl something else, blah, blah, blah. There were a couple symbols that looked like a capitol B with a tail (β).

"This mean anything to you?" I asked.

"No. Not really. He never mentioned...what is it, Cali-Plus. Seems strange."

"How about the picture?"

"It's some kind of organic substance," she said. "What, I don't know."

I moved down to the next page. There was a date at the top.

"That was a week before he disappeared," she said.

Under the date was an address: *Rua Sào Clemente 154, Minas Gerais, Brazil, SA.* Below the address was a list of a dozen names with Judkins at the top. There were two others I recognized - Trudy James and Syd Baxter both late and both supposedly killed by me.

"That second name," she said, "Bernard Meacham. He's...was Bruce's boss. A real egghead. Several degrees in biochemistry and stuff. Bruce used to call him Dr. Dork. They really had a battle about the South American project. It looks like Bruce knew more than he told me."

"You said this was just before he disappeared," I said. "Maybe he just found out, or didn't want to alarm you." She nodded. "Have you met this Meacham guy?"

"We went to a party at his place. He's about sixty. Odd duck. Lives in a fancy, older house in Wellesley. His wife is about thirty years younger than he is. Doris, I think, or Doreen. Something with a D. Maybe Dolly. She was built like a Dolly." She laughed.

"Was she one of his students?"

"I don't think she could *spell* chemistry."

"Doesn't sound like you like her very much."

"I didn't care much for either one of them. I behaved at the party because it was important to Bruce, but I would have loved to have thrown a glass of wine into Dr. Dork's face. He's a real cretin. With a capitol K, you know."

"I might be wrong, but this looks like a short list of people involved in the South American Project. When I met Trudy, she never mentioned it. Of course she was killed before she could tell me too much. Meacham--Dr. Dork as you call him--is listed right after Judkins. Second in command, maybe, and maybe he has some answers. I think we should talk to him."

"I'll call him and try to set up a meeting," she said. I nodded, and she picked up the phone and dialed. I could tell by the conversation that he wasn't available. She said she'd get in touch with him later and hung up. "He's not in today. I may have his home number if I didn't throw out the party invitation." She left the kitchen but was back in about five minutes with a lavender envelope. "Bruce always said I was a pack rat. Sometimes saving everything comes in handy, you know."

Margot dialed the number, listened for a few moments and then slammed the receiver down without saying anything into it. He's home," she said. "Started yelling into the phone as soon as he answered. Maybe we should surprise him with a visit."

~ 53 ~

That plan sounded good to me. It was just about noontime. Margot drove her car into the garage and I got into the back seat and crouched down. I was getting sick of lying on the back floor of cars, but it was bright daylight and all the cops in the world were looking for me. It took a little over twenty minutes to get to Dr. Dork's place in Wellesley. Margot had a lead foot and a couple times during the journey I urged her to slow down. I didn't want to lose everything over a crummy speeding ticket.

"We're there," she said. "I don't see anyone around. I think it's safe for you to come up."

"Fancy neighborhood," I said. She parked on a small lane to the side of Meacham's house. It was a two and a half story Victorian, mostly brick with vines crawling on it. It sat back off the road about 300 feet. There was a detached three-car garage with an ornate roof designed to look like the house. The lot was verdant with expensive looking plants and bushes and a lawn that wasn't maintained by the home owner.

"Let's go talk to the cretin," Margot said.

"I think it would be better if I went alone."

"Look, I have a score to settle with that moron. You don't think I can take care of myself." She had that pouty look that women get when they think men are putting down their abilities because of their sex.

"I'm sure you can handle yourself just fine, but he knows you and he doesn't know me. At least he doesn't know that we're together. I might get a little tough with him and if he reports me to the cops, it will be better to leave your name out of it."

She thought this over for a few moments and then said, "You're right, I guess. Here." She handed me a pistol. "In case he gives you a hard time, threaten him with this." It was a small 9mm Beretta. "Click the safety off and it's ready to go."

"How many guns do you have?" I asked, taking the Beretta from her. She ignored my question. "I'll take it with me but I don't want to use it. So far I haven't hurt anybody and I don't want to give the cops a *real* reason to be looking for me."

"If Meacham had anything to do with Bruce's disappearance, I'll come back and hurt him myself," she said. "Meanwhile, if you have to, I think it would be OK to inflict a little pain on the son of a bitch."

"Nice language," I said. "And with Pluto right there listening." I dropped the gun into my pocket. The Beretta was very similar to my own gun, a Walther PPK, that I was sure was in the property room at the New Stratley PD, along with who-knew-what-else of my belongings.

Chapter 9

I walked quickly to the front of Meacham's house. Two huge oak doors that probably cost more than my condo boasted of the home-owner's wealth. I rang the bell and waited. Shortly one of the giant doors was flung open and a man, I assumed to be Meacham, stood looking at me.

"You're thirty minutes late!" he snapped. "And where are the trucks?" He glanced past me towards the street.

"Are you Mr. Meacham?" I asked.

"It's Doctor. Doctor Meacham. Now where are the trucks?"

"I don't know what you're talking about," I said.

"Aren't you from Global? From the moving company?"

"No, I'm not," I answered. "I'd just like to ask you a couple quick questions."

"I don't have time now."

His intention was to slam the big door in my face. I put my foot inside and stopped it from closing. He cursed under his breath and opened it again, apparently to take a heartier shot at my foot. Before he had a chance, I pushed against the hard oak and forced my way into his hallway.

"Get out of here," he screamed. "Who are you? I'm calling the police." He turned and picked up a phone that was resting on a packing box.

I grabbed the phone from his hand and yanked the wire from the wall like they do in the movies. "You're not calling anybody," I said in my best tough-guy voice. "I have a couple questions and I think you have the answers."

"I'm not answering anything. I'm going to sue you for every penny you have."

It was an emptier threat than he could have imagined. He was a slender man, about my height. He was nearly bald but had combed a few remaining strands across the top and it gave his head the appearance of a dappled egg hiding under a couple pieces of straw. He glared at me with beady, close-set eyes reminding me of the huge river rats that skulked on the banks of the Charles and had caused me several childhood nightmares.

He stormed off into a room to the right of the entrance and I followed him. The house was like the doors, huge and expensive looking. Almost everything seemed to be packed in moving boxes that were everywhere. Everything but the tools that went with the giant white brick fireplace. Meacham chose a gold poker from the assortment. Brandishing it over his head he came after me. I might have been able to take it away from him. And then again he might have got in a lucky shot. Anyway, he had escalated it so I slipped the Beretta from my pocket and pointed it right between his beady eyes.

"Drop it," I yelled, and he did.

"Wh...who are you? What do you want?"

"I'm Jake Lawless," I said.

"Ah...the killer," he mumbled, his eyes widening with recognition.

"I'm not a killer," I said. "Not yet anyway. But I want some answers. Now."

"You're crazy. I have no idea what you're talking about."

"I'm talking about Heather Baxter, Dr. Dork." I couldn't resist using Margot's epithet. I enjoyed the mortified look that flashed across his eyes. "And I'm talking about Bruce Anderson and Trudy James." I hesitated, watching his expression change.

"And I'm talking about *Cali-plus.*" He shook his head in apparent denial, so I continued. "Did you know Bruce had an old laptop? Well he did, and he put some pretty interesting stuff in it. All about South America and *Cali-Plus* ...and *you.*"

"Bastard," he spat. "I don't know anything. I'm a chemist."

"You know plenty. You should read what Anderson wrote about you." I was lying. Only his name was in the file. That, and the fact that Margot hated him was good enough for me, though. I pushed the gun closer to his face. "Start talking!"

He wasn't talking. I pushed the gun even closer. For no apparent reason, his terrified look was replaced by a sinister grin. What was the matter with him? Was he going crazy? Too late I realized he was looking behind me. Before I could turn, something very hard hit me in the back of the head. His rat smile seemed to explode in a burst of white fireworks. And then, blackness.

***

I was standing by the river. Something was very strange. I couldn't see the opposite shore, like the ocean, and yet somehow I knew it was the Charles. I was holding three strings, fishing line actually that ran to my boat. My boat. Favorite toy of my childhood. But my boat was long gone, buried in a horrible landfill somewhere. And yet there it was. I had to be dead and in Heaven. But my head hurt and there was no pain in Heaven, was there? I couldn't afford a radio control so I used the strings; one to make it turn right and one to make it turn left. To starboard and port. Had to remember that. If I pulled the third string the small engine would shut off and I could haul it back to shore and start again. The Apollo, named after the Moon rocket, was sailing fine, turning sharply with the flick of my wrist. It was great. Something was swimming next to the boat, breaking the surface of the water gracefully and then submerging, like a small dolphin, only to surface again after a few feet. It wasn't a dolphin though. It was covered with slick black hair. What was it? Whatever it was it suddenly raised a hideous head from the water and bit into the Apollo's control lines. One chomp with two razor sharp teeth that I could swear gleamed like steel and the fishing line went

~ 58 ~

limp in my hands. I pulled furiously but there was nothing there. The boat was chugging away to the other shore, the shore I couldn't see. Gone forever. Again.

I was crying and screaming at the creature. Through blurry eyes, I saw it turn and head towards me. "Come on, you son of a bitch," I yelled, hoping my mother didn't hear me. It was swimming fast. I found a good size stick and hefted it. Perfect to crush the thing's ugly skull.

It swam faster and faster as it approached the shore. I was waiting. Then behind it. I saw two breaks in the water. Two more swimming creatures. A family of river rats. I'd kill them all. And then more and still more splashes as an army of the things thrashed through the water. There were too many to count. In seconds, they had turned the calm waters of the Charles into a roiling mass of white foam and black fur. The leader, the string cutter, clawed its way up the bank and charged me.

I raised the stick above my head and just before it reached me, I swung down with all my might. I looked at the creature just before impact and couldn't believe what I saw. It didn't have a rat face. It had a human face. Almost human anyway. It had Dr. Meacham's face. It caught my stick with its stainless-steel teeth and snapped it in half. I turned and started to run. I heard it chasing after me, the gnashing of its metallic teeth and the scratching of its paws on the dirt. Soon the creature was joined by its friends. Hundreds maybe thousands of them were chasing me. I held my hands over my ears to keep out the sound. They were right on my heels, so close I could smell their rancid breath. It was a foul smell that reminded me of rotten fish mixed with the outhouse at the old picnic grounds.

I turned to look at them. They stretched as far as I could see, a legion of Meacham faced rats, their eyes glowing in anticipation. I turned forward again, and there, dead ahead, was an old rotten stump. I tried to jump over it but it caught my foot and I began falling. They had me. I waited for the impact of the ground but it never came. I just kept falling... and falling...and then.. . blackness.

And then voices.

Chapter 10

"Soooooo whaaaaaaattttt wiiiilllllll," the voice droned. I couldn't tell if it was a man or a woman. Or if it was even human. It was like playing a 45 record on 33 speed. I had to concentrate. Keep my eyes closed and concentrate, try to hear the voices in real time.

My head hurt like hell, a throbbing hurt like a whole-head toothache. Things were coming back to me. I remembered talking to Meacham and I remembered the whack on the squash. That was a good thing, I thought, that I could remember things. The voices were clearer now, a man's and a woman's.

I heard a man's voice. "...coming too?"

That was followed by a woman's voice. "No. He's out like a light. I think you should kill him, Meach. He knows way too much."

Meach replied, "I'm not going to kill him. I've never killed anybody. I'm a chemist!"

Good boy, Meacham, I thought, Maybe you're not all that bad after all.

Meacham said, "I'll call Judkins. He'll send Luther over to kill him."

Then again, maybe you are.

The woman said, "Sometimes I think your balls are filled with cotton."

"Don't give me that," said Meacham. "In two weeks you'll be sunning yourself on the beach at Rio with more money than you could ever spend, and it's all thanks to me. Nobody could have engineered Cali-plus like I did. Ah, shit. The movers are here."

The woman asked, "Do you want *me* to shoot him?"

"Of course not. The movers will hear and there'll be blood everywhere. Maybe Judd will bring him down to Brazil like the other two. I'll call him and find out what to do. Give the movers twenty bucks for lunch and tell them to come back in an hour."

"What if they want to know why?"

He scoffed at that. "They're movers, for God's sake. They don't need to know why."

I heard her footsteps and the sound of the door opening, and her muffled voice talking to the men. I heard Meacham swearing about the damage I'd done to the phone chord. I wanted to try to get up, but I didn't know if I could. If they knew I was awake, they'd surely bop me again. His heavy footsteps thumped by me into another room. I opened my eyes. Bright sunlight streamed in through a huge picture window and magnified the pain in my head. I closed my eyes as I heard them both come back.

"Judd says to bash him a couple times more. He's sending Luther over. Be here in about twenty minutes."

"I suppose I have to do it," the woman said. "What's Luther going to do with him?"

"Throw him into the ocean. Luther knows a good spot where he'll wash up in a day or two."

It was time to give it a go. I opened my eyes and tried to get a location on them.

"He's awake!" Meacham squeaked. "Hit him."

I spun on my back trying to bring her into view so I could at least kick at her.

She was laughing. "Look at him," she said. "Just like an upside down turtle."

I spun around as fast as I could, kicking wildly, but I didn't connect with anything except a packing box. My gyrations were apparently making her laugh more heartily. I had to keep her away from me or else I'd be fish food within the hour. She kicked my side. The pain lanced through me and made me forget about my head for a moment.

"Stop squirming, you bastard," she said.

And then there was a tremendous *kee-rash*. I grabbed my head feeling for the injury, but it wasn't me that was injured. I heard a different woman's voice.

"Drop it, Dolly!" It was Margot. She had heaved a cement block through one of the side windows next to the picture window and was pointing her immense looking Ruger at Meacham's wife. The bat dropped harmlessly on the floor next to me. What ever did Meacham and Dolly do with an aluminum baseball bat?

"My name's not Dolly," Mrs. Meacham spat. From the corner of my eye, I saw Dr. Dork pull the pistol from his pocket. Margot saw it, too, and fired a round into the fireplace next to where the good doctor stood. The bang was deafening and echoed from every corner of the huge room. What was left of a couple white bricks crumbled to the floor. The smells of cordite and masonry filled the room. And something else. The disgusting aroma of human excrement wafted its way up from Meacham who had dropped the pistol and fallen into a fetal position when the slug exploded into the fireplace. Dolly, or whatever her name was, looked at the pistol but decided against it. I picked it up and pointed it at her.

"Don't move," I said.

I walked to the hall, keeping the gun trained on her and unlocked the door for Margot. "I didn't know what was going on," Margot said. "Two moving trucks came and went, and I figured I'd better have a look. When I saw her standing over you with the bat...."

"You did great," I said. I told her about Luther and about what I had heard Mr. and Mrs. Dork talking about while they thought I was unconscious. Margot walked over to the prone figure sobbing on the floor.

"Where's my husband, Meacham?" Margot shouted at him and then crinkled her nose. "Ugh. What's that smell?"

"I think he had an accident," I said and then looked at his wife. "Do you have to change him often?" She responded with a string of profanity that almost made me blush. Margot wasn't impressed either.

"Shut up, you bitch," she said and hit Dolly on the cheek with the barrel of the Ruger. It was a glancing blow, meant more to frighten than injure, but she fell screaming to the floor, holding her face as if mortally wounded. "What should we do?" Margot asked me.

"I think you should go home. I'll call the police and stay with these two and hope the cops get here before that Luther fellow."

"Do you think the cops will believe you? Or do you think they'll just add armed home invasion to your list of crimes?" I liked the way she said "armed home invasion." Spoken like the true daughter of an FBI agent. "I have to find out what happened to Bruce." She turned her attention to Meacham, who was still curled up on the floor but had stopped sobbing. "Okay, Dr. Shitty-pants, start talking."

"Don't hurt me. Don't hurt me. I'm just a chemist."

Margot pushed him onto his back. "I swear if you don't tell me what happened to my husband you'll be a dead chemist."

"Nothing happened to him. He ran away with that secretary."

"That's bullshit," Margot said. "You're just about out of time, now tell me the truth."

"I'm just a...chemist," he mumbled.

She fired the Ruger into the floor six inches from his head and then held the smoking barrel against his jaw. "Tell me," she screamed.

"My ears!" he screeched. Then: "He...He's all...right." He shook so badly, he could hardly talk. "He's in--Brazil...both of—"

"Shut up, idiot," Dolly said. I pointed the pistol at her, a stern warning to be quiet.

"Both of them are...in Brazil. Judd brought them...there...to the plant. They found...out too much....would have ruined everything. Please...don't hurt me."

Margot stood over him just staring. "Alive," she said. "He's alive?"

Before the Doctor could say more, there was a noise from outside, a car pulling into the driveway. We probably wouldn't have heard it if Margot hadn't opened the window with a brick. I looked out. It was a huge black station wagon like funeral parlors have. The windows were darkened, I was sure beyond the legal limit. But who would bother with a hearse. A tall man with a dark suit got out of the driver's side.

"This must be Luther," I said.

"What are we gonna do?" Margot asked.

"There are two of them, at least," I said. "I can't see if there are any more in the car. Can you hit a tire with that thing?"

"It's pretty far, but I'll give it a try."

The men were about ten feet from the car walking slowly towards the house. Margot knelt down at the broken window, aimed and fired. The blast of the Ruger sent the two men running for cover behind their car which was slowly sinking on its punctured front tire. The men pulled weapons and were looking around frantically for the source of the shot.

"Nice shooting!" I said. "You should've seen your pals scurry, Meacham. That was loud. The neighbors must have heard that one for sure." He was lying on the floor with his hands over his head. I walked over to Margot who was watching Luther and his buddy.

"I really think you should go home," I whispered to her. "I'll try to square things up with the cops when they get here."

"You really think they'll believe you?"

"Yeah. After they talk to these two, and the goons out there." I pointed at the black station wagon. As if on cue, the men jumped into the car through the driver's side and backed down the driveway. The car pulled into the street and ka-thumped away on its three good tires.

"They're not gonna hang around and talk to the cops," Margot said. "But they won't be far. These two will tell a totally different story to the police. Remember, down at police headquarters, they can't use our methods to get answers."

"I know. I don't want you to get any more involved, that's all."

"I am involved. Hell, I have been since Bruce disappeared. This is the first chance I've had to *really* do something."

"Isn't that touching," Dolly hissed. "Boo, hoo, hoo. Go home to your lonely life and leave us alone!"

Margot covered the ten feet in what seemed like a fraction of a second. She raked the barrel of the revolver across Dolly's face a lot harder than she did the first time.

"Okay," Margot said. "We can't stay here. Let's take these insects to a safer place where we can get some answers." With the Ruger in her right hand, she grabbed Dolly under the arm with her left and jerked her to her feet. "Grab him," she said to me.

Margot was in command.

"We better go out the back," I said. "I don't hear any sirens so I'm sure Luther will be back soon." I pulled Meacham to his feet. He was mumbling that he wasn't going anywhere. "Let's go."

I pushed him toward a door that headed away from the street. There was a short hall with an empty room, probably once an office on the right and two large empty closets on the left. Every couple feet, he'd try to stop and I'd have to give him a little shove. We came into an immense kitchen. Light streamed in through two skylights and a slider that looked out over the back yard.

"This is kidnapping," Dolly said. "I'll make sure you rot in prison."

Thwack. Margot biffed her again with the pistol.

"Shut up, I told you. There's certainly nothing wrong with taking a couple old friends out for a little drive, is there?"

Dolly moaned quietly. Apparently she'd finally gotten the message about not talking. I unlocked the slider and stepped carefully out onto the deck. Everything was eerily quiet. Still no sirens. No ka-thump of Luther's car. Not even a neighbor's lawnmower. The backyard stretched a good football field to a stand of trees that obscured any other houses. Small wonder nobody heard the shots.

"Why would you leave a spread like this?" I asked Meacham. "Rio must be some kinda place."

He turned and looked at me, a look of surprise and anger. Then he tripped over his feet. I had a good grasp on him, though, and held him up. We went across the yard as quickly as we could with the Meachams in tow. Once we got beyond the cover of the house, I could see the street. There was a brick mansion across the way, but it had bushes and trees all around it and it was unlikely that the residents could see us. Or that they would care about us if they did.

Then I heard it. The ka-thump was gone. The sound of the huge motor idling along had to mean only one thing. Luther had changed the tire and had returned.

"Hurry up," I yelled quietly, and pushed Meacham ahead. He had to run to keep up with me or he'd fall. We got to a group of lilac bushes just as the black station wagon cruised slowly by.

"Did they see us?" Margot gasped.

"I don't think so. Sounds like they're turning around. Let's get through these bushes." The lilac hedge was pretty thick and we all got scratched up a little, but we finally broke through to the little lane where Margot's car was parked. I couldn't see it, but I heard the station wagon pull into Meacham's driveway.

"Let's put them in the back seat," I said.

"He's not riding in my car smelling like that," Margot said, as she unlocked the trunk.

"Get in," I said. Meacham protested, but I pushed him and he fell into the trunk.

"I'm not going in there," Dolly said. "I'm catastrophic, I'll die."

"Your husband's a doctor. He'll save you," Margot said and shoved her with the butt of the pistol.

"Heeeellllp!" Dolly screamed louder than I thought a woman could.

"In," Margot said and crammed her into the trunk. Margot slammed the lid down and ran to unlock the car. I heard voices and footsteps running.

"Shit," I said. "They heard her." I jumped into the front seat and we were off before I could shut the door. I looked back just in time to see Luther crash through the lilacs.

"Catastrophic?" I said.

***

"Turn there," I said, pointing to the left. Margot spun the wheel and we hurtled around the corner. The tires screeched in protest. "Better take it easy, Margot. I think we have a good enough head start on them. Don't want to attract the cops." I had her make several rights and then another left.

She eased off the gas. "I'm not sure where we are. Those turns you had me make have got me discombobulated."

"Nice word," I said.

She smiled. "My Dad used to say it all the time." We came to a stop at an intersection. Cross Street and Walnut Avenue, the signs proclaimed. Which way?"

"Straight ahead, maybe," I said. "Think we're still in Wellesley and—" I was cut off by a tremendous wailing from the trunk. Apparently the doctor and his missus had sensed the car stop and were trying to get some attention. They sounded like two cats in a trash can with their tails tied together.

Margot turned right onto Walnut and then gunned it up to about thirty. 'Hang on," she said, and then jammed on the brakes. When she returned to normal speed there was no more noise from the captives. They were quick learners.

"We have to get them out of the trunk pretty soon," I said. "We don't want to kill them." I noticed a little smirk on Margot's face. "You seem to almost enjoy torturing them." That was the wrong thing to say. She pulled over to the curb, buried her head in her hands and started sobbing. "I'm sorry...really. I didn't mean it like that."

My apology did nothing to ease her sobbing. It was not a good place to be and it got worse quickly. A police cruiser drove by the other way and I saw the officer looking at us. "Wellesley Police" and "Dial 9-1-1" were painted on the side. "Shit! Margot," I said. "We gotta get out of here. The cops just went by." I looked through the back window and saw the cruiser turning. It was over now. His blue lights were on. He had us.

"Hide your face!" Margot said. I looked at her tear-streaked cheeks and then buried my head in my hands. I heard the cruiser door shut and the unintelligible noise of the two-way radio.

Margot rolled down her window.

"Are you all right, Ma'am?" the officer asked. It seemed like his stare was burning into my neck.

"No...I'm not," Margot stammered.

Bad answer, I thought. *Never tell them you're not all right.*

"What's the problem, Ma'am?"

There was an awkward silence and then she said, "It...it's my husband...Chad," she put her hand on my shoulder.

Chad?

"He...he...has a terrible tumor...pancreas..." and then she started to cry again.

Pancreas?

"Doctors...said," - she coughed- "two to...six months. What am I gonna tell the kids? Are you arresting us now, too?"

Kids?

"No, Ma'am. Just making sure you're all right. If you don't think you can drive I'll get you a ride."

"I...I'm...I'll be fine. I have a lot of driving to do now that Chad is...."

"You just rest here until you feel a little better. I know this is a bad time for you but your inspection sticker is expired. I'm just giving you a verbal warning, but try and get it taken care of."

"I will...thank you, sir." Margot said. "Chad always took care of that stuff before...."

I heard his boots scuff as he started to walk back to his cruiser. And then I heard Dolly, ever-resourceful Dolly, moaning from the trunk.

"What's that?" the cop asked. "It sounds like a woman."

"My cat," Margot said. No hesitation, no *ers* or *ahs*. She was good. "Poor Chad's cat actually...Snowball."

"Doesn't sound like a cat to me," the cop said. I really wanted to look at the expression on his face, but figured I'd better keep my head in my hands.

"She's hurt," Margot said. "Bad...Real bad...I ran her over with the car."

"Doesn't sound like a cat to me Ma'am. Maybe I'd better have a look. Would you mind opening the trunk?"

"No, in fact, maybe you can help me." She pulled the lever on her door.

"What?" the cop asked.

Can't open the trunk. We're busted for sure.

She slid out of the car keys in hand. "Maybe you can help me get Snowball in the back seat. She was a real mess, and she's a heavy cat. Chad was...too upset to help me. I had all I could do to get her in the trunk."

"Ma'am, I'd really like to help but...I just heard a call coming in on the radio."

"Please," Margot pleaded. "If you could just hold her intestines while I lift her?"

Enough already, Margot.

"Don't move her, Ma'am. Get that cat right to the vet's. They have cat stretchers and stuff." I heard him shuffling away as he was speaking.

Margot got back in and started the engine. "Nice going," I said. I watched her eyes looking in the rearview mirror as she pulled away.

When the cop car was out of sight, she jammed on the brakes. "Just a little tune-up," she said.

Chapter 11

Margot pulled the Toyota into her driveway and punched the garage door opener. She drove in until she just touched a plastic trash can and then pushed the down button. The lights had come on automatically. She and I got out and went to the trunk. Doctor and Dolly seemed no worse for the wear. They were both breathing anyway, and their eyes were wide open.

"I'm gonna see if I can find him some clothes." Margot said, pointing at the doctor. "Be right back." She went into the house and the lock clicked behind her.

"You can't expect to get away with this," Meacham said.

"What are you going to do? Tell the cops?" I asked. "How will you explain Luther to them. Do you really want to go over this *Cali-Plus* business with the boys in blue?"

He thought this over for a minute. "If you want money," he said, "I can get you plenty. Just let us go. You'll be a very rich man."

"Yeah. You'll have Luther deliver it and then take it back just before he throws us in the ocean. There's only one thing I want from you, and that's information. I heard you say some things while you thought I was knocked out. Something like 'bring them to Brazil, like the others.' Are the 'others' Heather Baxter and Bruce Anderson?"

He looked pensive, as if weighing different options and then blurted out, "yes!"

Dolly looked at him as if she couldn't believe what he was saying. She tried to kick at him, but I pushed her away.

"Mmmmmmmmmppphhhhrt," she said.

"I didn't have any part in it," Meacham continued. "I'm just a chemist. I just did some...well...lab things. Judkins took them to Brazil." Margot entered the garage and listened as he went on. "They found out about our plans and Judd...he...he had them taken away. They'll be released as soon as everything is over."

"He's all right?" Margot asked.

"Of course...we're not murderers."

"What about Luther?" I asked. "You were about to have him feed me to the fish. And what about Tommy Baxter's dad, the cop, and Trudy James? Who killed them and framed me?" My voice must have been rising. Margot put her hand on my arm apparently worried I was going to punch him. And punching him was a pleasant thought.

"Go on," Margot said. "Where are they?"

"They're at the plant in *Minas-Gerais*. They're fine."

"Somehow I don't believe you," I said. "You haven't explained the New Stratley murders yet."

"I don't know everything Judd does...I'm just a chemist...technical things. I told him I'd be no part of anyone getting hurt."

"Sure you did," Margot said, and I could detect the scorn in her voice. "Here. Clean up and put these on." She handed him a wet and a dry towel and some beat-up one-size-fits-all sweat pants.

"Could I have some privacy?" Meacham asked.

"Sure," Margot said. "Like I'd want to see that. Ugh. I'll take Dolly here into the house. You can change in that corner behind the garbage can. Put your pants and the towel in this bag." She handed him a green trash bag.

"No funny stuff," I said. "I'd love to use you for target practice."

I turned to Margot. "Well, whatcha think?"

"I think we're going to Brazil," she said.

***

Meacham went quietly about the business of cleaning himself up and changing his pants. I didn't want to watch the disgusting spectacle either, but I had to keep him in view from the corner of my eye. My brain was racing at the implications of Margot's last statement. Brazil! Surely she was kidding. How could we get to Brazil? I was wanted for a double homicide, one of which was a cop, albeit a bad cop who had probably needed killing. I didn't dare go to the store for a six-pack, never mind half way across the world... Although the six pack seemed like a good idea.

Meacham brought me out of my thoughts.

"What about underpants?"

"This isn't a department store, Meacham," I said. "You're lucky to get clean pants at all. Now hurry it up." He was mumbling under his breath, something not very nice I was sure.

Finally, he finished and stood with the green trash bag in one hand and his wallet and a ring of keys in the other. "Put the wallet and keys on the hood of the car and tie up that trash bag." He did as he was told. A couple times he looked at me, maybe wondering if he should give it a go, but then looked away.

The door opened a crack. "Is he done?" Margot asked.

"Yeah," I said. "What did you do with Dolly?"

"Her name's not Dolly," Meacham snapped before Margot could answer. "It's Delphine. From the Greek. It means 'calmness'."

Margot and I both started laughing.

"That sure doesn't fit her," I finally said. "She'll always be Dolly to me."

A look that I can only describe as sheer exasperation contorted his face which only made us laugh harder.

When she regained her composure, Margot said, "Whoever she is, she's locked in the bathroom. He can go in there with her while we think of what to do. Let's go, doctor."

He went to grab his wallet and I pushed him away from the car towards the door. "Hah," he said. "Now you're adding grand larceny to your crimes."

"Just move it," I said and pushed him again." He stumbled up the two steps into the kitchen and almost fell. Margot took his arm and steadied him. She led him to the bathroom, undid a barrel bolt near the top of the door and then shoved him inside. His wife was waiting for him and they immediately began sniping at each other.

Margot rapped sharply on the door. "Keep it down, you two, or we'll put you back in the trunk."

"Will they be all right in there?" I asked. "No way they can escape?"

"Nope," she said. No windows. Nothing in the medicine chest or under the sink. They'll be okay, if they don't strangle each other."

We went into the kitchen and sat at the table. Battle still raged in the bathroom, but the combatants fought quietly. Margot looked at the clock on the wall. "I have to tell my mother and sister I'm leaving for awhile and throw a few things together. That should take maybe an hour, then—"

"Hold on a minute," I interrupted her. "You're not serious about going to Brazil, are you. It's crazy. We'll never get out of—"

"It may be crazy, but it's the only thing we can do. You saw Dork's house. He was packed and ready to go. I'll bet Judkins's house is the same. Don't you see, this is almost over. They'll both be gone. It will be over...everything will be over."

"Meacham said they planned to release them after they—"

"Damn it!" she said and stood up. Her eyes blazed into mine. "I gave you credit for more brains than that. Why would they keep them alive? To come back and explain the whole thing to everybody? I don't think so." She sat down. "I'm quite sure...that...they're both already...dead." A tear trickled from each of her eyes.

"What if we turn those two over to the police?" I asked.

"We can't prove anything. It's our word against theirs and our word, especially yours, doesn't mean shit right now."

"You really know how to make a guy feel good," I said.

"Well, it's true. I think the answers to everything are in South America. And, if there's the slightest chance that Bruce is alive, it won't be for much longer. Do you know where the doctor was moving to?"

~ 73 ~

"While they thought I was knocked out, I heard him say something to her about sunning herself on...someplace...Rio, I think.

"That's what I thought," she said. "I read the label on one of their packing crates, to New York and then Rio. And that's in Brazil."

"You know, you should be a detective."

She smiled. "Like I said, my Dad was FBI and some of it rubbed off.

"What about your family? What if something happens to you. These people are obviously into something pretty heavy. You might not come back."

"My Dad lived with danger his whole life. He always talked to me about the possibility that some day he might not come home. He told me it was very important...his job... and that if he didn't do it, some other little girl's dad would have had to do it. And, he said...I was...braver than the other little girls. So I guess it runs in the family. I owe it to Bruce . . .to find out if he's alive and get him back. And if he's not alive...to find out why."

She got up and walked to the refrigerator and pulled it open. "Only one beer left. Wanna split it?"

"Yeah, sure," I said. I watched her open the beer and pour half into a glass. She handed me the glass and took a drink from the bottle. "What you say makes sense in a kind of wacky way. But how the hell are we gonna get to Brazil?"

"I've been thinking about that," she said as she sat down. There was a hint of excitement in her voice. "I have Bruce's passport and his international driver's license. You look a little like him. If you let your beard grow and I dye your hair blonde...I think you could get by."

"I can't grow a beard overnight," I said.

"You won't have to." She ran her fingers across my cheek. "It's been a couple days now right. It'll be fine."

"What about customs? I've only been out of the country once, and that was to Germany when I was in the service."

"Well then, it's about time you did a little traveling."

"What about them?" I said pointing at the bathroom.

~ 74 ~

"I figured we'd drop them off somewhere along the way. Keep them busy for a little while. My dad's best friend at the Bureau, Charlie Hamilton, is my godfather. Dad saved his life once. He said if I ever needed anything to come see him." She emptied the beer bottle. "He's retired and lives in Louisiana. If we drive down there ...to his house, I'm sure he can figure a way to get us to Brazil."

"Do you think we could get Charlie to go?" I asked. "Retired FBI. He might have better luck than us."

"He can't. He's in a wheelchair. Dad saved his life...but he couldn't save his legs." There was an awkward silence between us as we each thought about this impossible sounding mission.

Finally I said, "Time's wasting. We better get on with it."

"Great." she said and got up and hugged my head. "I knew you'd help me. I'm going over to Mom's. I'll get as much as I can from the ATM and we should be on the way in less than two hours."

"While you're doing that, I'll have a chat with the doc. See if I can get some more information from him about where this place is that we're going."

"Good idea." She grabbed her purse from the counter and went into the garage. I heard the Toyota come to life and the garage door rumble open. But she didn't drive out. A minute later she opened the door and tossed me Meacham's wallet. "Why don't you see if the doctor has anything to contribute to our trip." And then she was gone.

I brought Meacham into the kitchen at gunpoint and sat him at the table. I advised him that there weren't too many things I'd rather do than shoot him, so he'd better not try anything. Apparently his wife had gotten to him, and he just kept parroting his earlier statements that he was only a chemist and that Bruce and Heather were safe and would be allowed to return shortly. I questioned him for about half an hour and got nowhere. Frustrated, I returned him to the bathroom.

My head was killing me. I needed some pain pills but I'd have to wait until Margot got back. I held Meacham's arm with my right hand and unbolted the door with my left. When I opened it to push him inside, Dolly came charging out. She was holding the toilet tank cover over her head, just like Charlton Heston with the Ten

~ 75 ~

Commandments and her intent was obviously to smash it on my head. And she almost succeeded.

"Aiyeeeahheeee," she screamed, reminding me of the actress who shares my last name. I shoved the doctor into her, and the tank cover flew from her hands almost hitting my head and then fell harmlessly to the floor. They both toppled back into the bathroom, their heads clunking together as they landed on the tiles. I kicked their legs inside the room and slammed and bolted the door. I sat at the table and put my head in my hands.

My head felt like it was splitting open. I was beginning to wonder if Dolly had done any damage when she clocked me with the bat. And my bullet-wounded arm was throbbing. I needed a rest.

I closed my eyes for a good half hour. I didn't want to fall asleep in case they discovered a way out. Or in case Luther found out where we were. Luther was already on his way before Meacham found out that Margot was with me, but if Luther made contact with Judkins, and told him there was a female with me, and old Judd was as smart as Meacham seemed to think he was, it would only be a matter of time before they checked here.

Closing my eyes for a while helped my headache. It also made me sleepy. I had to find something to concentrate on until Margot got back. I found a jar of instant coffee, mixed a spoonful with tap water and put it in the microwave.

I went into the living room which was on the street side of the house. I looked out the picture window. Everything looked quiet, peaceful. *Was it too peaceful?* I was letting my imagination run wild. There was an upright piano in the corner of the room. It was an older one, but looked well taken care of. I lifted the lid and looked at the keys. They seemed to be brand new. I wondered how well she played. Or maybe it was Bruce who played. I thumbed through the sheet music resting above the keys: Pachelbel's "Canon in D major," "Songs from The Sound of Music," David Lanz's "Solos For New Age Piano" and "Sing Along With Barney." Interesting selections.

Next to the piano was a bookcase with a set of encyclopedia. I pulled out the Ber-Bug volume and went back to the kitchen to read about Brazil. Before I had opened the book, I heard a knock at the bathroom door.

"We're hungry," Dolly said. "We haven't eaten since breakfast. How long are you keeping us in here?"

"You should've thought of that before you tried to kill me with the toilet top."

"I was just trying to escape," she countered. "Even prisoners get to eat."

There was a loaf and a half of bread on top of the refrigerator. I took down the half loaf and looked inside the fridge. I found a package with six or seven slices of bologna in it. If they ate it, I thought, Margot wouldn't be able to feed it to me later. I took the bread and meat and walked over to the door. "Both of you, climb in the bath tub. No funny stuff. Remember I have a gun." I heard them scramble and the sound of their shoes scratching on the porcelain. I unbolted the door and put their supper inside. *"Bon Appétit,"* I said. Feeding time at the zoo. They noisily went about ripping open the food packages.

I sat back down with Funk and Wagnall. My knowledge of Brazil was minuscule at best. I'd slept through a good portion of high-school geography classes. It surprised me to read that it is the fifth largest country in the world after the USSR, China, Canada and the United States. If this book was written before the USSR divided itself up into smaller countries (I slept through geography, but I still read the papers a little) then maybe it was the fourth largest. It's the world's leading supplier of coffee, which also surprised me. I always thought the little guy with the donkey from Columbia had that market sewn up. The capitol is *Brasilia*, which I'd never heard of, and the two most populated cities are *São Paulo* and *Rio de Janeiro*, which I had heard about. Wasn't Rio big into Mardi Gras?

I made another instant coffee and read the twelve pages on Brazil. Then I got another book and looked up South America. I was starting to get a perspective of where we were headed, And it didn't look like it was going to be easy. I read the South America entry and then I looked up Central America. My head was spinning. Margot had been gone over three hours. Every fifteen minutes or so since they were fed, Meacham or Dolly would bang on the door asking for something or other: freedom, a TV, something to read, even a bottle of wine.

Threatening them with the "trunk" quieted them down each time. Finally, I heard the garage door go up, a car motor idle in and shut off and the garage door shut. I took the Beretta from my pocket and flicked off the safety. The door handle turned and Margot came into the kitchen. She was alone. And she looked like hell. I almost said something stupid, like "What happened to you?" but settled for "Hi." Her eyes were red and puffy and her nose was pink. Her hair was mussed up, as if she'd slept in it and didn't have a brush. She must have known what I was thinking.

"Mess, huh?" she asked. I smiled. "It was tougher than I thought. My mother is ripped. She said the things you did, but not as nicely."

There was a time when I would have had plenty to say. Probably one of the reasons I'm twice divorced. That's one of the things you learn as you get older: when to shut up. "Want some instant coffee?" I asked. Innocuous.

"I'd like a beer," she said. "I picked some up. It's in the car."

"I'll get it," I said, and started for the door.

"Wait..." she said and then was silent. I looked at her. "Would you hold me for a second. Like a friend. I feel really alone right now."

I put my arms around her and pulled her close. She nuzzled her head into my shoulder. We stood like that for several minutes. Finally, she pulled away.

"Thanks," she said. "Sorry I took so long but I figured we should wait until dark to leave. And my mother.... Guess we have to get going. How are our guests?"

"I questioned him for a while, got nowhere." I told her about the toilet top and about the bologna sandwiches.

"Oh, good," she said. "That was kind of old. I picked up some new at the deli. For supper. You like bologna, right."

"Love it," I said. I didn't have the heart to tell her that it was probably my least favorite food. I hoped she had lots of mustard.

She went to her bedroom to pack a few things. I went to the car and got two beers. She was back in about twenty minutes with a knapsack and a small soft-sided suitcase. We sat at the table and drank the beers. It was a refreshing taste after all the coffee. She handed me two bank-book sized folders. I took them: her husband's passport and his international driver's license.

"I got three hundred bucks from the ATM," she said. "We'll have to pick you up some clothes on the way. Guess we better get those two packed up for the trip."

"You don't plan on taking them all the way to Brazil, do you?" I asked.

"No. Course not. I just want to get them away from here. Give us a little head start. She handed me a roll of duct tape. "I'll cover them." She was holding the .357 at her side as she opened the bathroom.

"What's going on?" Meacham growled. "I demand to know when you are going to release us."

"Soon, if you cooperate," Margot said. "Now turn around." He hesitated. I spun him around and wrapped his wrists behind him with the tape. Dolly put up more of a struggle. She tried to bite me. Margot biffed her gently on the head and I got her turned around and trussed up like the doctor.

"Trunk?" I asked Margot. Dolly's eyes opened up wide like silver dollars.

"Back seat," Margot said. "But any funny stuff and they go in the trunk. Unconscious. Let's get going. There's a cooler in the garage, and—"

RAP, RAP, RAP. Three staccato knocks on the front door cut her off.

"Watch them," I said and went to the kitchen window. I couldn't see who was at the front door but I could see the car in the driveway. No mistaking it. The big black station wagon illuminated by the streetlight.

Luther.

The front door knob rattled.

"Shit," Margot said.

"Luther! Luther!" Meacham screamed and Dolly chimed in.

"Help us. Help us."

Margot pushed them both back into the bathroom. "How many are there?"

"Don't know," I said.

Thwummp. A shoulder against the door. One or two more like that and they'd be in. I shut off the kitchen lights and Margot did the same with the hall, plunging us into a very uncomfortable darkness. A sliver of light shone from the bottom of the bathroom door. Meacham and Dolly continued screaming for Luther.

Thwummp. And the sound of wood splitting. They were almost in. I held the Beretta in my hand. I wasn't sure if the safety was on or off. I couldn't remember if it should be up or down. My eyes were beginning to adjust to the pencil of light coming from below the door and from the streetlight that filtered in through the kitchen window. Then I saw movement through that window, two dark shapes behind the house.

"Margot," I shouted. "More of them. Behind the house." She didn't answer. "Margot! Where the hell are you?"

Thwummp. Keeraash. I heard the front door slam back against the wall on its broken hinges. Almost simultaneously I heard glass shatter in a room at the back of the house.

"Margot," I yelled. "They're in! Get out of the house."

"Give it up!" a man's voice, gruff, in control.

I realized I was about to die. I was never going to see my kids again. I'd take at least one of the bastards with me.

"Let's go." The man again. "We don't want to hurt you."

Where was Margot? Had she got out?

"Bullshit!" I yelled and fired once into the darkness in the vicinity of the door. The intruder returned my fire. Big caliber. Two quick shots, *blam, blam.* Then the hall lights came on. *Had he found the switch?* I heard a large body fall over some kind of furniture in the back room. Curses and then light from the back of the house. Then —

Blat-blat-blat-blat-blat-blat-blat-blat-blat-blat.

The guy at the front door screamed, more animal than human, like a dog hit by a car.

"Machine gun," one of the guys in the back room yelled.

Blat-blat-blat-blat-blat-blat-blat-blat-blat-blat.

Another blast and the door to the back room virtually disintegrated. My heart was hammering in my ears at about the same rate as the machine gun. The living room light came on and I saw Margot walk slowly towards the shattered back-room door. She was wearing ear protectors and carrying a very mean looking gun.

She looked at me. "You okay?" she yelled. I nodded, staring at her. "You look like you've never seen a girl with an Uzi before."

I edged along the wall toward the front door. I leaned against the broken jamb and tilted my head around so I could see outside. The goon who had busted in the door was crawling in the direction of the driveway. Actually he was pulling himself forward with his arms, his legs trailed uselessly behind him like a huge snail.

I aimed at the slithering piece of garbage, but I couldn't shoot. Not in the back as he was clawing himself away. His pals had apparently gotten out of the house faster than they got in.

They dragged their comrade into the back seat. One of them, the biggest one, looked back at the house, then shook his head and limped to the driver's side. I guess Judd hadn't prepared them for a crazy housewife with a machine pistol. I guess I was as surprised as they were. Almost.

"What are they doing?" Margot asked. "We gotta get out of here."

"Looks like their packing it in."

"Is the guy...the one at the door...is he dead?"

"No, but he won't be walking for a while. What's next? Have you got a bazooka hidden somewhere?"

"I'll explain in the car," she said. "Let's get going."

Luther and his pals drove away, maybe to regroup, maybe to call Judkins and ask for a raise. Bullies don't like being on the short end of the stick or, in this case, barrel. I helped Margot bring her bags into the garage. She opened the trunk and laid the Uzi on the floor, then covered it with an old blanket and her bags. I took the case of beer from the rear seat and slid it into the trunk. We wouldn't be thirsty for a while.

"What about the honeymooners," I asked. "Wanna just leave them?"

"No. I don't want them in my house. What's left of it. I still think it's best to dump them along the way, buy us a little time."

I heard a siren in the distance. Coming our way. She opened the door to the bathroom. Dolly and Meacham were cowering in the bathtub. The he-man was on the bottom, being shielded, probably unwillingly, by his loving spouse.

"Let's go," I said, and pulled them out of the tub. Margot grabbed Dolly's arm and I took Meacham's. They were both shaking and scared but smelled like they were able to control their bowels. They didn't put up much resistance. We rushed them into the car.

"Any trouble and you go in the trunk," Margot instructed them. "I'll drive."

She jumped into the car started it and pushed the button for the garage door. We were on the road less than two minutes after Luther had gone. We were only a block from her house when two New Stratley cruisers went by, sirens howling, lights flashing, headlights wig-wagging. I wondered if Bart was in one of them. I had to get a message to him before I got too far. Also Tommy. I had to find out how he was doing. I'd call them first chance I got after we dropped off the Meachams.

We drove for several miles in silence. Two more cruisers, an ambulance and a fire engine flew past us. Amazing what the sound of an Uzi will do to a quiet neighborhood.

Finally Dolly spoke. "Where are you taking us?"

"We'll let you go pretty soon," Margot said. "First I want the address of the place in Brazil where Bruce is."

"What if we don't tell you?"

"Then," Margot said, and the way she said it, I believed it. "I'll kill one of you and take the other one with us to Brazil."

Chapter 12

A light mist was falling as we drove down Route 20. The wipers beat an intermittent, peaceful rhythm. Boston's night lights lit the horizon like the beginning of a sunrise. The Meachams sat quietly, apparently thinking about Margot's threat.

After several minutes, the doctor broke the silence. "If I give you the address, will you let us go?"

"You don't understand," Margot said. "You *will* give me the address. I'm done playing games with you."

"Tell them," Dolly said. "They'll never get there. The police will have them in custody before they get out of Massachusetts."

Meacham exhaled, like he'd been holding the information inside him for a long time. "It's on the *Mariaña Road* in downtown *Belo Horizonte.*"

"What's *Minas Gerais*?" I asked. "You mentioned that at your house." It was also on Bruce's laptop.

"It's a state," he answered, "like New Hampshire or Connecticut."

"I know what a state is," I said. And I knew that was a good answer from my earlier reading. Margot told me there was a notebook and pen in the glove box. I skipped a few pages of mileage and gas gallons and wrote the doctor's directions on a blank sheet.

An "Entering Weston" sign flashed by and another proclaimed that Route 128/95 was just several miles ahead. I had no idea where we were headed and didn't want to discuss it in front of the Meachams. I assumed that Margot had a plan.

"I have to go to the ladies' room," Dolly said.

"You've been in the bathroom all day," Margot snapped.

"I couldn't go with him watching me...and all that shooting going on. How long do I have to wait?"

"Until we get to Brazil," Margot said.

"Brazil!" Meacham howled. "You said you'd let us go if I told you where the plant is."

"I think you're lying," Margot flashed a glance at me. "Don't you think so, Jake?"

"He's not lying!" Dolly's voice was shrill and hurt my ears, which were still ringing from the earlier gun shots. "Please let us go. He told you the truth."

I sensed a bit of panic creeping into her tone. I was feeling a twinge of panic myself. I wanted this whole thing to be over with. And I wanted Dolly and Meacham to be gone.

Brazil! What if he was lying? What if the whole thing was a wild goose chase?

Margot and I were silent as we drove. The Meachams complained about their situation but Margot ignored them. She turned onto 95/128. The mist had stopped and I rolled my window down half way. The smells of the road, the rubber and the asphalt, enhanced by the rain, mixed with the cool night air and took my mind away from it all. But just for a few minutes.

We had to do something with Dolly and the doc. About twenty minutes down the highway Margot signaled and got off on Route 2.

"There's a gas station," Dolly said. "Please stop, just for a minute."

"Hang on," Margot said, "just a little further."

I wasn't sure if she knew where she was going, but she seemed to. About a mile down the road, she took a left and then shortly a right. The last sign I remembered seeing said we were in Lincoln.

Margot took another left on a road that looked more like a path. There were no houses or lights. We bumped down a dirt lane for at least a half mile. She finally slowed down and stopped the car. "Here we are," she said.

"Where the hell are we?" Meacham asked.

"End of the ride for you two," Margot said as she turned to face the back seat captives. "I've been trying to decide if I should kill you. I'm sure you had a lot to do with whatever happened to Bruce. But if, as you say, he's all right, then I guess I'll let you live. If I find out you lied to me, then I'll track you down and kill you for sure. Now do what I say and if you try to run or scream or anything, I'll shoot you dead."

Margot got out, and I followed suit. She opened the back door and helped them out. She led Dolly, and I took Meacham's arm. About twenty feet in front of the car, Margot stopped.

Illuminated by the head lights, she undid the tape from Dolly's wrists. She took the Ruger from her waist band and a plastic trash bag from her pocket. She handed the bag to Dolly. "Take off your clothes," Margot ordered, "and put them in this bag."

"What?" Dolly and Meacham asked in unison.

"You heard me. You too, Doctor." She nodded for me to undo him and I did.

"I'm not going to—"

Margot shoved the revolver against his temple and pulled the hammer back. The click silenced the doctor. "I'm going to leave this bag with your clothes at the end of the road. Just buying us a little time. Now strip." They did as they were told. It was kind of comical to watch them shed their duds in the car's headlights on this deserted road.

"I'm not taking off my panties," Dolly said.

"Yes you are, or I will," Margot told her. "Now, hurry up."

When they were done they stood covering themselves as best they could with their arms.

"Turn around and walk away from us until we're out of sight," Margot said. "Then you can get your clothes."

"We'll die out here," Meacham said. "I'm gonna get you for this."

"Not if you die out here, you won't," Margot said. She picked up the bag of their clothes and began running to the car.

"See ya, Dolly, Doc," I shouted as I ran back to the car with Margot.

"It's Delphine!" was the last thing I heard Meacham say.

We jumped in the car and she backed down the road a good eighth of a mile and then spun around in a small clearing. We got back to the main road and she took a right. She continued driving, apparently retracing her steps.

"I saw you looking at her boobs," she said smiling.

"Hard to miss," I said. "What about their clothes?"

"I lied," she said, and we both started laughing.

We pulled into the gas station by the highway. Margot asked me to pump the gas. She brought the bag with the Meacham's clothes and tossed it into a "Goodwill" bin behind the station. Then she went inside. I filled the tank and then met her at the counter. She had bought a bag of food items which she paid for along with the gas, and we went back to the Toyota.

She pulled away from the pumps and stopped by a well-lit pay phone. "I have to call my mother," she said. "Have to let her know I'm OK. When she hears about the shoot-out at my house she'll freak."

We got out of the car and went to the phone. I took a few steps away to give her a little privacy. She was talking loudly, must have been a bad connection and I heard most of what she said. She was trying to reassure her mother that she was fine.

"Look, Mom, why don't you go to Aunt Ernestine's. You love the lake." There was silence for a few moments while I'm sure her mother protested. "Please...I have to do this...I'll be back soon. I love you." She walked away from the phone and handed me some change. "Do you have to make a call?"

"Yeah, thanks. I wanna check on Tommy, and let Bart know I'll be back in a few days, I'm not gonna tell them where we're off to."

"Good," she said. "I'm going to run into the ladies' room. It'll be a long ride."

I called Bart's number. He answered after two rings. I wanted to be careful what I said. "Hey, Bart. I'll be out of town for a couple days. I think I'm onto something."

"Where are you, Man?" he asked.

"Can't really talk right now. I should be back in a few days." I told him a little about Meacham and asked him to see if Wellesley PD could detain him for a while.

"I don't know how I can do that," Bart said. "I'm not supposed to be talking to you. You're a fleeing felony suspect, Dude. Remember?"

"Look Bart, There's some kind of huge scam going on involving that IotaTek place, and Meacham's at the bottom of it. And I think him and his pals are responsible for all the killings that are happening. I'm going to try and get some proof. Once they're out of the country, it'll be too late."

"Where are you going?"

"Can't really tell you. I'm not really sure myself but I'll be in touch."

"Hey, Jake?"

"Yeah."

"You're an asshole."

I could imagine his big grin on the other end of the line as I hung up. Next I dialed Shelly's number. She picked up after five rings and her voice sounded far away and hesitant. "Hi Shel, it's Jake."

She blurted out the where-why-what-are-you-going-to-do questions that Bart had just gone through. "I'm working everything out, Shel. How's Tommy?"

"He's pretty upset...he's been waiting to hear from you. Wait, I'll put him on."

After a long moment, I heard his voice. "Hi Jake...sorry I got you into this trouble."

"Don't worry about it, kid." I said. How are you doing?"

"I'm going to the cops tomorrow. I have to do something about my father's funeral. My mother would want me to. And look after my sister. She's...all alone now, too." There was a hesitation on the other end and then he spoke again. "Shelly wants to go with me but I'm afraid she'll get into trouble. I'll tell the cops I've been in a cave by the Charles River. They can't make me tell about you and Shelly."

~ 87 ~

There was a hitch in my throat, and it was hard to speak. "Tommy," I finally got out. I'm working...on some things. I don't wanna get your hopes up, but I think I may at least be getting some answers."

"About my Mother?"

"I still have a lot of stones to turn up...but I won't quit. Take care of yourself, kid. Let me talk to Shelly."

"Thanks, Jake."

There was a rustling with the phone and then Shelly's voice.

"He's a great kid," I said. "And he's right. If you go with him you could be in a lot of trouble. Drop him at the Oak Town Mall. That's only a couple blocks from the police station. Give him some money so he can have a pizza before the cops get hold of him, and I'll pay you back."

"In your life you'll never earn enough to pay me what you owe me."

"You're right, Shel. Thanks a million. I gotta run. Hopefully, everything will be cleared up shortly."

I hung up and started for the car. I stopped to wipe a couple tears off my cheek. I wanted to be with Tommy when he went to the cops, wanted to tell them that he probably had a better handle on what was going on than any of the adults involved. But, he'd be okay, and if Brazil worked out, he'd have some answers. *And maybe his mother?* That was too much to hope for. I was pretty sure, as was Margot, that both Bruce and Heather were dead. Answers, then, and closure hopefully were waiting in *Minas Gerais, Brazil.*

***

"It's great to have the Meachams out of our hair," I said as we had settled back into the flow on 128/95.

"I had to get rid of them." She was steering through the traffic, her hands at ten-to-two. I bet her dad had taught her to drive, too. "There was too much chance they'd give us away. I figured leaving them naked in the countryside would keep them busy for a while."

"It was a nice touch," I said. "So, what's the itinerary for our trip?"

~ 88 ~

"First," she said, "I'm starved. There's some bread and meat and mustard in the bag. If you want to make us sandwiches, that would be great."

I was pleasantly surprised to find ham and not bologna. I made us each a sandwich. I thought about the beer in the trunk, but it wouldn't be good to get stopped for something as silly as an open container of alcohol. I gave her a sandwich and she ate as she drove.

We had turned off onto the Massachusetts turnpike, a toll road, and she took the ticket from the automatic machine. "I figure I'd get us through New York City," she said, "and then let you drive for a while. It'll be a long ride."

"So we drive to Louisiana?" I asked. "What if Charlie isn't home when we get there? What if he can't help us?"

"Yes," she said, "we drive to Louisiana. I figure with both of us driving, we can get there in a day or so, maybe. I'm sure Charlie will be home. And if anybody can help us, he can."

"He's ex-FBI, right?" I was loaded with questions. "How can he help us in Brazil? Doesn't the FBI just do things in this country?"

"For the most part. But they also have over 50 international offices attached to U.S. embassies around the world. Remember about 10 years ago when that family from San Francisco was slaughtered in Mexico? Well my father and Charlie were down there for over a month."

"I don't remember that," I said. "Ten years ago I was going through a divorce with witch number one. Wasn't reading the paper much then, mostly drinking and fighting with lawyers."

"Was that why she divorced you?"

"Huh?"

"Because you were drinking too much?"

"No," I said. "No...I don't know. There were lots of reasons. The drinking was the result of the divorce rather than a cause of it."

"I'm sorry," she said. "It wasn't fair to ask you that."

"I don't mind. I've thought about it plenty over the years. You know, wondered what I did wrong...or didn't do right."

I made us each a second sandwich. After we ate them Margot suggested that I might want to take a nap.

~ 89 ~

"I'm not tired," I said. "Too much happened today. I'm wound up tight."

"Well then, why don't you tell me something about yourself."

"That's a good idea. That'll put us both to sleep."

She laughed. "No, really. I don't know anything about you. How did you get to be a private detective? What do you do for fun? Why do you call your ex-wives witches?"

"The last one's easy. That's the best description for them that I can use in mixed company." I could see the curve of her smile in the greenish glow of the dash-board. "There are two sides to every story though, and I can only imagine the names they have for me. I guess the only thing that really bothers me...I mean the dentist is loaded so that makes some sense...but they make it hard for me to see my kids. For that, I think of them as witches."

"Can't you do anything?" The smile was gone from her face.

"I tried. It takes a ton of money and better lawyers than I had. And the kicker was I had the same lady judge for both divorces. What are the chances of that?"

"That doesn't sound right. Seems like she should have excused herself from the second case."

"I know," I said, "that's what I told my mouthpiece. He mentioned it to the old bat and she threatened to hold him in contempt. 'How dare he question her?'"

"There was nothing you could do?"

"Lots of things you can do if you have the cash. About a year after my second divorce, I read in the paper that Her Honor Judge Pismire was arrested for drunken driving. Ran her Lincoln into a fire hydrant in Chinatown. I laughed for a week until I read that all charges were dropped."

"Pismire?"

"That's what I called her. Her name was something like that."

"So, sounds like two bad marriages and a mean lady judge have soured you on all women."

"I wouldn't say that. Maybe I've lost confidence in making the right choice."

"Do you have a girl friend?"

"No. Not right now. I'm pretty busy between the two jobs—"

"Two jobs?" she asked.

"Yeah, I tend bar part time at the White Stallion."

"That sounds interesting. You must meet lots of women there."

"Yes, Miss Lonely Hearts, I do."

"I was just asking. You don't have to get pissed."

"I'm sorry," I said. "I guess it's a sore subject. Most of the women that come into the Stallion are either with guys or carrying tons of baggage." We passed a sign that announced we were seven miles away from Connecticut. "How about you? Was Bruce your high-school sweetheart?"

"No, he wasn't. I didn't date much in high school. I was kind of a tomboy then."

"Then?" I was thinking of the Uzi.

She laughed. "Some habits are hard to break. When I was eighteen, I fell in love with an FBI guy. He was seven years older than me. He came to a party at our house and asked me on a date and I was hooked. My dad was really mad. He told me an FBI agent's job was too dangerous and demanding on the family. Naturally I threw it back in his face and reminded him about the sacrifices that Mom and my sister and I had to make. It was the first time I'd ever seen him at a loss for words."

We made small talk like that until we got through New York City. I took over the driving at a truck stop with the lights of Manhattan glittering behind us. We'd been on the road again for about twenty minutes when Margot dozed off. I drove on trying to keep close to the speed limit, thinking about the events of the past day and listening to the sounds of the tires on the pavement and of her gentle snoring.

***

We took turns driving and trying to sleep and, after thirty-two hours, we crossed the border into Louisiana. It felt like we'd been traveling for weeks. I was badly in need of some sleep and I was sure Margot was, too. The place we were going, Begnet Cove, wasn't listed on the map. Margot told me the population was under fifty not counting alligators and snakes.

"If you're lucky," Margot said, "Charlie might take you 'gator hunting."

"Great," I said, with as much derision as I could muster. "Right now, I'll settle for hunting down a pillow and a blanket."

I had tried to sleep several times during the trip. I almost dozed off while driving on route 85 in Georgia, but when I pulled over and got in the back seat, the sleep that had been so close just minutes earlier eluded me.

Chapter 13

We stopped near a place called New Iberia for gas, rest rooms and so that Margot could pick up a present for Charlie. She bought a huge bottle of Jack Daniel's that she said was his favorite.

"How much farther?" I asked as we pulled away from the Iberia Quick Stop.

"About an hour. Mostly bad roads. We're heading into Bayou Country. It's really quite a place."

"Sounds wonderful," I said. "When I hear bayou, all I can think about is swamp. Why would he pick a place like that to live?"

"You'll have to ask him."

She was right about the roads. Twenty minutes from the store, we were off the pavement and jouncing along on a rutty old path lined with what seemed an endless line of drooping trees, that Margot said were sycamores. It was hot and sticky and I had my window rolled down. The air was full of a strange smell, like flower blossoms mixed with mold. Not really unpleasant, just strange. It made me think of Chinese sweet and sour.

"Are you sure you know where you're going?" I asked. "Talk about boonies."

"Don't worry, I've been here several times." She laughed and patted my knee. "I won't bring you to the witch's house, little boy."

The path had narrowed and it seemed like it was about to end when it opened into a good sized clearing. Right in the middle was a cabin that was made of driftwood. It looked like what I imagined a bayou house to look like except for the white satellite dish on the roof. There was a shiny red 4X4 Bronco parked beside the house. Margot pulled in and beeped the horn, waving to a man who sat on a rickety looking porch with several dogs. He stood up and my first impression was "big."

"Magpie!" he yelled.

"Uncle Charlie!" she called back as she got out of the car.

Margot ran to him and he gave her a hug that swept her off her feet and looked like it could have snapped her spine. I began walking towards them. Charlie was wearing a cowboy hat and a khaki short sleeved shirt. His khaki shorts seemed to emphasize rather than hide his prosthetic legs.

"Charlie," Margot said as I reached the porch, "You're walking."

"Sure I am. I woulda told you about my new feets but I wanted to fly up to Boston one day and surprise you."

"Charlie," she said, "this is Jake."

"Glad to meet you, son," he said as he grasped my hand in his huge paw and shook with vigor. He looked at Margot. "I'm so glad you decided to move on, honey."

There was an awkward silence and then Margot spoke. "I haven't moved...I mean...Jake's not my boyfriend. We think Bruce may have been kidnapped along with that woman from his work. Actually, that's why we're here. We were hoping you could help us."

Charlie raised his eyebrows and stared into her eyes. It was the same facial expression I remembered that New Stratley Junior High principal, Mr. Muthrose, used to elicit the truth from wayward students. "Let's open up this Jack," Charlie said, taking the bottle from her hand, "and then you tell me what's going on. I'll get us glasses." He pushed the screen door open and hobbled into the house. He left us standing on the porch with the dogs, two good sized bloodhounds and a small poodle. The poodle and one of the hounds got up to sniff us. The hound was growling quietly, not real menacing, just enough to advise us we weren't formally welcomed yet.

"Knock it off, Bozark," Charlie bellowed as he came out of the house. Bozark stopped growling and plopped himself back next to the other hound. "He's a good dog. Little high strung, but he loves to chase 'gators."

He opened the bottle and half filled three plastic tumblers that had "Best Western" printed on them. I was having a hard time keeping my eyes open and Tennessee sour mash whiskey was about the last thing I wanted, but it was apparent that refusing Charlie wasn't an option, so I took the glass and dutifully sipped from it. Charlie led us to the end of the porch where there was a wooden chair swing and a couple folding lawn chairs. He and Margot sat on the swing and I on the chair that had the most straps still attached.

"Well," Charlie said, "let's have the story."

"I never believed that Bruce left me," Margot began, "but I had no proof. No one would listen to me. They said I was in denial, that it was normal when one gets dumped. I was starting to think maybe they were right. Then Jake popped up at my house."

She told him about how Tommy had hired me, about the New Stratley murders and Bruce's laptop. Charlie chuckled as she related our adventures with the Meachams. His chuckles turned to laughter when she got to the part about the Uzi, and I thought he was going to fall out of the swing when she described Doc and Dolly naked in the woods.

"That's quite a tale," Charlie said when Margot had finished. "You're your father's daughter all right. I need some more firewater. He opened the bottle and refilled his tumbler. Margot and I still had most of ours left. "Drink up you two. Young folks today sure don't drink like *we* used to." He looked at me. "So the law's after you?"

"He didn't do anything!" Margot spoke before I had a chance to answer. He just tried to help and wound up in a pile of horseshit."

Charlie broke into another fit of laughter. "I sure do miss your old man," he said grabbing her around the shoulder and giving her a big hug. "Boy, you remind me of him."

"I miss him, too," Margot said.

"Neither one of you looks like you're in any shape to travel anywhere, tonight. I'll jump on the net after you go to bed and see what I can find out about this Brazil deal." Charlie paused and drank half his whiskey. "Mmmm, that's some good stuff. Let me put out some feelers about how to get us down there."

"Us?" Margot asked.

"You don't think I'm gonna let you two go down there alone, and leave me out of all the fun, do you? No, you get a good night's rest while I put things in motion. Tomorrow, while we're waiting we can go for an air-boat ride."

"That sounds great," Margot said.

"Maybe even catch us some 'gators," Charlie said.

The inside of Charlie's house was as modern as the outside was rustic. Pelican droppings on the tin roof made me think of "Dr. No" and his fantastic fortress hidden underneath a mountain of bird shit. The temperature was cool and dry and a welcome relief from the sweltering Cajun evening.

"Feels like I fell through the looking glass," I said.

"All the comforts," Charlie said with a huge smile on his face. "I keep the outside shabby to appease my neighbors. Some of them don't even have electricity and they'd be pretty unhappy about 'new-fangled' buildings springing up. Hey, pardon my manners, but you two must be starved."

"We had a burger a couple hours ago," Margot said. "What I could really use is a shower."

Charlie held his face close to her and inhaled deeply. "You smell fine darlin'. Did your dad ever tell you about the time we were holed up in a closet-sized room in Beirut for two and a half weeks. No running water. No indoor plumbing. That was some stink."

"That's disgusting," Margot said, scrunching up her face.

"Have a seat in there, Jake." Charlie pointed at a room to the right of a big-screen TV. I'll get her set up and be right in."

I walked into the room, and the light came on as I crossed the threshold. A large table loaded with computer and electronic equipment took up one wall. Above it was a sign that read "Charlie's War Room." I sat there in awe of the gizmos, afraid to touch anything. I was sure it had to be alarmed. He came in after about five minutes.

"Amazing what you can buy on an FBI pension, ain't it?" he asked. He was carrying Bruce's laptop, and after moving a mound of books and papers he was able to put it on the counter. His big hands hooked a couple wires to the back of the small computer. "Let's get things fired up and see what there is to see. Have a seat in front of the big monitor."

There were two padded stools in the room and I wheeled one over in front of the screen. It was bigger than my old Zenith back at the condo which the New Stratley cops had probably seized or smashed. Charlie pushed a few buttons and the monitor started to crackle. "See anything, yet?"

"No," I said. I watched intently for several seconds wondering what the big deal was about a computer screen coming on. Maybe, I thought, he'd been in the Bayou too long.

"There," I said. "I see a small green dot, right in the center."

"Good, good," he mumbled quietly and pushed another button.

The small green dot was growing very slowly. I craned my neck forward to study it. Suddenly the green dot exploded into an alligator head coming right at my face. Jaws wide, teeth gleaming, it was screeching a blood-curdling alligator (I think) screech. I threw myself back from the screen and tipped over my stool and down on the floor I went. Charlie roared. I started to pick myself up when Margot appeared at the door.

"What's going on?" she demanded.

Charlie was laughing too hard to talk. I was embarrassed and more than a little mad. I pointed at the screen without looking.

"Flamingos?" Margot asked.

I looked and there was a flock of the pink birds floating quietly over a still lake.

"Just," Charlie choked out between guffaws, "just a joke, son. Little ice-breaker. Know what I mean?"

"What 's going on?" Margot was losing patience.

Charlie pushed the buttons that made the monster appear again. Of course the surprise was lost on her. She was trying to keep from laughing herself after she realized what had happened.

I was at a loss for words. In a way I wanted to belt the old man with the prosthetic legs, and in a way I wanted to laugh with them.

Break the ice. All right, I thought, I'd laugh with them, but I'd get even.

"You kids must be dog tired. I'll buy you a nightcap and then let you get some sleep. I'm gonna stay up awhile and do some investigating on this Brazil problem." He led us into his kitchen and poured three more glasses of Jack Daniel's. Margot mixed hers with Coke and I did the same. Charlie looked at us like we'd just poured ketchup on a hundred dollar *chateaubriand* but he didn't say anything.

While we drank and feasted on boiled hot dogs, Margot filled Charlie in on more of the details of the mystery. His eyes glistened with excitement as she unfolded more and more details of the bizarre disappearances and the strange IotaTek. I looked at the clock as she was finishing: 10:30 p.m.

I tried to add up the hours since I'd slept, but couldn't concentrate enough to do it.

Margot showed me where the shower was and handed me a plastic bag. "I hope this stuff fits" she said. "I got it all out of Bruce's drawer, but he never wore it."

"That's fine," I said. "I'm surprised you had time to get me anything."

"There's a new toothbrush," she said. "I got it when we stopped in Memphis."

"Thanks," I said as I took the bundle from her. "Where am I sleeping?"

"I'll check," she said and then yelled, "Charlie, where do you want us to sleep?"

He came out of his war room sporting a huge grin. I don't know if I'd ever met anyone that laughed and smiled as much as that guy. "Well, I hadn't given it much thought," he said. "I only have one guest bedroom. Do you mind sharing it?"

"The couch will be OK with me," I said.

"Well," Charlie steepled his index fingers under his chin. "That's where the dogs sleep. Bozark and Claude, anyway. They might take to your sleeping with 'em and they might not. Course sometimes Bozark finds himself some strange stuff to eat and stinks for all get out." This set him into another fit of laughter.

~ 98 ~

"We'll be all right," Margot said. "We need a good night's sleep in case you find us a way to get to Brazil." They were both looking at me as if they felt that my uncontrollable hormonal functioning was the only thing that would hinder our sleep.

"I'll be in dreamland as soon as my head hits the pillow," I said, "wherever it is you want me to be."

"Not if your nose is in the same room as Bozark's butt," Charlie said and headed into his war room laughing.

"I told you he was a character." Margot smiled.

"He's a real riot. Just what I needed to cheer me up before they send me off to prison."

"I bet tomorrow morning he'll have everything figured out. Now go take your shower and let's get some sleep."

I opened my "suitcase" in the bathroom. She had packed a pair of gray sweats, a Red Sox tee-shirt and a new package of briefs that Bruce hadn't opened. There were two pink plastic disposable razors, a new toothbrush, a travel-sized bar of soap and a small plastic bottle of English Leather. She had also left me out a bath towel and wash cloth. The shower felt great. Even the bayou had more water pressure than my "Green Ledges" Condominium. I let the water run on my wounded arm which looked like it was healing well. I shaved with one of the pink razors and brushed my teeth. Disguise be damned, I couldn't stand the itchiness my stubble was making. The Red Sox shirt was a little tight, as were the sweats, but they'd do. I folded up Bart's clothes and put them in the bag. They were badly in need of a Laundromat. Or a dumpster.

I'd been in the bathroom dawdling for quite a while. Spent minutes folding Bart's smelly duds when I usually didn't even fold clean ones. And finally the realization hit me, I was nervous. No I was going-on-a-first-date-with-a-real-girl scared to death about sharing the bedroom with Margot. Nothing to be afraid of. She was sleeping when I got into the bedroom and, as I had promised, I was asleep as soon as my head hit the pillow.

***

I awoke to the delicious smell of bacon cooking. Margot was gone. I brushed my teeth with my new toothbrush and then followed the aroma into the kitchen. Margot was busy at the stove. "Good morning," I said.

"Hi, sleepyhead. I was beginning to wonder if Charlie and I were going to have to eat this all by ourselves."

"What time is it?" I asked.

"It's almost eight thirty. I've been up since six, and I'm not sure if Charlie slept at all."

She put three heaping plates on the table and reloaded the toaster that had just popped. Charlie came into the kitchen and, for the first time since I'd met him, he wasn't smiling. His hair was messed up and his eyes were red and watery. He grunted a greeting at us and then headed to the refrigerator. He poured a tall tumbler full of tomato juice and broke an egg into it. He added several dashes of Worcestershire sauce and about a hundred dashes of Tabasco and stirred the concoction with a knife. Then he downed half of it in one gulp.

"Ah," he said, "That's better. I'm beginning to get my appetite back." One more gulp and the tumbler was empty. He sat opposite me at the table and eyed the plate Margot had filled for him, and a hint of a smile crept onto his face.

Margot sat down and we ate in silence for several minutes. Bozark and his pals sat and eyed the floor intently hoping to clean up any spilled morsels.

Finally Charlie spoke. "Jack Daniels and I were up late last night working on the net, and we came up with some pretty interesting stuff. You," he looked at me, "are hotter than my morning pick-me-up. In addition to the murders they think you committed, you're wanted for the kidnapping of Margot."

"That's crazy," Margot said. "I'm not kidnapped."

"We know that," Charlie continued, "but we're the only ones. I was hoping that Magpie and I could take a commercial flight down to Brazil, but she's hot property now, too. She'd never even get on the plane." He crammed a strip of bacon into his mouth and went on between chews. "But the most interesting thing, and probably the scariest is how little I could get on that company, IotaTek and on some of the stuff that's in Bruce's file, especially that chemical

~ 100 ~

formula. I faxed a copy to a chemist friend of mine. Said he'd get back as soon as he could. Seems like one big mystery."

***

After we'd finished breakfast Margot shooed us out of the kitchen and set about doing the dishes. Charlie and I went outside, followed by the dogs. The humidity hit me like a warm shower. It didn't seem to phase Charlie or the poodle which raced off yapping after some small swamp creature. Charlie laughed at the antics. He took a pack of Camels from his pocket and offered me one. I declined.

"One a day," he said as he lit up. "Doctor'd like me to give that up, too, but I'm down from three packs a day to one lousy butt. I figure that's a 6,000 percent decrease and the sawbones should be happy with that."

I wasn't sure about his logic but I was sure he was enjoying the one lousy butt. I wondered what his doctor thought about the whiskey. We walked along quietly as he smoked. He ambled along pretty well on his artificial legs. We got to an opening in the trees where the river widened. There was a short quay of hewn planks where an airboat and several smaller boats were tied up. A weather-beaten, wood-burned sign announced we were at "Charlie's Landing." We sat on a bench made of railroad ties and Charlie finished his smoke.

"Watch," he said and flicked the butt into the murky water.

Before it hissed itself out, something below the water gobbled it up. "I'm not sure what it is, but every morning it has a Camel for breakfast." He looked at me. "You don't talk very much, son. What do you think about this whole disaster?"

I wanted to remind him it was hard to speak when someone else talked constantly, but I figured I'd use the opportunity to express my concerns about Margot. "I think this Brazil thing is too dangerous to bring Margot along. I've seen her in action and I know she can handle herself . . . but these people don't play by any rules. They killed at least three people up in New Stratley. What are the chances that her husband is still alive? Not very good, I'd say. Can't you have somebody from the Bureau check this thing out down there?"

~ 101 ~

"I made a couple calls, but I've been out too long." He got up off the bench and began to pace slowly. "There's absolutely nothing to go on to get the Bureau to commit to an investigation down there."

"They must have a field office or someone in the area who could check."

"We're dealing with a foreign country here, son, and a rather large one. There's all the diplomacy crap to get through before they can even begin an investigation. If we had a little more to go on... ." He pointed at the river as a huge pelican dove straight in and came up with a wriggling silvery fish. "Always amazes me. Anyway, unless we can get something more up here, and soon, I think we have to get down to Brazil and find out for ourselves what's going on."

"Okay," I said, "but can't you talk her into going back to Massachusetts. For her sake. I know her mother's worried silly."

"I'm gonna try to talk her out of it." He shook another Camel from his pack and lit it. I was going to comment about that being his second, but I could see he was getting agitated and probably needed it. He went on, "I'm gonna tell you a story. Between you and me. If you ever tell her I told you, I'll cut you up and feed you to my friends in the river.

"This pains me deeply," Charlie began. "Margot's dad was my best friend. Best damn field agent the FBI ever had. But that was his life. Husband and father came second to the bureau. About two years before he was killed, we were holed up in Istanbul working with the DEA on a brown opium pipeline to the states. We got word that Margot's brother, Sammy, was badly injured in a car crash. I told him to go home, but, no. We were too close, just another day. But it turned out to be a week.

"And you know what we got? Twenty pounds of brown sugar. Fuckin' brown sugar!

"Well, he just made it home for Sammy's funeral. They kept him on support a couple days longer than they should have. Margot and her mom and sister stayed at the hospital the whole time. He was in a piss hole in Turkey when he should have been home with his family."

"That's pretty sad," I said, "but what has it got to do with now?"

"I'm getting to that. So, two years later he was killed. I lost my legs. The bureau went on without us. Margot asked me if I'd give her away at her wedding, and I was pleased as could be to take her down the aisle even in my wheelchair. She talked to me the night before. Cried an awful lot. She knew the damage her father's indifference had done to her mother. And to her. And she vowed to me that she would never make that mistake with her new husband. Always put him above all else. She plans to keep that vow and that's why I don't think I can talk her into not going. I need one more of these."

He lit another Camel and then looked away from me towards the opposite shoreline. I thought I saw a watery glistening in his eyes before he turned. I didn't know what to say so I just watched the brown river gurgle slowly past while he smoked number three.

Chapter 14

When we got back to Charlie's house, he went right to his war room to finalize details. I found Margot in the kitchen, staring out the window at the stand of eucalyptus trees that shaded the back of the house. Her eyes were wet and she turned her face away from me. She was trembling. I put my hand on her shoulder, but she shrugged it off.

"You, okay, Margot?" I asked.

She nodded. Except for her crying jag after Meacham's house, I'd never seen her like this, too upset even to speak.

"Can I get you something, some water maybe?" I asked and then felt stupid. *Sure, Bozo, get my life back,* was what I'm sure she wanted to say. I'd never been able to console upset women, witches one and two were proof of that. I didn't want to leave her alone and I didn't want to stay there without a clue what to do. I put my hand on her shoulder again. Had to try something.

This time she left it there.

"Why don't you go back to New Stratley," I said. "Go back and stay with your mom for awhile. Charlie and I will go down to Brazil and find out what's happening down there. You'll take some of the kidnap heat off me, and you can tell the cops all about IotaTek.

Besides I'll move along a lot quicker without a girl in tow." We both knew that was a lie. It did get a tiny grin out of her. She turned and put her arms around me, pressed her face into my Red Sox tee shirt. I returned her hug.

She sobbed quietly for several minutes. Finally she spoke. "I have to go there. You wouldn't understand." She pulled away and snuffled into a paper towel. "I just want this to be over . . .want to find out . . . what really happened."

I thought she was going to cry again but she didn't have a chance.

Charlie burst into the room. "I did it," he shouted, "three tickets to Brazil!"

"Great," Margot said. "When do we leave?"

"Soon as we can get ready," Charlie was looking at the paper. "My housekeeper's coming to take care of the dogs. Anyway, you two are flying out of a small airport near Baton Rouge. About two hours drive. I'm taking United. I figure at least one of us should be in Brazil legally. I plan to be there waiting for you. Better make some sandwiches for your flight. It's gonna be a long one. There's stuff in the fridge."

"How long a flight is it?" I asked. I didn't like the way he said 'long.'"

"Well," he made a U with his thumb and forefinger and cupped his chin, "I think Yodel's plane does about 160 knots..."

"Like in Star War?" I interrupted.

Charlie began laughing and it was several minutes before he could speak again. "No," he finally said, "like in Matterhorn. He likes to yodel while he flies. You know, yodel-ay-hee-hoo." Which was followed by another fit of laughter.

I wasn't laughing. I'd only flown a couple times, at Uncle Sam's expense, and I wasn't crazy about being taken half way around the world by a pilot friend of Charlie's who yodeled while he flew. "Can't we drive there?"

"Too many borders to cross. You aren't afraid of Old Yodel's flying, are you?"

"I'd rather be on the one with 'United' on the sides and a fifty-five year old guy making a quarter of a million a year in the pilot's seat," I said. "What kind of plane is it, a crop duster?"

"One of the best aircraft ever built, son, a Douglas DC-3." His eyes lifted toward the ceiling as if one was just now flying overhead. "Hey, times a-wastin' you two. I'm going to pack. Better get those sandwiches made."

Margot opened packages of meat and cheese and I spread mustard on the bread. Shortly there was a knock on the door and Charlie ambled from his bedroom and opened it. A beautiful young girl came in. She had shoulder-length, auburn hair, gorgeous almond shaped eyes and a red and white checked shirt that was tied in a knot beneath her breasts. *Hello, Miss Clampett*, I thought. Charlie introduced her as Alma-Lou, which fit her perfectly, and then took her into his bedroom to help him finish packing.

I watched as Charlie shut the door, lost in all kinds of thoughts until Margot spoke. "Don't drool on the sandwiches, please."

"Housekeeper, my foot," I said. "Why that old buzzard could be her grandfather."

"I'm sure she's old enough to . . .clean his house." Small blotches of crimson were creeping up Margot's neck to her cheeks.

Sensing her embarrassment, the gentlemanly route would have been to change the subject. I chose another route. "So, whatcha think they're doing in there?"

She punched me in the arm. Very unladylike. "None of my business or yours. Finish wrapping the sandwiches while I pack."

I picked up a glass tumbler from the counter. "Wanna listen at the door?"

She huffed away from me but I caught a tiny smile beginning to form. Twenty minutes or so later, Charlie and Alma-Lou came out of the bedroom. He was carrying a large suitcase. She knelt down and began patting the eager dogs. Charlie ran down some last minute instructions. Margot and I both had our passports, mine fake, which hopefully we wouldn't need. He told us it was too dangerous to bring weapons on either plane. He was pretty sure the DC-3 wouldn't be searched, but guns would be hard to explain. I wondered about the two illegal fugitives, but didn't say anything.

Charlie said he'd get some weapons in Brazil. He gave us a six pack of Coke for the flight, in case we got thirsty, and a bottle of whiskey in case Yodel's flying made us nervous.

***

If there were any paved roads between Charlie's and Baton Rouge, he avoided them. He drove the Bronco like a man possessed, laughing and screaming at everything he nearly hit and at the creatures that just made it out of his way. The knuckles on Margot's right hand were white squeezing the grab handle above her door. I think we both knew that any comments from us would make him go faster.

"Wheeee-hah," he bellowed, "lookit that possum scamper."

Somehow even the thought of flying in Yodel's plane seemed more appealing. Margot looked at me, a look of panic and exasperation on her face. I smiled back my best macho-tough-guy smile, but I don't think it reassured her. We finally made it to the James B. Elder Memorial Air Field. I wondered if James B. had been killed flying with Yodel.

We got out of the Bronco, almost happy enough to kiss the ground. Charlie went into the control tower, a little tin roofed shack and Margot and I unloaded our meager belongings.

"He's crazy as a shit-house rat," I said to Margot.

"He's just a little wild," she said. "Kind of like a kid who never grew up."

"You can make excuses for him if you want, but you're still white as a ghost and look at your knuckles. He should be put somewhere where he can't hurt anybody, especially us."

"My dad told me his craziness pulled them out of some tough scrapes."

I let it drop. Her dad had been killed in one of those tough scrapes and I didn't want to say something real stupid. I looked around at the airfield. There was a quarter-mile long stretch of tarmac maybe forty feet wide. Orange wind socks hung off poles on both ends. I counted seven small planes tethered to the ground behind the control shack. One larger plane stood near one end of the runway and three guys were loading something into it from an old pickup truck. *That can't be the plane.* I don't really know what

I'd been expecting. At least a jet of some kind. This thing looked older than I was. A lot older. It was no longer than a bus and it had a propeller on each wing. Two propellers. To get us to Brazil.

"I was only kidding about a crop duster," I said to Margot.

A few minutes later, Charlie came out of the hut with a very short bearded man that he introduced to us as Yodel. Despite the heat, the pilot was wearing a knitted cap with a New Orleans Saint's emblem. His beard did a pretty good job of covering a face that had been ravaged by malaria, or something equally as horrible. His eyes bulged out and when they focused on Margot, never left her. Peter Lorre would have played him in an old movie. He reeked of garlic and motor oil.

We walked as a group to the plane. I took Margot's arm in an attempt to ward off Yodel's stare. She gave me a quick smile to show she appreciated it. The men had finished loading and we were introduced to one of them, the co-pilot, a tall Hawaiian-looking guy named Sham. Charlie and Yodel and Sham climbed up a small ladder into the plane and the other plane loaders drove off in the truck which expelled enough bluish smoke to kill half the mosquitoes in Louisiana.

"That guy is spooky," Margot whispered to me. "I hope Charlie knows what he's doing."

"It's not too late to back out, Margot," I said half-heartedly, knowing that it really was. "Maybe we could call in an air strike on that flying garbage truck while the three of them are in there."

"Shhhhh," she said. "Don't want to piss them off. Remember, they're on our side."

Before I could reply, Charlie appeared at the door and motioned us to climb aboard. Margot went first and I grabbed our baggage and followed. Yodel just about pushed Charlie out of the way so he could help Margot aboard. Nobody helped me. The inside of the plane was grubbier than the outside. Pull down seats ran the length of the passenger cabin and there were clips and rails on the ceiling which explained the small block letters above the door: *Sham's Skydiving School.*

Charlie led us around a pile of crates that had been lashed to the floor and took up most of the compartment. In the back were four fairly normal looking airplane seats, a pair on either side mounted facing the aisle.

"Here you go, kids," Charlie said with a laugh, "first class. This baby even has a working head." Then he almost whispered, "You don't know how lucky we are. Yodel only makes about one trip a month like this. Brings some stuff to a couple resorts in Cancún. He filed a flight plan that calls for a day-or-two layover in Mexico. Plenty of time to get you down to *Minas Gerais*."

"I don't like the way he looks at me, Charlie," Margot protested. "I wish I had my .357."

Charlie laughed. "You wouldn't shoot old Yodel, wouldya? He's harmless. Just naturally horny. He loves women. Don't worry. He'll get himself straightened out down in Cancún. There's a senorita down--"

Margot kicked him in his plastic leg almost hard enough to knock him down. "I don't care how he *straightens* himself out," she said. "If he keeps looking at me, I'm gonna poke his Kermit-the-Frog eyes out of his head." This made her smile that quickly turned to a laugh.

Charlie and I joined in. I guess all our nerves were stretched to the limit. Before we finished laughing one of the engines started spinning and wheezing. Sham came from the front to see Charlie off and close the hatch. Listening to the engine trying to cough itself to life reminded me of an old movie I'd seen as a kid. It was about some World War II bombers on an aircraft carrier, getting ready to blast Japan. If the planes didn't start right up, the crew had orders to push them into the Pacific. I was half hoping the crate wouldn't start. I was getting the overwhelming feeling that I was about to be pushed into the ocean.

Sham helped us buckle into our seats and headed back to the cockpit.

Shortly, half my prayers were answered and both engines were spinning away happily. I was sure I heard them both missing and I was equally as sure that Yodel didn't care. The plane shook and rattled as the engines increased their speed. All I could see was a dust cloud through my little window.

I looked at Margot and couldn't believe how green her face was. I felt her trembling.

"Never really cared for flying," she said.

"It'll be all right." I took her hand and held it. She didn't resist. "Try closing your eyes."

We had taxied around and were pointed down the runway. It didn't seem very far to an ominous stand of trees. We were poised at the end of the tarmac. The plane was shuddering like it was ready to come apart. Margot's eyes were clamped shut. Then the pilots voice clicked on a speaker which must have been close. I could hear it over the screeching engines. We started moving down the strip.

"Pilot to passengers. Charlie said you were nervous about this here old Gooneybird. Let me show you what she can do."

The plane veered sharply off the runway. Margot screamed. I probably did, too. Then it fish-tailed several times. I was afraid it was going to spin around or flip over. But Yodel was able to bring it under control and we bumped along on the grass and dirt parallel to the runway. We bounced along, going faster and faster for what felt like a very long time. Then suddenly the jouncing stopped and we were off the ground. The pilot's Alpine singing blared over the speaker. I've never wanted to choke anyone more than I wanted to choke Yodel at that minute.

The plane shook as it lumbered into the sky. Once we were airborne it felt like It was going too slow to stay up. I looked out and watched as we slowly rose above the trees. Yodel had the plane banked to the right as he was apparently circling the airstrip. The cargo crates shifted slightly but the heavy straps held them. Then, apparently waving to Charlie and his ground crew he jerked the plane back and forth, wagging his wings. It was like a bad carnival ride gone worse.

Margot and I were thrown against our belts and then back into our seats several times. I looked at her just as she began to vomit. She tried to hold her hand to her mouth to stop it, but couldn't and soon she was covered in bile-smelling breakfast bits. No airsickness bags on this flight.

Margot was crying, obviously mortified. I felt my stomach churn from the ride and from the throw-up smell. I fought to keep it down.

I undid my seat belt and pulled a tee shirt from our bag and handed it to her. Then I walked around her headed for the front of the plane. She grabbed my arm, but I shook her off. I edged along the crates and got to the cockpit area. There was a canvas flap separating it from the main compartment. I pushed the canvas aside. The pilot was yodeling and Sham was doubled over with laughter.

"Very funny," I said, and then slammed my open hand against the side of Yodel's head as hard as I could. The blow knocked him sideways and cut off his awful caterwauling.

"Hey, Man, You're crazy," the big Hawaiian said as he unbuckled his belt and began to get up. I smashed the heel of my hand into his jaw with all my might. He fell backwards, his head hitting the window and then crumpled onto the stick. His weight made the plane nose downward and I almost lost my balance. I pulled him back into his seat. Yodel pulled back on his stick and we began climbing again.

"What's wrong with you?" Yodel screamed over the howl of the engines. I grabbed him by his beard and pulled his face to mine.

"That wasn't necessary," I said. "You made that poor girl sick. Any more stunts like that and I just might kill you."

I pushed back on his beard and his head bounced off the back of his seat. I turned, ready to punch Sham again, but his head was back and his eyes were rolling around. I don't think he knew where he was. I walked out of the cockpit with Yodel swearing at me in a language I didn't know.

When I got back to Margot, she had cleaned herself up pretty well with the tee shirt. I took a bottle of Coke from the travel bag and handed it to her. "Here, have a few sips. It'll make your mouth taste better."

"Where did you go?" she asked. She was watching my hand shake as I handed her the Coke.

"I guess I flipped out and did something really stupid. I punched out the pilot and the co-pilot."

"That was pretty dumb," she said. She took another drink of Coke and smiled a weak smile at me. "But, Thanks."

I guess I expected the plane to return to the airstrip and Yodel to kick us off. It was stupid what I had done. All the tension of the past few days had finally gotten the better of me and I vented on probably the only two people who could get us to Brazil. Margot's eyes were closed, her head bowed and she was supporting her forehead with her right hand. *Stupid!* I Thought.

How could I jeopardize this trip for her, too? But the old plane didn't head down. It just kept rattling upwards into the sky. From the tiny window I saw a vast expanse of blue that had to be the Gulf of Mexico. Maybe Yodel was going to throw us into the sea.

My hands were shaking. I reached into the travel bag and got the bottle of Jack Daniel's that Charlie had given us. I asked Margot if she wanted some.

"Yes, please," she said.

The way she looked, I figured she could use the whole bottle. I took two of the plastic cups she had packed and poured in about an inch and a half. She took hers and filled it with Coke. I drank mine straight. Took me three gulps to get it down. It was hot in my mouth and burned going down. I was about to pour another when the canvas parted and Yodel pushed through and came into the cabin. He walked toward us and edged around the lashed down crates.

"Who's driving this thing?" Margot whispered to me.

Yodel had reached us before I could answer. I couldn't tell from the look on his face if he had come to fight or explain the amenities his charter passengers could expect.

"I'm sorry about that," I said. "I'm pretty stressed out."

"You hit hard," he said, and a broad grin flashed beneath his beard. He held out his hand and we shook. "I like a guy who hits hard. Like Charlie, now there's a puncher. I'm the one who should be sorry." He looked at Margot who had cleaned herself up pretty well but still smelled like vomit. "I'll see that the lady gets a nice hot bath in Mexico. My treat." He paused as if waiting to see if she'd smile. She didn't. Then he changed the subject. "Charlie tell you about me?"

"He told us you were a pretty good pilot," I said.

"Pretty good?" His grin widened. "Shee-it, I'm the best damned pilot alive. And he knows it." He grabbed a large sack that had "chutes" stenciled on it and dragged it in front of us, and then he sat on it. "Let me tell you a story about Charlie and me."

~ 112 ~

"Shouldn't you be flying this thing?" Margot asked.

"Thing?" Yodel laughed. "Don't let her hear you call her a thing. She knows the way without me. And old Sham, he's almost as good a flyer as I am." He rearranged himself on his makeshift seat. "I met Old Charlie about fifteen years ago. I was flying this same route back then. Only times were tough in those days and every once in a while, I'd bring back a shipment I probably shouldn't have. Only ganja though. Nothing heavy."

This made him laugh and snort and for a second I thought he might break into a yodel. But he didn't and continued with his story. "Well, I thought I was pretty smart. Never a snag. That's cause I wasn't greedy. But old Charlie, he got onto me somehow. The bastard'd never tell me how. He loads me and Sham in this truck under arrest and hauls us away somewhere. I figured I'd lose my plane and go to prison. But Uncle Sam, he didn't want me. He was after some bigger fish."

He paused for a minute and his eye lowered to the bottle I was still holding. Against my better judgment, I offered him some. Margot dug her elbow into me. But I had just punched him, and the Hawaiian *was* flying. I poured him a couple fingers and put the bottle back in the travel bag.

"Used to drink this stuff with Charlie," he said and downed the whiskey. "Now there's a guy can drink even harder than he can hit."

"Macho bullshit," Margot mumbled under her breath.

Yodel didn't hear her or ignored her and went on with his tale. "So he's got me and Sham chained up in this rat hole somewhere. Bet it was illegal what he was doing. Course I ain't complaining. Has us there for three days. Woulda sold my soul to get out of there. So he lays this plan out for me. Wants me to help him haul down some heavy hitters. Using me and Sham and Old Gooney here as bait. I suggested I'd like to talk to an attorney and Old Charlie off and punches me. Lots harder than you did. Said he was the only one could save me and by the time I talked to a shyster it'd be too late."

He paused and held up his empty cup. I reached for the bottle and poured him another. I was waiting for Margot's elbow but I guess she'd given up. He gulped it down and threw the cup in a corner behind more bags labeled "chutes." I was sure I heard Margot's sigh of relief over the whine of the Gooney's engines.

"I don't understand," I asked, "how can you be a pilot after a drug conviction?"

Yodel laughed and snorted. "Hell, there was no conviction. Almost got killed, but no conviction. Had to make three flights with these bad hombres. Even Sham was scared and he don't scare easy. First flight was a passenger trip. Guess they wanted to check us out. Second flight they brought suitcases back. I didn't yodel once when I had them on the plane. Third flight we had cases loaded on almost as big as these." He pointed to the crates lashed down. "I was sweating the whole flight. Charlie'd put tracking and bugging devices on the plane. Didn't tell me where. But I was sure he'd be waiting when we returned. Had to land Gooney on a stretch of grass barely long enough to play football on. And it was dark. I had to land almost blind. Only the lights of two pickup trucks to guide me. The bad dudes' men. Then a really bad thought struck me. What if Charlie and his pals weren't there. These guys might not need us any more and kill us right on the spot. I usually carried a couple guns with me but Charlie and his men took 'em when they checked the plane. Sham and me was both sweating. Well I landed all right. Little bumpy, but I kinda like that." He smiled and nodded slightly at Margot.

I don't know how she did it but her head had dropped and she was sleeping.

"So what happened?" I asked.

"Well, the two pickups drove over to us and shined their headlights on the hatch. The three goons all had their weapons drawn. Big time artillery, too. They made me open it up for them. I was sure I was gonna get it. One of the trucks backed up to the hatch and the one they called Hun jumped into it. Well as soon as he hit the truck, the shooting started. I hit the deck. Sham was still in the cockpit grabbing as much floor as he could. It was over in no time. Hun was dead. Killed instantly. I'd call it an execution, Charlie called it self defense."

He chuckled at that and looked at the spot where he'd thrown the cup, but didn't ask for more.

"The other two fired a bunch of rounds but couldn't see what to aim at. Finally they gave it up and surrendered. Well, I figured that would be just the beginning for me and Sham, testifying in court, death threats, everything. But Old Charlie took care of it. Filed the reports like Gooney, me and Sham never existed. Let me keep my plane, my pilot's ticket and I even ended up with the grand I woulda got for the shipment.

"Don't know how he did it. Or why. But I'm really beholding to that guy. Course, he did tell me he'd be watching me and if he found out I was doing anything illegal, he'd shove old Gooney up my ass." He started roaring with laughter. Margot stirred but didn't wake up. "So that's why when Charley asked me to get you two to Brazil I said 'no problemo.' That's also why I didn't let Sham kill you after that stunt up front. Hey, how 'bout while the missus is sleeping, I let you fly the greatest airplane ever built?"

"I don't know how to fly," I said. "I don't even like flying."

He laughed. "There's nothing to it. Follow me. He pulled back the flap to the cockpit. Sham glared at me as he got up and walked by me. "He'll sleep on a pile of 'chutes," Yodel said, "and when he wakes up, he'll have forgot all about that little love tap. Just sit here in the pilot's chair."

The seat was ripped and had been patched with duct tape, but it was quite comfortable. I felt the wheel and looked at the controls.

"She's on autopilot right now. You just have to sit back and enjoy the ride. Check the altimeter and air-speed indicator once in a while." He pointed to them. "They should remain steady, but if they don't, wake me up. Here." He handed me a book that he pulled from a pocket by his seat. "This will explain anything you don't know about old Gooney." And with that he closed his eyes and began snoring almost instantly.

I couldn't believe it; the snore was more like a yodel. The bastard even yodeled in his sleep. I looked at the altimeter; steady at 4,047 feet. The air speed was steady at 230 knots. I couldn't remember what a knot was but I guess that didn't matter as long as it stayed steady. The book he'd handed me was a dog-eared old manual that had been printed on yellowish paper that was turning brown in spots.

I noted a penned inscription inside the front cover, Col. Jonathan S. Blane, December 1945. Maybe the plane's first pilot. I looked out the windows for a while, nothing but blue ocean and blue sky and an occasional wispy white cloud. I took the wheel, and it felt good. I watched the gauges and the sky for a while. Nothing changed. Boring. I figured I'd read the manual.

It was an interesting little book, "Pilot Training for the Skytrain C-47." On each of the 107 pages, the word "Restricted" was printed. There was a drawing of a five-star general (five stars on his shoulder anyway) on the first page. He looked a lot like Ike. Part of the introduction read:

> Shortly after the landing of our marines on Guadalcanal, C-47s, making their final approach over the Japs who held the edge of Henderson Field, flew in anti-personnel ammunition when not a round was left among our forces.

Rah, rah, rah, boys! I guess they weren't politically correct back in 1945. Then I came to my favorite part:

> It's an easy plane to handle, has no bad flying characteristics and gives maximum performance under the most adverse conditions. However it is an airplane that you can't stunt drive.

Right. Like I was gonna flip off the autopilot and wake Yodel up with some loop-de-loops. I watched the gauges and read the book and looked at the sky and the ocean for a good three hours, until Yodel woke up. He seemed happy I hadn't found a way to crash us.

"She sure is fun to fly, ain't she?" he asked.

"Oh yeah," I said, "It was as exciting as watching grass grow."

We swapped seats. And Yodel fiddled with knobs and switches. "Look ahead, there," he said. That's Mehico."

The view was spectacular as we approached Mexico at 5000 feet. Yodel pointed to a plume of smoke billowing skyward to our left and said it was from Cuba. Probably a sugar-cane field. Ahead purple mountains loomed over sparkling sand that crept into the cobalt-blue ocean.

We were in a gradual descent. Yodel sent me back to my seat and I helped Margot buckle in and then buckled myself. Margot closed her eyes tight and gripped my hand. I turned my head to watch out the small window. We were getting low and the plane was vibrating. I heard a clunking which must have been the landing gear. Margot heard it too and tightened her death grip on my hand.

I expected a thump when we touched down, but there was none, just the change in noise as the tires gripped the tarmac and began rolling. We taxied for about five minutes and then came to a stop. The Hawaiian was out of the cockpit before the plane had stopped rolling. He rushed to our seats.

"You two will have to hide in the head," he said, "until Yodel finds out who's working and makes arrangements." He led us to the little compartment and we squeezed in. Just before he shut the door, I spotted a Jeep heading toward us. I probably would have enjoyed being stuck in the tiny space with Margot except it was about 130 degrees in there and the smell of vomit mixed with the chemical-toilet aroma was about the worst combination of odors I'd ever experienced.

"I'm so sorry, Jake," Margot whispered. "I know I smell awful."

"Don't worry about it kid. We'll be out of here real soon. Until then, I'll just imagine that lilac perfume that you wear."

Chivalrous.

We heard the hatch clang and then the muffled exchange of Spanish. Shortly, the door opened and we were greeted by Yodel's smiling face. "The men will unload the plane," he said. "We will leave in three hours. Paco will bring you to a nice inn where I have arranged a room and a hot shower. Again my apologies to the lady." I thought he might take her hand and bring it to his lips, but he didn't. She probably would have socked him.

We climbed in the Jeep with Paco. Sham loaded our traveling cases. The Inn was about a mile from the airport. *Mesón De Paco,* said the sign.

Paco took our bags and led us to room Number 6. He had a key and opened the door. "Two hours," he said *Comprenda?"*

"Si," I said. It felt good to talk the language.

It was a small room, clean and cool. The air conditioner under the only window was running on full. Margot took her shower first. Then I got into the hot water, letting it run over the wound on my left arm. Charlie had done some doctoring to it at his place and it felt like it was healing well. Even the *Mesón De Paco* had more water pressure than my condo.

After my shower, Margot put some salve that Charlie had given her on my wound and re-bandaged it.

"Thanks," I said. "That feels nice."

"I was thinking of joining you in the shower," she said, her brown eyes staring at me.

I didn't know what to say. *Shut up and listen, idiot.*

"When we first met, I was planning a way to seduce you, or have you seduce me." She paused. "At the doctor's, when he said that Bruce was alive and well and had been kidnapped, I was ashamed. That's why I have to find out what happened and get him back if he's alive."

I hugged her. "I understand," I whispered. I was thinking of how much this woman differed from my exes. Hell, Witch Number two was with the dentist getting her cavity filled, while I was working hard to pay the rent.

Oh, well. We lay on the bed, holding each other, silently, for a good hour, lost in our private thoughts. Paco tap-tapped on the door and we left our little room.

Outside was like a sauna. I was soaked with sweat just walking to the Jeep. Paco chattered away in Spanish through the whole ten-minute ride. He stopped at a cement block building. Yodel's plane was fifty yards away. Men were refueling it and loading heavy-looking blue drums on board. Paco exited the Jeep and ambled to a soda machine by the front of the building.

I looked at Margot. "About back at the Inn--" I began but she cut me off.

"Let's not talk about it now, Jake. I'm so totally messed up with everything that's happened. And will happen. I don't know if I'll ever get home again."

"Don't talk like that, Margot." I put my hand on her arm, but she pulled it away. "Why don't you just head home now? Tell everyone I kidnapped you."

"I have to do this. Let me be alone for a few minutes, OK?" She got out of the Jeep and began walking slowly toward the plane.

I went into the building. I saw Yodel in a room to the right. He was standing at a table with a very thin man dressed in a khaki uniform. They were staring grimly at a large chart. Yodel managed a weak smile as I walked in. He introduced me to the man, *Señor* Able Cortez, the manager of the airfield. He shook my hand, an unexpectedly firm grip from such a wiry *hombre.*

"Señor Cortez doesn't think much of my flight plan," Yodel said.

"What's the matter with it?" I asked as I watched the thin man shake his head from side to side.

"Look," Yodel said and flattened the chart out on the table. "My official flight plan is to take two American passengers to *Punta de Aragua.*" He pointed to a small dot. "It's not much more than a big rock in the Lesser Antilles. Has a weather station and a makeshift airfield. Ten years ago I wouldn't have had to tell them anything. Now I have to fill out fancy forms *ala* Uncle Sam. Put you two down as professors from Louisiana State going down to count birds."

Cortez was still shaking his head, speaking to Yodel in Spanish.

"What doesn't he like?" I asked when Cortez finally stopped.

"Ah, he can be an old woman at times," Yodel said to me. "*Vieja Señora,*" to Cortez. Anyway, we start descending like we're gonna land, but instead, we turn south and fly at about 200 feet until we cross into Venezuela. We should be just below their radar. We'll fly right between these two small towns."

He pointed to *Rio Caribe* and *Güiria.* "The only one who might see us is the old man with the burro loaded with coffee beans.

Him again. "I thought that was Columbia," I said.

Yodel looked at me like my father did when I had tried to correct him. "All these countries down here have old men with coffee-loaded burrows. Only two things to worry about at this point. We'll be real heavy with all the extra fuel. That makes it difficult to fly so low. Second are these little bumps." He ran his finger along a half-inch section of the coast of Venezuela. "Mountains." He smiled at me. "*Montañas.*"

"*Imbécil,*" Cortez muttered and stomped away.

"Can he cause trouble?" I asked.

"Nah." Yodel waved after him. "He's well paid for the little he does. I don't think the bastard's flown anything with more than one engine in his life. I've done stuff like this many times. Nothing to worry about. We fly due south until we cross into Brazil and then southeast, almost in a straight line until we get to *Belo Horizonte,* right here." He thumped the spot with his finger and then traced the imaginary line back up to Venezuela. "Not much here but mountains and rain forest."

"Where do we land?" I asked.

"That," Yodel said without smiling, "Could be our biggest problem. We have to depend on Charlie to get down there and establish an LZ."

"LZ?"

"Landing zone. We can't fly into a commercial airport. We'll circle in a fifty mile radius around this point," he tapped the chart, "and wait for Charlie to contact us."

"What if he has problems?" I asked. "What if he can't find an LZ or if he doesn't even get to Brazil?"

"Well, I trust old Charlie. But if he can't hook us up . . ." He shrugged, "I figure we can circle for an hour and a half. Two hours tops."

"And if we don't hear from him?"

"Then we head back. I can't stop for fuel in Brazil."

I must have looked pretty discouraged. Yodel put his hand on my shoulder and squeezed. "Don't worry mister bird-counter, Charlie's pulled off a lot more complicated operations than this."

"I hope so," I said and walked out, not acknowledging Yodel's rare moment of compassion.

Despite the oppressive heat, I began to shiver when I walked back into the sunlight. I had a tremendous urge to just run, to run until I reached the bone-white sandy beach I'd seen from the plane, to run right into the ocean, as if the ocean would cleanse me of this whole mess and flush this Brazilian nightmare into a bottomless abyss.

A half hour later Margot and I sat strapped in our seats ready for the next leg of our adventure.

Chapter 15

The Gooney Bird shook with a vengeance as it rolled down the runway. I had the image of an old hawk trying to fly holding a very large sheep in its talons.

"Why aren't we taking off?" Margot asked, a note of panic in her voice. "Why isn't he howling?"

"Don't worry," I said, but I didn't feel confident. "We have a heavy load of extra fuel. And if I never hear him yodel again, it will be too soon."

The palm trees were whizzing by us and I knew the Caribbean Sea was looming dead ahead. I felt Margot's fingernails digging into my leg. *Sing, you bastard!* I said to myself. It seemed like an eternity, but finally the noise of the wheels on the runway quieted and I knew we were off the ground. A minute later I heard the clunking sounds as the landing gear was retracted.

"We're off," I said to Margot. Her eyes were shut tight and her fingernails continued biting into my leg. "That should be the toughest part of the flight." I was trying to reassure myself as much as I was her. The plane stank of oil and aviation gas. Twenty hours, Yodel had estimated. It was unimaginable.

After we'd been in the air about an hour, Yodel came back to see us. He was smiling but it wasn't the usual broad grin he sported.

"No yodeling?" I asked him.

"Saving it for the ride home," he said. "Goonie knows how to handle take offs like that. We'll be okay. We should be light enough by the time we get to the mountains to make it over."

"Mountains?" Margot asked, her eyes widened at the thought. "What mountains?"

"Nothing to be concerned about," he said grinning a little larger now. I was glad *he* was happy. "Lucky for us the best route is over some of the smaller mountains. Should make it with feet to spare."

"I hate you." Margot said and it sure sounded like she meant it. But it got Yodel laughing and Margot and I soon joined in. I wondered if some of Custer's men laughed at the "Last Stand."

Yodel unfolded our chart and explained what the trip would be like. He wanted to cross the coast of Venezuela while there was still daylight. That would be the most dangerous part. After that, it was just mountains and rain forest until we were almost at our destination. He set up a couple crates and he and I played cribbage. Margot read a magazine that she had packed back in New Stratley.

We'd been in the air for several hours when the Hawaiian came back into the cabin. He said he was going to take a nap and then began arranging himself a bed of parachutes. Yodel motioned for me to follow him. Margot's eyes were shut and her head tilted back. She was snoring very softly and I hoped she was dreaming about something more pleasant than this plane ride. I got up as quietly as I could so I wouldn't wake her. I made my way around the drums of fuel and went into the cockpit.

"Take a seat, *Amigo*," Yodel offered.

I took the co-pilot's seat. I much preferred this to the claustrophobic cabin. All I could see in every direction was blue ocean with sunlight sparkling off it, almost as bright as the sun itself.

"So how much longer?" I asked, like the little kid in the family sedan.

"I've been thinking about that since we took off," Yodel said. "I'm changing the route a little. I'm a little nervous about the Venezuelan Coast Guard. Also some of the mountains can be tricky, especially after dark which is when we'd be going through them."

He handed me a chart that he'd folded into a manageable size. "See, here we are right now." He pointed. "And right about here," pointing again, "I was gonna head due south. Would be the most direct. What I'm gonna do is stay on this course to here." He unfolded the map once and pointed to two small land masses. "We'll go right between Kingstown and St. George's Islands. Then we'll arc around here and enter South America right here into Guyana about 100 kilometers west of Georgetown."

"Guyana will be better?" I asked.

"Hell, yes!" He laughed and almost broke into a yodel. "The Guyana Air Force consists of two biplanes they bought from the French after World War I."

I knew he was kidding, but I was also sure he was right about the border crossing being much safer. Hell, I'd never heard of Guyana before Jim Jones killed his whole flock with smiley-faced pitchers of poisoned fruit punch. I remembered I'd looked it up on the map after that. It seemed so far away and unapproachable. And I *had* been thinking about Venezuelan jets swooping down and blowing us out of the sky.

"Anyway," Yodel continued, "We'll get to Kingstown in about six hours. Maybe less if this tail wind continues. And then another nineteen hours and we'll be smack dab over old Charlie, waiting for his landing instructions."

"That's twenty-five hours," I said. "We'll be in this old crate for more than a day."

"That's pretty near what I figured." He patted the planes instrument console. "And please watch what ya say about Gooney here. She's sensitive." And then he began to yodel.

I closed my eyes and, luckily, dozed off.

I slept for a while before Sham shook me awake. "Get some food," he said. I went into the cabin. Margot had opened the bag of sandwiches.

"Guess we both slept a while," she said.

"I feel like I could sleep for a week." I took the sandwich she handed me and bit into it. We ate and made small talk trying to control the tension we both felt. An hour later, Sham came out of the cockpit.

"Yodel says one of you should go up front," he said and then lay on his bed of parachutes. He sure knew how to pass the time flying. Margot didn't want to be alone with Yodel, so I went into the cockpit. The sun was just setting on the horizon and it was a spectacular view. I was beginning to get used to the thrum of the engines, although I wished they'd been jets.

"Why do we have all those drums of fuel on board?" I asked after a long silence.

Yodel laughed. "This isn't a trip to the corner store, Sonny. I have extra tanks built into Gooney 'cause I've done a few long trips. But there's no place to refuel in Brazil, so when we drop you off, we have to get back to Pago Island and we'll be using that extra fuel to get there."

"Seems kinda dangerous to pump fuel from those drums," I said.

"It sure is. One small spark, even static electricity and kablooey! Off we go to the big hangar in the sky." Yodel looked at me to see what reaction this had. "But you don't have to worry. You'll be safe on the ground eating roasted llamas with Charlie when we do it. We've fueled like this before without problems. everything is well grounded and I have a special pump just for fuel."

I was a little relieved that the refueling would take place after we'd gotten off. I still didn't like the idea of all that gas sloshing around back there. At least it would be quick, I thought. We flew into the dusk for about an hour. Yodel had a small transistor radio that he kept fiddling with. Once in a while he'd find a station that came in pretty well. There was nothing in English and the music wasn't like any I'd ever heard before. But it really seemed to please him.

"There" he said suddenly, surprising me. "Dead ahead. Can you see it?"

"What am I looking for?" I asked.

"That's the coast of Guyana."

I strained my eyes and finally I could make out just the shadow of a hump seeming to rise from the ocean.

Yodel dimmed the lights in the cockpit. "We're going in kind of low," he said. "They don't have much for sophisticated radar in this area and there are many small planes that fly around out here. Showing the tourists the sunsets. We shouldn't even be noticed."

And It seemed like we weren't.

We had been over land for about ten minutes when Yodel swore under his breath. Then there was a great roar as something flew by us on our left side. I wasn't sure how close but it was near enough that Yodel had to fight to gain control.

"What the hell was that?" I asked.

Yodel peered through the windscreen following with his eyes the fiery jet of a marauder. "That," he finally said, "was a fighter plane. I'm just not sure whose."

Sham came into the cockpit just as the fighter disappeared from our sight.

Yodel was putting on a head-set. He turned a knob on the radio apparently searching for the other jet's frequency.

Sham looked at me and I wasn't happy with the frightened look on his face.

"What are we gonna do," I asked.

Just then Yodel began speaking into the headset's microphone. It was Spanish and I didn't understand a word, but Sham did and his eyes grew wider as the conversation went on. After a minute of this, Yodel flipped a switch and turned to us. "It's Venezuelan," he said. "Shocks the hell out of me. An F-16, too. A Fighting Falcon. Must've hit their airspace somehow."

"Shit," said the Hawaiian.

"Gonna have to do some serious acting here," Yodel went on. "Remember how we did that fake crash in Colombia back in seventy-seven?"

"I remember," Sham said. "But . . . I don't know--"

"Stop yappin' and get moving, we have about three minutes to make this happen."

Sham backed out of the cockpit and Yodel turned the radio dial and flipped a couple switches.

"Oscar time," he said.

"I don't like this, Yodel. Maybe we should give up."

"Shhh." He put his fingers to his lips. "Trust me, South American prison food sucks, and that's on a good day. Now get ready to call the Academy." He turned another switch and began speaking into the mike. "Mayday! Mayday! This is flight 7177 bravo sierra from Honduras. We are lost and experiencing engine problems."

He had turned on a small speaker so I could hear the conversation. He was enjoying this.

"7177 bravo sierra this is VAC Tower. We copy you. You must change your heading 170 degrees west. Copy, flight 7177?"

"Unable to. Have lost the starboard engine! We need to land now, Tower." The panic in his voice sounded real. He moved a lever and I heard the right engine sputter and stop. "We're losing the port engine, too." He whispered to me. "This will crackle it up. Sounds real good, like we're really in trouble." He fiddled with a dial on the radio.

From where I was sitting it felt like we *were* really in trouble.

"Flight 7177 bravo sierra, this is VAC Tower, interceptor confirms your starboard engine is out."

"No shit, Tower." He pointed over his shoulder and I could see the fighter had come around and was off our wing. Yodel looked out the window and made some frantic hand gestures to the other pilot. "He can't go as slow as us for long."

"Five hundred feet," Yodel said over the intercom. "Hurry it up, Sham."

"What if he's not ready in time?" I asked.

"Then," Yodel glanced briefly at me. "We crash, or they shoot us down."

Yodel was working the controls frantically and screaming into the microphone. If he wasn't scared, he *was* a great actor.

"Go back and help him," he ordered. "We have less than two minutes."

The plane was angled downward and I grabbed what I could hold onto and scrambled to the rear compartment. In the dim light I saw the big Hawaiian strapping two Jerry cans together.

"Two minutes," I yelled at him. Margot remained in her seat, her eyes wide. "It'll be fine," I called back to her but she didn't respond.

"What can I do?" I asked Sham.

"Tie this." He handed me two ends of the rope that he had wrapped around the cans. I began tying them. Just as I was finished, he was back holding something in his hand. A hand grenade. "Here," he said, "tie this to the cans. But don't pull the pin."

I did as he said. *Why did they have a hand grenade on board?* I didn't have much time to wonder. Sham swung open the big door. The rush of the air made a frightening sound. I was just able to hear a moan from Margot over the wind noise.

"Sixty seconds," Yodel came over the loud speaker.

Sham checked my knots and when he was satisfied, we picked up the cans and carried them to the door. I was just beginning to understand what we were doing.

"Thirty seconds."

Margot was screaming something but I couldn't tell what it was.

Sham and I stood at the open door, and it was then that I realized how really low we were. It was dark out but I could make out the shapes of the tree tops that we were skimming over.

"Fifteen seconds. You better be ready You crazy Hawaiian bastard." Yodel's voice was scratchy over the loud speaker.

Sham looked at me with a nervous smile. "I hope we're ready," he said. "And, I hope this grenade isn't a dud."

"Me, too," I said.

"Ten seconds! Nine."

Sham and I each held a handle. He pulled the pin on the grenade.

"Seven . . . six."

Sham nodded at me and we picked the cans up. "When he says three," he yelled over the howling wind.

"Four . . . three."

We heaved the cans out the door.

"Two . . . one." All the lights in the plane went out. We looked out the door and for a very long second or two there was nothing. And then a flash of fire illuminated the sky behind us.

We were just above the tree tops and running on one engine. Shan shut the door and the back of the plane was in total darkness.

~ 127 ~

I felt my way over and sat next to Margot. She grabbed my hand so hard I thought she might break a finger. "What's happening?" She asked.

I explained to her what I had seen and what I was sure Yodel had hoped to accomplish with his fire bomb. "We'll just have to sit tight and hope it worked."

A minute later, Yodel's voice came over the loudspeaker "They bought it. They think we crashed." I felt like cheering until I remembered how low we were and how much danger we were still in. One tall tree or high power line stretched across the forest, even a hill and it would be all over.

I kept saying things to Margot, trying to reassure her. When I heard the second engine start, I did let out a little whoop.

"Why are the lights out?" Margot asked. "I hate this."

As if on cue, the cabin lights came back on. I told Margot I was going to find out what was going on and headed for the front of the plane. The cockpit was very dimly lit but I saw the huge smiles on the two men's faces. There were urgent voices over the radio.

"Worked like a charm," Yodel said. "They're trying to get a chopper in to inspect the crash site but that will be an hour or two away. We're picking up altitude slowly so I'd say we're out of any danger. Couldn't have done that in daylight. By the time they find out we fooled them, we'll be over the rain forest of Brazil. That is *if* they ever find out. Lots of rough terrain down there."

With that, he reached under his seat and took out a bottle. He took a big gulp and gave it to Sham. "One snort for good luck," he said. Sham drank and handed it to me. I took my snort and it sure felt good as it warmed my mouth and throat.

I asked Yodel if I could give Margot a drink of the whiskey. He nodded but told me not to let her have too much. I brought the bottle back into the cabin and offered it to her. She wiped the top with her sleeve and took a giant swig. And then another.

"Easy," I said. "Yodel said you could only have a little."

She made an unladylike comment about the pilot and took another gulp. Then she handed the bottle back to me. I sat down next to her. "Looks like we dodged another bullet."

"This is crazy, you know," she said. "We might as well be going to the moon. Maybe there won't be anything down there in Brazil. What will we do then?"

"Well I've thought some about that. I can't go home if I can't prove who's behind the murders in New Stratley. And if I can't do it down in Brazil I don't have the foggiest idea where to look next. In that case, I might just get myself a used sombrero and head into the hills to write my memoirs."

"Very funny," she said.

Just then Sham came back. "Yodel wants the bottle," he said.

I took one more swig and Margot took two and handed it to him. He frowned when he saw what was left.

"Hey, he drank most of ours," Margot said.

"He wants you both to sleep for awhile. We have a long ways to go and he'll want some fresh eyes with him in the morning."

After he went back up front, Margot and I agreed that we should try to sleep. I leaned my head back, sure that there was no way I'd be able to doze off. Several minutes later, I was somehow fast asleep.

Chapter 16

The next thing I knew, someone was shaking my shoulder. It was the Hawaiian. "Wake up, sleepy head," he said. "Your snoring's louder than the engines." He laughed at this. "Your turn up front." With that he went to his bed of parachutes and fell into it. Margot was still sleeping. I was surprised his voice and laughter hadn't woken her, but I was glad she was getting some much needed rest.

I went to the head and then into the cockpit and was greeted by an amazing sight. It was just about dawn and stretching out in all directions, as far as the eye could see was a sea of green.

"Rain forest," he said. "It's like the grand canyon. I never can fly over either without getting this feeling inside."

"Warm and fuzzy?" I asked.

"No, more like the feeling when you hear some great jazz and the guy plays notes that you couldn't imagine he could play, but there they were and you just never want him to stop. Know that feeling?"

"I don't, but my friend Bart does. Or at least he tells me he does."

I guess I was surprised that Yodel would have feelings like that. There sure was a lot to this crazy little pilot from Cajun country.

"One more hour," he said, "give or take a couple minutes, and we'll be over the Amazon River. I'm gonna close my eyes and let you fly awhile. Wake me up when we get there."

"How will I know the Amazon?"

"You'll know," he said.

***

Yodel was right. The Amazon was like a giant blue snake slithering through the green forest. I woke him up. He wiped his eyes and inspected the instruments and then the view of the great river.

"Ya done OK, Sonny," he said. "I'll make a pilot out of you yet."

I went back into the cabin where Sham was snoring on his makeshift bed. Margot was awake and she and I had a sandwich and a Coke. The Coke was warm but it tasted wonderful. Margot asked if I wanted to borrow her magazine but I declined.

"I've got a lot to think about," I said.

I sat there thinking for a while and then somehow fell asleep. I slept for a long time, dreaming about flying and crocodiles and all kinds of crazy things that I couldn't remember. Margot woke me and said Yodel wanted me in the cockpit. I rubbed the sleep from my eyes and joined him.

"Where are we?" I asked.

"We're about a hundred miles from *Belo Horizonte*, according to my calculations. We should be hearing from Charlie any minute."

I noticed his music radio was turned way down and his plane radio was making crackling noises. Everything looked the same to me, all green and brown.

Several minutes later a familiar voice broke through the static. "Come in Bird-Dog. This is Charlie. Over."

"Wahoo," Yodel yodeled. "Good to hear you, Charlie. Bird-Dog is here awaitin' instructions. Over."

Sham came into the cockpit, a huge grin spread across his face at the sound of Charlie's voice. Charlie gave Yodel some coordinates that I didn't understand. Yodel made a few adjustments and we flew in silence for about ten minutes.

"Why isn't he talking?" I asked.

"We agreed that once we made contact we'd keep radio transmissions to a minimum. We're using a frequency that isn't very common, but no sense taking extra chances. This is a covert mission, you know."

"Yeah," I said, "I know, and I'll be happy as hell when it's over."

"Bird-Dog, come in. You're looking fine. Got a nice patch of pampas here for you to set down on."

"Roger, Charlie. Let me know when you have visual."

Three minutes later, Charlie advised that he had sight of us. We were pretty low at that point, about 500 feet. Yodel pushed some levers and there was a clanging as the landing gear deployed.

Lights flashed on the instrument panel. "Shit," said Yodel.

"Bird-Dog, this is Charlie. Your port-side gear is up."

"Roger that, Charlie. What does it look like for company?"

"We're pretty barren down here. No sign of any locals. A half-hour should be safe. Over."

"What did he mean?" I asked Yodel.

"He means," he said as his fingers kept flipping levers back and forth, "that there's no sign of any local army or cops so we can circle here for a little while to see if we can get the gear down."

"Can't we land with the gear up?" I asked.

He looked at me and there was frustration in his eyes. "You ask a lotta damn questions. Yes, we can land with the gear up. On our belly. But we can't take off like that and I ain't gonna leave Gooney down here in Brazil." Anticipating my next question, "And if I can't get the gear down in the next half hour, I'm heading back. If we gotta go in belly first, I want friendly faces around when we do."

With that he got up. "Take over Sham. Keep us in a tight circle at about 1,000 feet while I see if I can find out what's wrong with the gear."

He looked at me. "Come on, Mr. Questions, give me a hand with that landing gear."

Yodel and I went into the back, behind the cockpit and he opened a panel on the floor and peered inside with a flashlight.

"What's going on?" Margot asked. She had walked over to see what we were doing. "Sham said we should be landing soon."

"Another one with questions," Yodel spat and then cursed.

Margot looked at me.

"One of the landing gear won't go down," I said. "We only have a half hour or so to get it fixed or we have to turn back."

"No." Margot shouted. "We can't. We've come too far."

"Hopefully, Yodel can get it fixed," I said trying to sound reassuring but I sure didn't feel that way. Tears were streaming down Margot's cheeks. I put my arm around her and gave her a hug.

She pulled closer to me and put her face against my shoulder. I could feel the wetness of her tears through my shirt.

Yodel's head was jammed into the hole where the panel came from. When he looked up at me, I knew it wasn't good. "There's a hydraulic leak somewhere," he said. "I can see fluid coming from the port side. Could take hours to fix it. If I can get to the leak at all." He shook his head. "I'm sorry." He actually sounded sincere.

I looked at Margot's tear-streaked face. I wanted to cry myself.

"There is one way," Yodel said. "Might be a little risky but Sham's a good teacher."

"What way?" I asked.

"We'll give you a crash course, and you can parachute in."

"Parachute? You must be crazy." Margot's face had turned bright crimson, reminding me of the Caribbean sunset. "I don't even do stepladders."

"It's the only way," Yodel said matter-of-factly. "You parachute in . . . or you fly back with me."

Margot looked at me. "I don't want to do it, either," I said. "I only do three rungs on a stepladder, myself. But, he's right. It's that or we go back."

"And we have to get going right now." Yodel said. "I'll go relieve Sham and let Charlie know what we're gonna do. Here." He handed me a duffel bag. "Put what you can of your stuff in this bag. Anything else, I'll get back to Charlie's."

Margot and I hurriedly filled the small bag with as much as it would hold. I had often wondered what kind of a nut would jump from a plane with nothing but a parachute, and now I was going to find out. The big Hawaiian came back, reached into one of his big sacks, and handed us each a parachute. He was smiling broadly, the sadistic bastard. Revenge for the punch in the mouth. He helped us on with the chutes.

"How will we know when to open the chute?" I asked.

"You won't have to," Sham said. "I'm using seventeen-foot static lines. They will open the chutes for you shortly after you jump." He cinched up the straps on my chute and then began helping Margot. I don't know what he did but, from the corner of my eye, I saw Margot belt him in the head. And it was a pretty good belt, too.

"Watch it, Buster," she said.

"Ow, Lady," Sham complained. "I was only tightening it up for you."

Apparently a hit to the head wasn't unusual for the big guy and he carried on with the tightening. He walked away to get something and I whispered to Margot.

"I hope you didn't get him too mad. If he forgets to cinch us up . . .."

Shan came back with the static lines and began hooking them up. He gave us quick instructions on how to land. "There's no water down there and Charlie will be watching for you. You can steer the chute a little by pulling on the strings but I don't have time to teach you that. Just try to avoid getting caught in a tree. They're sport chutes and they'll let you down pretty gentle. Try to land with your knees bent a little and you should be all right." He bent for us to show us the proper landing procedure.

"What if the chute doesn't open?" Margot asked.

"They do... almost always." Sham said with a smile. He was enjoying this too much. "You'll feel the chute when it opens. It will really slow you down. If for some reason it doesn't open, this is the emergency chute. Pull this handle."

At that minute, Yodel came back. "Are we ready?"

Sham nodded. Yodel shook our hands. "Give my regards to old Charlie. And good luck." With that he was gone and Sham opened the side door of the plane.

"Ladies first," Sham said. Margot didn't budge. "Almost out of time, lady."

She edged over to the open door and put one foot on the edge. "I can't," she said.

"Yes you can," Sham said and he pushed her out the door. He watched and after several second, announced that her chute was open. "Okay, it's your turn."

Well, if Margot could do it I guess I could. But I wasn't about to give him the satisfaction of pushing me. I walked to the door, closed my eyes and jumped into nothingness.

As soon as I exited the plane, the wind caught me and spun me. All I could see was a dizzying kaleidoscope of green. I was sure at that point that I was plunging head first to my death. And there was nothing I could do about it. Then, there was a huge snapping noise and I was jolted upright. The chute had opened and slowed me down. Maybe I wasn't going to die after all.

I saw Margot's chute a couple football fields off to my right and several hundred feet below me. I looked down trying to spot the landing area but all I could see were trees. I was hoping that Charlie was watching and could get to us when we landed. I don't think we were very high when we jumped because soon after the chute opened we were almost down. I wasn't sure how to steer the thing. I tried pulling a couple of the chords but nothing happened. I looked down and all I could see was the biggest tree in Brazil rushing to meet me. I lost sight of Margot before we hit the tree line and I was hoping she landed all right.

The next thing I knew I was crashing through tree branches. I covered my head and face as well as I could. Then I was jolted again as the chute caught in the top of the tree. I was dangling at least fifty feet in the air. My first instinct was to yell for help. But then I wasn't sure who was around, if anyone. I was about ten feet away from the tree trunk. I began swinging back and forth and soon was able to grab a branch and pull myself next to the trunk. I tested my weight on the branch and it felt secure, so I undid the harness and pulled it off me. I'm not sure what kind of tree it was but it had many branches and was easy to climb down.

The branches stopped about ten feet from the ground. I hung by my hands, monkey-style, and then dropped to the forest floor. And it felt good to touch the ground again. I heard a noise and looked up. It was the C-47 flying tight circles with one wheel up and the other down like a huge wounded bird. I could imagine Yodel and

Sham laughing at me dangling from the tree. And then it flew off. I listened as the plane's sound diminished and then vanished.

But it wasn't quiet. The jungle was full of noises, caws and chirps and clicking sounds. And it was hot. Sweat rolled down my forehead and into my eyes. I was in Brazil. And even though Margot and Charlie were nearby, I had no idea which direction they were in. And I felt very alone and very, very lost.

***

I began walking in the direction I thought I'd last seen Margot's chute. The forest floor was covered with ferns and what looked like large pine needles. As I walked slowly along, something was skittering and slithering underneath them. I felt almost barefoot in my sneakers. I tried to remember the kinds of snakes I'd read about that live in South America. I was pretty sure that most of them were poisonous and that the worst ones were probably here.

I don't hate snakes, but I don't like them enough to get up close and personal. After a while, I got to a little clearing covered in a brownish saw-grass. Things couldn't hide in it too easily and I figured I'd stay there until Charlie, hopefully, found me.

About fifteen minutes later, I heard the rumbling of an engine. I looked over some kind of a leafy thing and there was an old beat up Jeep with Charlie driving. I couldn't believe how happy I was to see that crazy old guy.

"Charlie!" I yelled and started through the brush towards him.

"Hoy, Jake," he yelled back.

I pushed my way through the brush onto the dirt area where the Jeep was stopped. And then it got me. I must have stepped on it or scared it somehow. I felt this awful, biting pain in my ankle and looked down in time to see the black and red creature slither away.

I saw two blurs of khaki as Charlie and the man who was in the Jeep with him jumped to the ground and ran towards me. Charlie was waving a huge machete and my first thought was that he was going to slice my leg open with it. But he hobbled right past me. The other man took my arm and urged me to sit. He was speaking in a language I didn't know. I didn't see any more snakes on the ground so I warily obliged him and sat down in the saw grass. He took a knife from his pocket and slit the leg of my pants up past my ankle. I could see the two pink dots where the fangs had pierced my skin.

"*Sinto muito, Senhor,*" the man said. "*Meu nome — Sexta-feira. Silenc—!*"

I heard a rustling in the brush and Charlie came out holding half a snake. He held it just below the head. The bottom was writhing and splashing blood even though half was missing. The Brazilian man looked at the snake and then muttered some words as his fingers marked the sign of the cross on his chest. I was beginning to feel faint and his actions weren't helping.

"It's a coral snake, I'm pretty sure," Charlie said. "Course there's a lot of snakes that mimic them."

"What does that mean?" I asked not sure if I really wanted to know.

"Well, corals are pretty poisonous."

"Well are you gonna suck the poison out?" I asked.

Charlie laughed. "First of all, I don't like you enough to suck poison out of your leg. Second of all, it wouldn't do any good."

The snake had stopped writhing and Charlie laid it on the ground. My nostrils were filled with the stench of its blood and I almost puked. "Am I going to die?" I asked.

"Raul thinks so." He laughed again as he looked at the Brazilian who was poking at the dead snake with a stick. "I think you'll make it, but you might be sick for a while."

"Shouldn't I go to a hospital?"

"Closest one is a good four hour drive and they might not even have any anti-venom there. Besides I have to find Margot."

"Margot!" I said. *How could I have forgotten her?* "She's missing?"

"Probably hung up in a tree like you were. I had a nice field all picked out. I don't know why you two had to jump in the trees."

"*Posso? Senhor* Charlie?" Raul asked still poking at the snake.

Charlie nodded his head. "He wants the snake for supper. *Sim, Hombre.* It's your stomach." This time I did puke. My fingers were beginning to tingle. I could feel a throbbing pain in my leg near the bite. Raul got a burlap bag from the Jeep and put the snake's body in it then went off in search of the other half.

~ 137 ~

Charlie grabbed me under the arms and dragged me to a tree at one end of the clearing. Actually I could see two Charlies and the tingling in my hands was worse and had spread up my arms. I told Charlie about this.

"Yep it's a bitch of a poison. Hits the CNS, central nervous system, almost immediately. I'm gonna lash you to this tree." He tied a rope under my arms and then secured it to the tree. "I want to keep you upright, keep your leg as low as possible."

"Are you leaving me here to die?"

"Nothing more I can do for you now. I'll be back as soon as I find Margot.

Now I could see four Charlies and my field of vision was dimming.

"Try to stay as calm as you can," he said and, with that, got into the Jeep. Raul with his bag of snake meat joined him, and I watched four Jeeps carrying eight men rumble off in a cloud of dust and oil smoke. I had never imagined the journey would end like this, killed by a coral snake, my final smells, snake blood and vomit. I guess that was my last thought before I leaned against the rope Charlie had tied around me and passed out.

Chapter 17

I remember waking up a few times for brief periods while I was tied to the tree. I couldn't move my arms or legs and I remember sweat streaming down my forehead and into my eyes. I could blink and I recall being happy about that. I remember thinking about my breathing and hoping it wouldn't stop. Crazy things run through one's mind when they are close to dying, which, despite Charlie's lack of concern, I was sure I was.

Every breath became a constant reminder of how fragile my existence was. I tried to control my breathing and I could. Breathing and blinking were all I could do. I'm not sure how much later, but I heard voices.

"Is he alive?" It was a female voice. Margot's.

"Yep. See? He's breathing." That was Charlie's voice.

The Brazilian was speaking under his breath in Portuguese and I wasn't sure what he was saying. Hands grabbed and roughly shook my shoulders. I opened my eyes and they immediately filled with sweat. Margot was next to me and she wiped my forehead with something cold, and it felt great. I tried to talk but nothing would come out. Then it hit me that I might be like this for the rest of my life, however long or short that might be.

Charlie said, "Let's get him into the Jeep." The three picked me up, kind of dragged me to the vehicle, and then hoisted me into the back seat. I was dead weight and couldn't help them at all. And I was burning up. Margot must have read my mind as she started swabbing my forehead with the cold cloth again. *Would that be the greatest pleasure I'd ever know?*

"What will happen to him?" Margot asked and it sounded like she was choking back tears.

"Say something encouraging, Charlie," I thought.

"Well he might die."

"Not what I had in mind."

"But I don't think so. I've seen snake bites before and usually if you live this long you'll recover. The poison wears off after a time and the paralysis will gradually go away. I wish I'd thought to pack some anti-venom but I didn't think we'd be crawling through the jungle."

"You dummy, where did you think we were going, Palm Beach?"

The ride in the Jeep seemed to last for days. I kept fading in and out of consciousness. Margot tried to keep me on the seat, which was a chore. I wasn't sure who was driving, Charlie or the Brazilian, but I made a mental note that if I recovered, I'd kill whoever it was. We hit every possible bump and were airborne as much as we were in contact with the road. I remember Margot screaming to slow down a few times. None of my senses came back on the Jeep ride and that was probably a good thing.

We arrived at a small town. I could tell because the road dirt was smoother and I saw electric wires strung across the street. They carried me into a shack and laid me on a sleeping bag in the corner of the room. A robust lady with a red and white checkered apron came in and saw me and began clucking at Raul in Portuguese as only a wife could do. The universal language of matrimony. He clucked back, and they went into another room to continue. It was then that I felt a tingling in my fingers. Margot was bending over me and saw my fingers moving.

"Look, Charlie. I think he's coming out of it."

"Sure he is. I knew that he would," Charlie said.

"No thanks to the Jeep ride," I said. I think I surprised myself by talking more than them. They were smiling at me and I tried to smile back. I attempted to lift my head but it wouldn't budge, and then I felt dizzy.

"Try not to overdo it," Charlie said. "It'll take a day or two before you're feeling yourself again."

Margot brought me something cold to drink and dripped it into my mouth. She was a great nurse. Soon I closed my eyes and drifted off to sleep.

***

I awoke to a variety of small noises. It was the half-light of just before sunrise. I was lying on the sleeping bag on the floor. Margot was lying next to me which surprised me but made me feel kinda nice. I got up slowly trying not to wake her. I had to find a bathroom and I wanted to know what all the small noises were. My legs felt rubbery as I got up, but I was able to stand on them. The first of the noises was coming from a back room.

Stereo snoring. Raul and his wife still battling in their sleep. Chirping noises came from outside, birds and small critters just waking up. And there was the small scratching noise that was just audible but very different.

I walked slowly to the front door, holding chairs and the wall to steady myself. I pushed open the front door and there on the porch was the source of the sound. It was Charlie sitting at a rickety table working with a rat-tail file on three dismantled guns.

"I see you're still alive," he said quietly.

"Yeah. I've felt better, but this is a big improvement over yesterday. I gotta find the men's room."

Charlie pointed behind the shack where there was a small building barely visible in the dim light. I headed for the outhouse, clutching the wall of the shack as I went. There was a bare bulb in the outhouse and a real toilet. Not as primitive as I thought. When I was done, I walked back to the porch, this time not holding anything, and took a seat in a cane-back chair next to Charlie. I asked him about the guns.

"Well," he said, a smile indicating I had posed a question he'd enjoy answering, "I had some trouble with my weapons supplier

~ 141 ~

down here. Figured I'd get us some real firepower. But that fell through. These are Tokagypt 58s, 9mm parabellums. Made by the Hungarians for the Egyptians in the early fifties. They're based on the Russian Tokarev TT 30-33. I'm fixing up the slide and the action, don't want any jams. These should work fine."

The confidence in his voice made me feel a little better. "I'm starved," I said.

"There's some of that snake that bit you."

"Thanks, anyway, Charlie. I'll pass on that."

"I'll be right back," he said. "Watch the guns and enjoy the sunrise."

Five minutes later, Charlie came back carrying two pineapples and his machete. The morning haze was burning off as the sun just peeked over the top of a far off purple mountain. "Beautiful, isn't it?" he asked.

"Sure is." I said. And for a moment I was caught up in the spell of the sunrise, as if all the things that had happened in the past week were just a bad dream that would evaporate with the new day. I was dashed from my reverie by a wet *thwunk* sound.

Charlie was using his machete to chop up a pineapple. He handed me a couple pieces.

"Thanks," I said. "Uh, you did wash that thing after you chopped up my snake?"

This made him laugh, a muffled laugh so as not to wake the others. "Best germ fighting agent in the world is snake blood," he finally said.

I took a bite of the pineapple and it was about the best tasting thing I'd ever had. It didn't taste at all like the canned stuff or even the fresh ones I'd gotten at the store before.

"This is great, Charlie." I finished my two pieces and he handed me more.

"Jake." It was Margot who had just come through the door. "You're awake." She came towards me as if she was going to give me a hug but then thought better of it. "You look great. I was afraid you were going to die."

"Take more than one snake to kill this guy," Charlie said.

Margot left to use the outhouse and when she was gone, Charlie spoke to me in almost a whisper. "I think she's sweet on you."

"Nobody's sweet on anybody anymore. My grandmother used to say that. I think she just tolerates me until we get this thing over with. Even if she was, there's the matter of her husband who we're going to rescue."

Charlie looked at me, a serious look this time. "There's only a one-in-a-million chance Bruce is alive. Unless he's involved in the underhanded business with IotaTek. She knows it, too. Either way, he's lost to her. She needs some closure is all, and she's gonna need somebody to help her get through the tough times."

"I'm starting to like Margot a lot," I said, not believing I was saying it to this peg-legged old FBI agent. "I want her to get through this, but I also know it's a vulnerable time for her."

"Vulnerable, shmulnerable. She needs some lovin'. You young folks watch too much of that Oprah stuff." The outhouse door banged shut and we stopped talking about her as she came back.

Charlie handed her some pineapple and she seemed to enjoy it as much as I did. We finished both pineapples and then Charlie opened up a map on the small table.

"We're here," he pointed at a dot in a large blotch of green. "About 250 kilometers from *Belo Horizonte*, on the other side of these hills, here." The hills were brownish-red blotches. "*Belo Horizonte*, Portuguese for Beautiful Horizon, is capitol of *Minas Gerais.*"

He paused as if admiring the far off hills. "And then right here on the northern edge of the city is where I believe the IotaTek factory, or whatever it is, is located." He poked the area with the tip of his machete and the sharp point penetrated the map's paper. Give me a half hour with these guns and we'll have breakfast."

***

We ate biscuits and had strong coffee that the Brazilian's wife made us. After serving us, she headed to her bedroom carrying a straw broom. I wasn't sure if she needed it to sweep or to rouse her husband. I was starting to feel much better, still a little weak, but the affects of the snake bite were definitely wearing off. It was

~ 143 ~

getting hot, even though it was still early in the morning. Charlie had put the pistols in a knapsack and he handed it to me.

He took a similar one and pointed to the forest. "Let's get a little practice with these," he said, "and we can be off as soon as Raul has his breakfast."

Charlie led the way. Margot followed and I went behind her. My attention was focused on the ground as we walked. Guess being bitten by a snake makes one much more aware of the creatures. We went about a quarter of a mile into the woods and came into a clearing.

"This should be just fine," Charlie said. He took three boxes of bullets from his pack and then took the pistols from the pack I was carrying.

Margot was smiling like it was Christmas morning. "I love this," she said. "Shooting always makes me feel so alive."

"Hopefully," I said, "we won't have to do any shooting to *stay* alive."

Charlie handed us each a pistol. He spent the next half hour showing us how to load and unload the clips, how to field strip the gun and how to clear it if it jammed. Then he produced three small cellophane packets with disposable ear plugs in them. He had wanted muffs, but these were the best he could do on such short notice. We fired at trees and pineapples and coconuts. I was hoping to get a shot at a snake but I didn't see one.

Charlie was an excellent shot but Margot was even better, which seemed to make him proud and piss him off at the same time.

I was way outclassed by their shooting but at fifty yards, I could hit the coconut next to the one I was aiming at.

"Just remember," Charlie said, "when you shoot like you do, if you aim for the heart you'll probably hit the lung, but in most cases that's good enough to win. Just don't try any head shots unless you're real close."

We cleaned the guns and loaded the clips and then headed back for the house. Charlie figured the ride to *Belo Horizonte* would take the better part of the day. When we got back we put the knapsacks in the Jeep and then walked to the house. There was no sign of Raul.

"Damn him," Charlie said, "I told him to be ready."

We walked up the steps and into the house. A banging noise came from the back somewhere. Charlie raised one hand motioning for us to stop and drew a pistol from his waistband with his other hand. It took several tense seconds before we realized what it was, Raul's bed banging against the wall. We retreated as quietly as we could until, about twenty feet from the house, we broke into laughter.

"Guess he must've told her he might not be coming back," Charlie said. Then he yelled a few words in Portuguese toward the house.

We went back to the Jeep to wait for Raul. I was, and I'm sure Charlie and Margot were wondering, if it was going to be as dangerous a journey as Raul had told his wife.

***

It was about nine in the morning when we left Raul's place. There were several other houses not too far from his but not close enough to be real neighbors. Raul was talking away in Portuguese and Charlie was doing his best to interpret.

"He says his village is called *Escoballo,* and that we were northwest of *Belo Horizonte.* He can make it in six hours if everything goes perfectly. He likes to take his wife to a couple places in *Barro Preto* once a month where they drink beer all night and listen to *sertaneja.*"

"What's that?" Margot asked.

"It's a kind of Brazilian country music. I got pretty fond of it myself once when I spent a lot more time down here than I wanted to. Ran out of Jack after two weeks, but the local beer saw me through."

"How do you know Portuguese so well?" I asked.

"I actually can speak seven languages quite fluently. Besides English and Portuguese, I speak French, Spanish, Ukrainian, Mandarin and Thai. Always came easy to me. And it has been most useful in my work."

I was impressed. But I wasn't happy with the ride. Raul was doing about forty and the Jeep bounced along as if it was almost ready to tip over. Charlie seemed to be enjoying it. The day was

~ 145 ~

sweltering already and the movement, though scary, felt good. And it kept the bugs off. Charlie had told us he wanted to give us shots when we got to his room in the city. "The bugs down here spread all kinds of bad diseases," he had said.

We drove on for about three hours. The road got increasingly smoother as we went. Raul kept talking and Charlie translated when he wasn't caught up in his own thoughts. Margot and I sat quietly in the back, except when she occasionally complained about her butt being sore or yelled for Raul to slow down.

We pulled into a little village where Charlie said we could get lunch. He gave Raul money to buy gas for the Jeep and then led us to a roadside stand. There was a hand-painted sign over the tin roof and several men and women were working over an open fireplace. A dozen tables stood under a grove of trees, all mostly full with people eating.

"Where's the menu?" I asked Charlie.

He chuckled. "Where do you think you are? Pizza Hut? They serve only one dish here. Some days it's different, but not much."

We went to the counter and a huge woman wearing a multi-colored dress gave us each a plate. Charlie ordered two pitchers of beer from a man standing next to her. He paid the man and we took our plates to the only empty table. Some of the natives stopped eating and stared at us but most didn't seem interested. Raul joined us with his plate and an empty glass and Charlie poured us all a beer. It was warm and I didn't like it at first, but after three or four swallows found it passable. Margot picked at the food on her plate.

"What is it?" she asked. Her tone was such that if the answer was wrong, she wasn't eating it.

"It's *tutu à mineira*," Charlie said. "Roast pork served with *tutu.*" He took a mouthful and began chewing.

"I thought that was a ballet dress," I said.

Charlie almost choked on his food. When he was finally able to stop laughing and swallow his mouthful, he explained that *tutu* was a thick bean sauce that they made by mashing uncooked beans and cooking them with manioc - spices - and yucca, which is flour. He said he had learned the recipe once and still made it on occasion.

Margot seemed to like that explanation and began gingerly eating hers. I dug into mine and it was really very tasty.

Charlie said the dish originated with the mule trains that traveled in the area over a hundred years ago. Meat was scarce and the spices were used to preserve it and to kill the taste when it became rotten. Margot gave him a quizzical look, and he just laughed.

Raul ate his plate with gusto and Charlie gave him more money to get another one. The only time when he was quiet was when he was eating and I think we all enjoyed the respite. The Brazilian went to pour himself a third beer but Charlie stopped him. He nodded, grudgingly agreeing that Charlie was right. There were outhouses behind the trees. Not as modern as Raul's, but they worked.

Soon we were in the Jeep and on the road, the aroma of the *tutu à miniera* following us for quite a distance.

"Next stop," said Charlie, "*Belo Horizonte.*"

***

The afternoon sun beat down on us unmercifully as we deove along the dusty road. Plenty of trees and green plants abounded on both sides but none close enough to offer any shade.

"Are we there yet?" I asked in my best brat imitation. "It feels like a blast furnace in this crate."

"About two kilos," Charlie said. "Right around that rise." He pointed straight ahead to a purplish–green mountain. "And when we get there, I know a great little place that serves the best Argentine steak. I can almost taste it now."

"That sounds okay," I said, "as long as there's a couple gallons of beer to wash it down. *Cold* beer."

A short time later the Jeep was huffing up around the rise. I don't know what I was expecting, maybe a large village, but what I saw was amazing. Stretched out before us in a natural bowl lay the city of *Belo Horizonte.* Numerous skyscrapers climbed heavenward and presented a scene reminiscent of Boston in the seventies.

"Wow," Margot said. "It's huge."

"Over two-and-a-half million people live there," Charlie added.

Raul drove us to an airport at the outskirts of the city. The sign said *Pampulha Aeroporto.* Charlie told us to sit tight and he ambled into a Rent-A-Car place. The Brazilian was chattering away to us,

~ 147 ~

but we had no idea what he was saying, except when he said "*Senor Charlie."* Senor Charlie appeared about twenty minutes later driving a green compact Ford.

"I hope it has air conditioning," I said to Margot and she nodded her head in agreement. Charlie gave Raul some money and a small pager and, after a few instructions in Portuguese, bid him farewell. The Jeep roared away with Raul clucking and waving until he was out of sight. We loaded our baggage into the rental's trunk and then climbed in the car, Charlie behind the wheel, Margot shotgun, and me in the back. Miraculously the Ford had a great air conditioner and Charlie cranked it.

Charlie drove us to an outside eatery where they brought beers to the car and we could sit inconspicuously and plan our raid on the IotaTek plant. Charlie turned on his laptop computer and, after pushing a few buttons, had a map of *Belo Horizonte* on the screen.

"I figure," Charlie said, "we should drive by a couple times to get the lay of the land and then go in after dark. We're about here," he pointed to a spot a couple streets over from a train station. "If we drive down here," a street marked *Avenida Afonso Pena,* "and then hook a left on *Avenida Brasil,* by my count twelve blocks and we'll be in the area. I'll need you guys to keep your eyes peeled."

We finished our beers and Charlie drove off. We hadn't gone a block before both Margot and I scrambled for our seat belts. The Brazilian drivers were crazy and Charlie was as bad if not worse. "You have to drive like this down here," he said, "or they'll run you over."

I wasn't sure what we were looking for. I was imagining a small scale version of the IotaTek-Waltham building. We had driven for about twenty minutes when Charlie pointed to the map on his laptop.

"Should be right around here," he said.

We were in a run-down section of the city, the kind where you make sure your doors are locked, especially if you're still in the car. The buildings were older here, dirtier looking. Many of them board-ed up. A man with a straggly beard stared at us as we drove slowly by.

"This place is creepy," Margot said.

I agreed with her. Charlie pointed to a building that we were just passing. It was an old three story red-brick mill building and it looked vacant. "I think that's it," he said.

"It can't be," Margot said in almost a whisper. "Not after all this."

We drove around a block, and the next time by I spotted a sign fastened to the third floor. It was painted on a four foot by eight foot sheet of plywood. Red letters on a cream background. It was in Portuguese and I couldn't read it, but I made out one word. *IotaTek*. The third time by, the bearded man was sitting on the curb, still staring at us or through us, the hollow stare of despair I'd seen so many times on homeless people in Boston.

Charlie made a couple turns and we got onto another street where we could see the back of the IotaTek building through an opening where a fence in a vacant lot had been knocked down.

Charlie stopped the Ford and took out a small pair of binoculars. "Three stories," he said, "bars on the windows, most of the glass is broken. Doesn't look like anybody's been there for a while. There's two sets of railroad tracks that go by the dock in the back of the building. I think that will be the best place to get in."

"What for?" Margot said, tears streaming down her face. "There's nothing here. Nothing. All this way for nothing."

"Easy, Magpie," Charlie said, but she ignored him and began pounding her fists on the dashboard. Charlie put the Ford in gear and drove off. "Let's get her to the hotel and calmed down."

I was feeling almost as low as Margot. The disappointment at finding the abandoned mill at the end of the journey was disheartening to say the least. What would we do next if there was nothing here? I guess Margot and I had expected it to finish in *Belo Horizonte*, that all the loose ends would be tied up, and that we'd find her husband and Tommy's mother, or at least discover what happened to them. But it all seemed like it was crashing down, like the long dangerous journey had been for nothing. It felt like all our hopes had come to an end at a dingy, abandoned mill building in the dirtiest part of a far-away city. Again, I felt like crying too.

Chapter 18

Charlie had gotten us two adjoining rooms at a hotel about ten blocks from the old mill building. We took the elevator to the fourth floor and went into one of our rooms. Margot sat on the edge of the bed. She was crying softly, her shoulders bouncing up and down gently.

Charlie got her some pills from his suitcase and she took them. "These will make you rest," he said. "Jake and I will go to the factory at dusk and see what there is to see."

"I want to go, too," she said through her tears.

"Trust me, Magpie. If there's anything to see we'll come right back and get you. Meanwhile I've got to give you guys some shots." He had hypodermics in a small valise and gave us each a shot. "Should have done this back in the states."

Within minutes of taking the pills Margot fell asleep. I pulled a blanket over her.

"We better get a little rest, too," Charlie said. "It could be a long night."

I closed my eyes but there was no way I could sleep now.

***

At dusk Charlie and I left the hotel. Our plan was to park on the street behind the building and approach it from opposite directions, Charlie from the front and me from the back. I had one of the pistols and an extra clip and Charlie gave me a flashlight and a spare key to the car, in case only one of us got back. Charlie told me there was a bar across the street. He'd park by that and we'd meet there later if we got separated at the factory. I got out of the car and walked towards IotaTek.

I felt like I'd been beamed down into an alien world. The smells of the city were different than I'd ever experienced, sweet and sour with a smoky tang. *Belo Horizonte* is in a natural hollow and the smog settled down over it like a peaceful blanket that hinted it could smother you at any moment. Even the last rays of the sun that glittered up over the high rises were a different shade of red than I'd ever remembered seeing.

I was shaking. I could feel panic surging through my body. What was I doing! I had a gun, sure, but who was I going to shoot? Brazilian cops doing their job? A factory worker or a poor slob of a night watchman who didn't know anything about IotaTek?

I stood on the dirty sidewalk and pressed my back against the brick wall. I forced myself to take slow, deep breaths. After a few minutes the panic subsided, gone with the last rays of the sun. I heard a noise. Two men walking and talking loudly. One was laughing and patting the other on the back. They went into the bar on the other side of the street. If they saw me they paid no attention, just two laborers after a hard day's work beginning a hard night of drinking. That was a familiar sight.

I began walking toward the alley that led to the back of the IotaTek building. The streets were very narrow in this part of town which was probably why there was hardly any traffic. I moved along slowly, looking in every direction. I kept close to the buildings trying to blend in. I got to the alley and it looked deserted.

I saw a few trash cans and I could hear little feet scurry away. Rats. About half-way down the alley, I heard a noise that wasn't rats but that came from a human. A muffled voice speaking.

Then, two men stepped from the shadows of a doorway. It was the same guys I'd seen go into the bar. They stood arms folded, blocking the alley.

"Get out of my way," I said.

The biggest one said something in Portuguese and the other one laughed. Then they both unfolded their arms to display very large knives.

"No speak Portuguese," I said, and I started backing out of the alley.

I was stopped by a voice behind me. "He say, give him your money, pig-face or he slice you like a chicken."

"Look. I have no money. Now tell them to get out of the way."

"You stupid, gringo, you should no be here. So you pay or you die."

"Not alone, I won't," I said and pulled the pistol from its holster. The three men shouted various things that I didn't understand, but they held their ground. I was really glad that Charlie had taken us shooting that morning. I flicked off the safety, like I knew what I was doing and fired a round into the trash can next to the biggest guy. The shot was deafening. Like a cannon in a valley, it echoed off the brick walls of the old factory buildings.

My intent had been to scare them but the slug must have hit the can just right and it ricocheted and hit the big guy in the leg. He dropped and the knife clattered onto the stone alleyway.

His partner's eyes were wider than I'd ever seen eyes get. He bent to try to help his pal up. I turned quickly and the English speaking one stopped dead in his tracks.

I pointed the pistol in the general direction of the bridge of his nose. "Who's a pigface?" I asked with as much menace as I could muster. His eyes went wide also, and he turned and ran like a scared chicken, squawking into the dark street. I turned again and the big guy was up and hobbling away with his friend helping him. And once again I was alone in the alley in the *Belo Horizonte* night.

I expected Charlie to come running after the shot, but there was no sign of him. I climbed up on the loading dock at the back of the building. The huge door was bolted solid, but I found a small window to the right with several bars missing. One more bar and I'd be able to squeeze in. I wiggled it around and chipped away at the concrete holding it, and finally I got it pulled away from the bottom. A couple more wiggles and the top came free.

That left me a space just big enough to crawl through. I imagined myself half in and half out of the window, stuck, when Charlie came to find me, and I could almost hear his laughter.

I was sweating profusely in the tropical evening heat. Maybe that would help me slide through more easily. There was no sign of the police or the robbers, or of Charlie. Maybe gunshots in this area weren't a rarity. I pulled myself up onto the window ledge and slid between the bars. I stopped and listened and all was quiet. I turned on my flashlight for a quick burst to make sure there was a solid floor to come down on, and that there were no bad guys there waiting for me.

The coast looked clear and the floor looked solid so I let myself down from the window into the IotaTek building. I was in a large room that took up the back of the building and extended up three floors to the roof. Slivers of light trickled in from cracks in the walls and through the broken windows. My eyes were adjusting and I could make out most of the room. I saw maybe a dozen large crates that took up most of the floor space. I pushed at one and it was heavy. Using the flashlight I found a tag on the side of one of the boxes. It was mostly in Portuguese but I did make out IotaTek, so I guess I was in the right place. But, would I find anything?

The ceiling was high and blanketed in darkness. The floor area of the room I was in was about a 100 feet by 100 feet. I stood there trying to be quiet and listen. I heard my heart beat, felt it vibrate in my ears. There was another noise in the room but I didn't know what it was. It was like the sound that many small saws would make if they were all sawing through wet wood.

The place smelled awful, sickly-sweet like rotten fruit. It mixed with the odor of my sweat and brought the taste of bile into my throat.

Maybe five minutes had passed since I'd come through the window. I was certain that the sawing noises were coming from the crates, like they were alive. I found a metal bar on a workbench and broke the straps off one of the crates and then I opened the top. I

~ 153 ~

listened. No sound of anyone coming. I turned on the flashlight and shined it into the crate. It was three-quarters full of greenish-brown leaves. They were rotting and the cause of the smell. Hundreds of green colored slugs were eating them. They were shaped like, and as big as hot dogs and they were chewing away. The sawing sound.

This time I couldn't control the bile and I vomited onto the floor. I had to get out of there. My mouth burned with the sour taste of puke. I planned to head back to the car and wait for Charlie. Find a bar and have a beer or three. Maybe the ex-FBI guy could make some sense of this. I started for the window I'd come through.

I stopped when I heard a noise. Then the ceiling lit up with fluorescent lights. I reached for the pistol in my waistband. And then I heard a familiar voice.

"Drop it! You're surrounded." It was a voice I thought I'd left behind in the Massachusetts woods.

"Dr. Dork," I said. "Fancy meeting you here. Come to join your feasting relatives?" I thought that was cute, but it got me a whack in the head from behind.

The blow knocked me to my knees and my pistol fell on the floor. The guy who had hit me kicked the gun away. I tried to grab for him but he backed away and hit me again with some kind of club. I fell onto my stomach. Armed men were pointing guns at me, and all I could think of was the slugs. I had to get up before they crawled on me.

"You're a very stupid person," the Doctor said. "Did you think I'd never find you? Well I have, and this time the numbers are in my favor."

I was on my knees again. Dr. Dork was standing with one man by the door. I recognized him as one of the guys from the alley. There were at least two behind me.

"What do you want Dork?" I asked trying to spit the words.

"I want you to die, Mr. Lawless, and you will. Very soon. And so will your girlfriend and your gimpy partner."

"Everybody knows we're here. The gimp is FBI and he has friends on the way."

He chuckled. "He's washed-up FBI, soon to be late FBI. Tie him up, men."

The three guys moved in on me. I tried to fight, but they were too much. One put a bandanna in my mouth and tied it behind my head so I couldn't speak. They tied my hands behind my back. I felt the guy behind slip a rope over my head and tighten it around my neck.

"String him up boys," Dr. Dork said, and then laughed. The three lifted me onto the top edge of the crate and then threw the rope over a wooden beam. They tied it to something and I could feel it biting into my neck.

"I see terror in your eyes, Mr. Lawless, or can I call you Jake? I don't imagine you can balance there much more than an hour. That will give you enough time to think about how stupid it was to mess with me and, with IotaTek. Oh, Armand and Rojo are both excellent marksmen and they'll be waiting upstairs for your friends. Unless they come soon, you won't hear the shots." He chuckled again and I wanted to strangle him.

"Bet you're wondering what this is all about," he went on. "What you are down here for, and what you are going to die for. If this was a movie, I'd tell you all about it, but it isn't a movie, and you're never going to know why you died. And when you do slip off the box try to fall inside, my little friends are waiting. Good night, Jake." With that, he shut off the lights and left the room.

One hour, I thought. I'd be lucky to last ten minutes balanced on the rim of the crate. I heard footsteps. Men climbing creaky stairs slowly in the dark. Armand and Rojo heading for their perches to wait for Charlie. With the bandanna tied tightly around my mouth I wouldn't even be able to warn him. Not that I'd even be alive when he got there.

There were a couple inches slack in the rope. I found if I leaned slightly to the left, it would actually support me a little, help me keep my balance without cutting off my air. The ropes tying my wrists were tight. I kept working at them trying to get them undone, but to no avail. I had read a book once about Houdini and I was trying to remember if he'd divulged anything that would help me. I seemed to remember he'd used a special rope that had a removable center and that when he pulled out the center the rope would get slack. I was sure that wasn't the case with this rope. But there was nothing else I could do so I kept trying to work the knots loose.

I'd been there for what felt like hours but was probably closer to ten minutes, when I heard a popping noise. Then I heard a scream and a crashing noise above me. Then yelling in Portuguese.

I heard another pop and then glass breaking overhead. Three more loud shots rang out. My inclination was to duck but the noose around my neck prevented it. I heard running down the stairs and then all the lights blazed on. I think it was Rojo running toward me screaming and swearing. He got about five feet from me and then spat at me. Then he raised his pistol.

Before he could fire, there was another popping noise, louder this time. A small black hole opened up neatly in Rojo's forehead. His eyes turned in as if looking at the object that had invaded his head. Then, before he dropped, his pistol went off.

The shot was low and hit the crate, but it was enough to make me lose my balance. The noose bit into my neck. Before I could think, the rope went slack and I fell to the floor. The first thing I saw as I lay there was the alligator skin cowboy boots that Charlie wore on his prosthetic legs. I never thought I'd be so happy to see alligator hide in my life. Charlie was laughing as he cut the bandanna away from my mouth.

"I don't think this is very funny," I said.

"Well if you saw yourself like I do, you'd be laughing too. And how about a 'much obliged.'"

"Sorry, Charlie." And I thanked him profusely.

Rojo lay on the floor, his dead eyes open but not seeing. A pool of blood was expanding in a slow circle from the back of his head. We both looked at him for a minute.

"You gonna be okay, Charlie?" I asked. "About killing him?"

"This piece of shit?" Charlie said and he drove his boot into Rojo's side. "He was just about to kill you, and he was waiting upstairs to kill me. I've swatted insects I've felt worse about killing." He finished cutting the ropes off my wrist. "Now let's see what we can find and then get the hell outa here."

"How did you manage it?" I asked Charlie. I couldn't figure out how he could do the shooting upstairs and then get downstairs to kill Rojo.

He smiled. "Well, I'm not the magician you might think. After you got out of the car I drove around the block a couple times. I saw three guys who were very intent on watching you. I called Raul and told him to get over here in a hurry. Raul is a very talented man. He shoots better than I do and climbs like a monkey. By the time he got to the second story, they'd already strung you up."

"How did you know they'd go upstairs?"

"We didn't. But that played right into our hands. Raul was going to cover me from above and they went right up into his sights. We would have had them all if I could have gotten through that window quicker." He looked around at the crates. "So what have we got here?"

"Some kind of rotten plants with big bugs eating them," I said.

"Interesting." He walked over and looked into one of the crates. "Those are some ugly critters. Don't let Raul see them. He'd probably want to eat them." He laughed.

"Yuck," I said. I could still remember Raul dining on the coral snake.

Charlie used a pocket knife to remove one of the labels from the crates. "Let's see if we can find an office or someplace where they keep files," he said.

"What if Dr. Dork comes back with help?" I asked.

"Raul's up there," he pointed toward the second floor. "He'll keep watch. They'd better bring plenty of help to get by that old Brazilian."

The building was made up of the large room that had the crates and several smaller rooms near the front that were under the second story. Charlie and I walked toward the rooms in the front.

"You take the left and I'll take the right," Charlie said.

"Okay," I said, "but let's hurry. This place gives me the creeps and I really could use a cold beer."

Charlie nodded and walked into the first room. He flipped on a light switch. I did the same on the left. Several cockroaches scurried into hiding when the lights came on. I was wondering if it was wise to use all the lights but it sure made it quicker and easier. I found two ancient wooden file cabinets in the first room.

The files in them were old and yellowed. I pulled a couple papers out. The writing was Portuguese but I made out the dates - 1951 and 1952. I assumed they belonged to a company that used to own the place. We searched the rooms finding nothing new or that mentioned IotaTek.

We were about to leave when I thought I heard something. I put my finger to my lips to signal Charlie to be quiet and listen.

He heard it, too. A very faint thunking sound.

"Raul?" I asked.

"No," Charlie said quietly. "He's up above and that's definitely coming from below us." There was one door we found that had a new hasp and padlock on it. "Go get a hammer or something."

Chapter 19

I ran and got the bar and the flashlight I'd dropped in the fight with Dr. Dork's pals. Charlie took out his pistol and then told me to break off the lock. The lock was sturdy, but the wood was old and it gave way with a crunch as I pried the bar against it. I pulled open the door and Charlie pointed his gun into the opening. No one there. A stairway led down into blackness. Charlie fished around for a light switch but found none. I trained the flashlight onto the opening. The stairs went down to a landing and then turned downward. My flashlight lit up a bare light bulb with a pull chain about halfway down the first course.

Charlie led the way and we walked slowly down the stairs. The thunking noise had stopped. The bare bulb illuminated the stairs but left most of the basement in darkness. I played my flashlight across the area. Several rats and mice scurried away.

"Think they were making the noise?" I asked.

"No, I don't think so. It seemed almost rhythmic like it was made by a human or a machine."

Bombs and booby traps ran through my mind. The cellar was strewn with numerous pieces of junk and debris. "Let's get out of here," I said.

"Wait. Shine the light that way." He pointed to the front of the building where there was something shiny. I pointed the light at it and we saw it was a padlock, very similar to the one I'd just broken. It was on a door to a very little room in the corner of the building. "Let's check it," Charlie said.

We went over and I rapped on the door with the bar. No response.

"Break it," Charlie said. He took the flashlight from me and pointed it and his pistol at the lock. This door was much sturdier and I had to work harder but finally pried it off and pulled the door open. Charlie scanned the small space with the light. It smelled awful, bad human smells like sweat and worse. Then we saw a woman - at least it looked like a woman - crouched in the corner.

There was a wild look to her, like an animal trapped and scared. But there was no mistaking the cobalt blue of her eyes. Tommy's eyes.

"Heather?" I asked. "Heather Baxter? We're here to help you."

Just then we heard Raul yelling from above. "*As poliicia! As poliicia!*"

"Ahh shit," Charlie said.

My sentiments exactly.

"Let's get the hell out of here," Charlie added. He pointed the light at Heather who was crouched in the corner of the room. "Help her."

I went over and took her by the arm to help her up, but she pulled away and forced herself tightly against the walls. "We're trying to help you," I yelled.

She began to wail like a cat whose tail was caught in a meat grinder. Charlie was swearing, and then several gunshots sounded from above.

"Raul," Charlie yelled, "Run, Get the hell out of here. *Funcionamento!*" Then to me, "What's the matter with her?"

"She's scared, I think."

"Smell that?" Charlie asked.

"All I can smell is her and I'm trying not to. What is it?"

"Gasoline. Let's go. Somebody's about to torch this place."

He put the flashlight in his pocket. The beam bounced off the ceiling, casting eerie moving shadows in the small space. Charlie grabbed her right arm and I grabbed her left and we hoisted her to her feet. Even in the dim wavering light the look of terror in her eyes was unmistakable. She was fighting us now, clawing with her fingers at us and trying to dig her feet into the dirt that was the floor.

Charlie said, "I hate to do this." He let her arm drop and, before she could scratch him, belted her in the jaw. She went limp and would have slumped to the floor if I wasn't holding her.

"Can you carry her?"

"I think so," I said. Charlie helped to boost her onto my back. She probably weighed about a hundred pounds, but it was awkward trying to walk and carry her in the dim light. I went up the stairs first with Charlie pushing us and supporting us as best he could from behind. At the top of the stairs I realized that Charlie had been right.

Flames licked up the wall near the window where Charlie had come in. A red five-gallon can lay on the floor and was being devoured by the growing fire. The lights flickered and then went out. The room was beginning to fill with an acrid smoke. Charlie ran to the loading dock door. I hobbled after him as fast as I could with Heather on my shoulder. She was starting to move.

We didn't have much time left. Charlie tried to lift the overhead door, but it was jammed. There was a small door at the far end of the building. It opened about a half inch. Charlie shined the light into the space. "Padlocked," he said.

"She's coming to, Charlie. We gotta get out of here."

Charlie pointed his pistol at the opening in the door and fired. Nothing moved. He fired again and again. Still nothing. He was cursing now as he aimed again and fired. The fourth shot hit metal and the door flew open. We ran out onto the loading dock. I let my lungs fill with fresh night air. There was an explosion inside, and a ball of flame burst through the window on the other end of the building. I heard faint sirens in the distance, heee-yaw sound like in foreign films.

We went gingerly down the steps to the ground, Charlie leading the way with his pistol pointing in front of us. The fire was beginning to light up the area. We made it to an alley across the street just as another explosion ripped the night.

The first fire truck was arriving at the scene when Charlie pointed at the top of the building. Two men stood on the roof, silhouetted like phantoms in the fire-lit smoke. They seemed to be looking at the roof of a building about twenty feet away from the IotaTek warehouse.

"Raul," Charlie said under his breath.

First one man ran along the roof and jumped into the blackness. Then the second man ran, but he never made the leap. Another explosion tore upwards through the roof and he disappeared into the inferno.

Flashing lights and screaming men filled the area. I looked at the building. The IotaTek sign had broken loose on one end and was swaying slowly back and forth. Then as the fire started to engulf the red letters the sign dropped and fell into the flames.

"Let's go," Charlie said. There was a sadness to his voice that I hadn't heard before.

"I have to put her down," I said, and eased Heather off my back. We picked her up by her arms and started walking away. "Stay in the darkness as much as we can."

Several people ran past us hollering and pointing at the fire.

Heather was becoming conscious and actually started stumbling along with us. We got to the car parked about three blocks away. The smell of smoke was still strong in my nose. Charlie unlocked the door and we loaded Heather into the back seat.

"Buckle her up and sit with her," Charlie said.

I did as he asked and soon we were driving away. I saw the orange glow in the rear-view mirror as we turned a corner and then just the headlights of oncoming cars and the flashing lights of a fire engine. Heather was moaning and I hoped she wouldn't fully come to until we got her back to the hotel.

"Hey Charlie," I said. "I'm sure that was Raul . . . the guy who jumped."

"I hope so," he said with a sigh. "But we don't even know if *that* guy made it."

It was a twenty-minute drive back to our hotel. Charlie was silent the whole way. I wanted to try to reassure him that Raul was all right but I couldn't imagine how he could have survived even the jump. Heather had gained consciousness but she wasn't talking either.

"How are we going to get her into the room?" I finally asked as the hotel loomed into view.

"I've been wondering that myself," Charlie said. "We don't want to make a scene. See if you can talk to her."

"I'll try." And then to her, "Heather, you're safe now. We're going to get you home. Get all of us home but you have to help us a little."

She stared straight ahead, her eyes wide.

"Tommy is waiting to see you," I continued. "He's the one that hired me to find you." I told her how Tommy had come into the bar and how he had saved fifty dollars to hire a private investigator. I told her about the shoebox of pictures and facts that Tommy had gathered. Charlie pulled the car into the underground lot. "You have to help yourself and us so you can see Tommy again. He's waiting."

"Tommy," she said, almost a quiet sob. The more I talked about him and mentioned his name, the more she seemed to comprehend that maybe she was really being saved.

Charlie parked the car. I got out and opened her door. Tears streaked down her cheeks, but she took my hand and slowly got out. Her first steps were wobbly, like a newborn colt. I took one arm and Charlie the other and we made our way to the elevator.

"This elevator stops at the lobby," Charlie said. "I'll go up first and make sure the coast is clear. If it comes back empty, you bring her up. There's about thirty steps to the main elevator and we'll have to make them as quickly as possible."

I nodded and Charlie pushed the *up* button, the doors closed, and he was gone. I gave him enough time to get off and then pushed the *down* button. I supported Heather there and it seemed like a very long time but was probably only a couple minutes. The elevator came back empty and I helped Heather on. She seemed scared but came with me and I pushed the button that said "Lobby." I was a little surprised that the buttons were in English.

We rode up and when the door opened, Charlie was there waiting for us. He took her other arm and we made our way to the main elevator.

Soon we were on the fourth floor. Charlie led us to the room, knocked and then used a key to open the door. Margot was lying on the bed with her eyes closed, the flickering colors of the TV the only light.

"Hey, Magpie. It's us," Charlie said.

Margot opened her eyes slowly and then jumped out of bed when she saw that we had Heather with us. "What did they do to her?"

"She'll be okay," I said. "Needs a little cleaning up and a good meal or two."

"You poor thing," Margot said. "Let's get you washed and changed. She took Heather by the arm and led her to the bathroom.

"Go easy with her, Magpie. She's still in shock."

Margot shot him an I-can't-believe-you-said-that glance and shut the door. I heard water running and Margot's voice speaking softly.

Charley unwrapped a couple plastic glasses and began pouring from a Jack Daniel's bottle. "If you need ice, there's a machine just off the lobby."

"No ice is fine," I said. He poured us each three fingers and we both drank about a finger and a half immediately. I walked over to the window with my drink. Off in the distance I saw the red glow in the sky that was the burning IotaTek building. "All the evidence is going up in smoke," I said.

"Maybe not all of it," Charlie said with a grin. With his right hand, he took some crumpled papers from his jacket pocket and placed them on the small table. From his left pocket, he extracted a handful of green vegetative material. "Hope there's no caterpillars in it." He chuckled. "And, our most important evidence is right in there. Tommy's mom."

Just then the phone rang and Charlie answered it. He listened for a minute and a huge smile broke across his face. "You snake-eating son of a bitch, I knew you'd make it," he said. Then to me, "Here's to a successful mission," and he hoisted his plastic cup of Jack.

"I'll drink to that," I said and I tapped his cup with mine.

Charlie's mood had gotten much better since he received the call from Raul. The Brazilian had called from the hospital where he was being treated for burns and a broken arm, but nothing life-threatening. I had begun thinking about the process for our return to New Stratley. Charlie called room service and ordered us some food.

"I got a little of everything," he said. "We have to get some good food into that poor lady."

Margot came out of the room just as the room-service tray arrived. It smelled great. I hadn't realized how hungry I was until the aroma hit me.

"How is she?" I asked Margot.

"She's okay, I got her cleaned up, and she'll be out soon."

I noticed something funny, like a hitch in Margot's voice. I think Charlie noticed it, too.

"And you, Magpie?" he asked. "Are you okay, too?"

"Oh, Charlie," she said and tears began streaming down her cheeks.

"Easy, honey," he said and put his arms around her. "What is it?" A question that we both knew the answer to.

"Bruce," she said and began sobbing louder. "Bruce is dead."

She pushed slowly away from Charlie. "I need to be alone now. Please." She went into the adjoining room and closed the door.

Heather came out of the bathroom. She was wearing a tee shirt and shorts of Margot's. She sat in a chair and Charlie put the room service tray in front of her. She ate ravenously.

I finished my drink and poured another one. I offered the bottle to Charlie and he nodded and I filled his cup. I had completely lost my appetite. We had all known that the chances of finding Heather and Bruce safe and well, as Dr. Dork had promised, were almost non-existent. Heather being alive was fantastic, but it made the fact of Bruce's death that much harder to take. I looked out at the city. The glow from the IotaTek fire was gone. Thousands of lights shone from the high-rise buildings and gaudy neon signs flashed and pandered their wares four stories below.

"You know, Charlie, I feel like a general who's just won a battle but has lost half his men." He didn't respond, just took another sip of his drink. I finished my drink and thought about pouring more. My head was spinning and I decided I'd had enough.

There were double beds in the room and I laid down on one. I heard Charlie fiddling with the food tray. I fell asleep wondering if he was just eating so he could drink some more.

***

I awoke to a shadowy hint of pre-dawn light. Charlie was sleeping in a chair that he had moved in front of the door. Heather slept quietly on the other bed. I hadn't thought about it, but she was technically our prisoner at least until we could get her to the authorities. If she had wandered off in the night, who knows where she would have ended up. My respect for Charlie and his knowledge went up another notch. I looked out at the city, which was quiet now. It seemed so much like Boston in many, many ways and yet it was so far away. *We* were so far away. How were we ever going to get all the loose ends tied up and get home?

I needed some fresh air. Charlie didn't think it was a good idea for me to be wandering around, but I had to get out of the hotel room. I assured him I'd stay close and not arouse any suspicion. I took the elevator to the lobby. It was 5:45 a.m. and there was no activity there, not even a desk man although I figured a bell would summon one. I was hoping to find a place where I could get a coffee.

The air was city air but it was refreshing. I took a few deep breaths and headed in the direction where I had seen a coffee place.

The first time the car went by, I just barely noticed it. The second time it went much slower and really stood out because it was so large. It was a dark gray Lincoln Continental. The windows were tinted but I saw the shadows of heads inside. I was sure they were looking at me. Maybe I was getting paranoid. It turned at the next block. Was it circling me? I picked up my pace and soon came to the little shop I'd seen earlier. A neon sign in the window advertised "*Barzinho de Maria.*"

~ 166 ~

A half dozen small tables with chairs took up most of the floor space and at the far end, I spotted a counter where a large smiling lady was waiting to serve. "*Bom dia,*" she said.

"*Bom dia,*" I said. She smiled, and I could tell she knew I was a foreigner. She prattled on for a while. I finally made a gesture with my arms indicating I had no idea what she was talking about.

"*Café?*" she asked. I nodded my head and pointed to a biscuity-looking thing beneath a glass cover. She identified it as a *bisnaga*. She poured me a coffee. I waved off the cream. She put the pastry on a dish with two wrapped pats of butter. I gave her an American five. She looked at it and then disappeared for a few seconds into a back room. She came out and handed me three coins with a big smile.

I smiled back, took my *café* and *bisnaga* and sat at an open table where I could see into the street.

Seven or eight other patrons sat in Maria's, all busy with their breakfasts and their morning chatter. A few glanced at me, the stranger, but didn't seem too interested. The *café* was the best I'd had in a long time and the *bisnaga* was delicious. I had it half eaten when the gray Lincoln cruised by again this time even more slowly. The driver of a small green car behind it tooted his horn and then screeched around it. Hands and arms in both cars made obscene gestures.

Then the Lincoln was gone around the block again. I finished my buttery pastry. The smiling lady was making the rounds with a pot of coffee in each hand. I smiled back and nodded, and she refilled my cup. I thanked her in English, couldn't remember how to say it in Portuguese, although I was sure I'd heard Charlie say it numerous times.

I sat sipping my coffee and watching the morning lighten the street. Traffic was getting heavier. Then I saw the Lincoln again. It was taking five or six minutes to make the circle. This time it was barely moving. It went by the hotel and then pulled over to the curb. Three men got out. Two looked like Brazilians. The third was well over six feet and even though he was about 500 feet away, I recognized him. He was one of the guys that had been shooting at us back in Massachusetts. I had to get back and warn Charlie and Margot.

I watched from inside the *Barzinho de Maria*, waiting for the three men to go into the hotel. But they didn't. The Lincoln pulled away leaving them on the sidewalk. One of the Brazilians crossed the street and began walking in my direction. The other one started walking toward me on my side with the tall guy about twenty paces behind. My detective's brain jumped into gear and I realized they didn't know we were at the hotel.

They must have been driving around looking for us and they spotted me. Now they were on foot hunting me down.

They moved quickly, looking in alleys and doorways. They would find me in here for sure. I walked out the door onto the sidewalk and turned to the right. I had a three-hundred foot head start. They had the advantage that they knew the area. I heard a crash and the picture window of *Barzinho de Maria* exploded.

Another advantage. They had guns with silencers. I began to run, zigging and zagging as much as I could without losing ground. I heard their footsteps running behind me.

At the first side street, I took a right. I ran about a block and then started to cross the street. A guy in a black BMW almost ran me down. He swerved and mashed his horn. I heard profanity of some sort coming from him.

I made it across the street and took another right. I had no idea where I was going. My thoughts were just to head away from the hotel and try to lose them. About two blocks ahead, I saw a Brazilian police officer standing on the sidewalk. I thought about running up to him. But I didn't speak his language and I wasn't sure if he was friendly with the guys who were chasing me.

I took a left and ran down a short alley. Luckily, it wasn't a dead end. I was starting to get tired. It felt awfully hot and humid for so early in the morning, but I had to keep going. I came out of the alley at a very narrow street and I took another right. I stopped for a second and looked behind me. The men weren't in sight. My shirt was soaked with sweat. I slowed to a jog. Traffic was getting heavier and heavier as *Belo Horizonte* awakened. Which was probably a good thing for me. I slowed again to a fast walk. I kept to the pattern of taking the next left and the next right for several blocks. I looked back every hundred feet or so, but there was no sign of them. And there were no more windows shattering. Finally, I had to rest.

Chapter 20

I came to a place that looked like a drug store. A long counter ran along one side of the store from front to rear. A row of round stools on chrome pedestals, just like the old Woolworth's in New Stratley center that I patronized as a youth, were almost all taken but I found one near the end. Some of the customers looked at the sweaty foreigner who was panting, but none seemed overly interested. A counter man approached me, and I pointed at the Coke sign on the wall. He asked me a question that I didn't understand, maybe drink size. I pointed at the glass of the guy next to me, and the counterman nodded. The guy moved his drink to the other side. Guess he thought I wanted his.

The counter man brought my Coke and I gave him a ten. He showed it to another guy, and then he brought me change, several bills and some coins. I pushed back one of the bills and mimicked dialing a phone. He understood and brought me more coins. I took a big gulp of Coke. Delicious. I kept watching the door for signs of my pursuers. I looked around the store for things I could use as weapons if they did come in. But they didn't. Should have taken a Tokagypt with me.

I finished the Coke and went to the front of the store. There were two pay phones there. I put in a coin and dialed '0'. I got an operator who didn't speak English. She finally hung up on me. I tried again and got another Portuguese speaking lady. I was finally able to convince her I could just speak English and she put me on hold and another lady came on.

"Can I help you?" she asked. I gave her the name of the hotel and she connected me. The man at the hotel understood me and rang our room.

Charlie answered after two rings. "Where the hell are you?"

"I'm not sure, to be honest. Some drugstore about two miles from you."

"I told you not to go out," he said.

"Hey, I had three goons chasing me and they were shooting."

"Yeah. I saw them."

"Thanks for jumping in," I said.

"I figured you could outrun them. Or they'd kill you. Wasn't much I could do from here. Besides, I couldn't leave the ladies."

"Well, are you coming to get me?"

"I don't know where you are. Just grab a cab they all know where the hotel is. But come in through the garage and make sure nobody's following you."

"Okay," I said. I could hear him laughing. "Thanks for nothing." And I hung up.

I went back to my seat and ordered another Coke. I'd give it a little time before I went searching for a taxi. Just to make sure the coast was really clear.

***

I walked around for about half an hour, before I hailed a taxi. I was sure nobody was following me. The cabbie didn't speak English but did understand my pronunciation of the Hotel's name.

The meter was running and it was apparent he was taking me the long way back, but that was all right with me. We finally arrived at the hotel. I motioned to a side street. He turned down and then stopped. He looked at the meter and gave me the price. "*Por favor.*"

I showed him three bills, and he went to take them. I shook my head *no*. He took two of the bills and drove off smiling.

~ 171 ~

Take some money from the stupid gringo. He's got plenty.

I walked around a couple blocks and then ducked into the hotel garage. All looked good, no sign of the gray Lincoln or the bad guys. I took the stairway up to avoid the lobby. I knocked and Charlie let me in. Margot and Heather were sitting at the small table finishing up their room service breakfast. Heather looked like a different woman. It was amazing what a good night's sleep, a couple showers and some good food could do. I smiled and greeted the ladies, and they smiled back, Margot a big bright smile and Heather a more anemic curl of the lips, but still a smile.

Charlie motioned me into the other room. He was chewing on a toothpick.

"How's she doing?" I asked.

"Much better than I expected after how she was last night. I gave her a mild tranquilizer."

"I was glad my near brush with death didn't interfere with your breakfast."

"Hey," Charlie said as he spat the toothpick into a wastebasket. "You're the one who insisted on going. I didn't tell the girls about it. Didn't want to upset Heather anymore."

"I've been thinking," I said. "Dr. Dork knew we were headed down here, but at the factory, he mentioned the gimpy ex-FBI guy. We never said anything about you when he was with us."

"Shit," Charlie said. "I made some inquiries into this back at home. I never figured this company would have the kind of resources to track me down. One of my sources must be a rat."

"The crazy fly-boy?" I asked.

"I don't think so," Charlie said. He sat on the bed and steepled his fingers under his chin. "I'm going to have to investigate that when we get back. Meanwhile, we've got three people in this country illegally. There's Brazilian laws and American laws to deal with. Hopefully, Heather will be able to talk soon and she'll remember the details of her kidnapping. If she can tell a convincing tale, I'm going to the American Consulate and see what I can do."

"Maybe we could say we were all kidnapped," I suggested.

"A possibility. I'm leaning more towards trying to smuggle you all back into the U. S. of A." He looked at me and smiled. "Course it won't be anywhere's near as comfortable as your trip down here."

***

Six hours after my adventure with the gray Lincoln, Margot, wearing a big straw hat, and with a pistol tucked into her belt, as the least identifiable of our band made a trip to the market and to the drug store. Charlie and I took turns watching out the window for any signs of Doctor Dork or his cohorts, or for any unusual police activity. Margot picked up a couple local newspapers which Charlie translated. The article on the IotaTek warehouse fire was especially disconcerting. Charlie translated.

> A blaze gutted the *Biscatero Factario* on *Madielena Avenida*. One unidentified body was removed from the scene. The building is leased by an American company and has been a major developer in new-age pharmaceuticals. A spokesman for the company, Dr. Bernard Meacham, says several million dollars worth of an experimental medicine was destroyed. The *Arsoniero Unita* has been assigned along with the police to investigate this fire.
>
> Dr. Meacham believes the fire was set by a group of industrial terrorists, working for a rival drug company, and led by a felon named Jake Lawless who is wanted for several murders in the United States.

The article went on to speculate that the body was a night watchman and that murder would most likely be added to the arson charges.

"Well, at least they made me the leader," I said. It was a poor attempt at humor, and no one laughed. Margot and Charlie and I sat around the table trying to come up with a plan of action. We were all edgy from sitting and waiting. The only positive, besides the fact we hadn't been caught yet, was Heather's progress. Her appetite was great, and we fed her as much as she could eat. She had wanted to call her kids but there was no safe way to do it.

Margot had picked up some clothes for both of them on her trip. She was beginning to look more and more like the picture Tommy had given me what seemed like ages ago.

~ 173 ~

We were sitting there sipping beer around three in the afternoon when Heather came out of the bedroom. She was wearing jeans and a bright yellow shirt with red Portuguese writing on it. She smiled at us and then took a chair at the small table. "Could I have a beer, please," she asked.

Charlie got her one from our cooler. It was the first time she had asked for anything alcoholic. She knew our return home hinged on information that she alone could provide. After taking a sip of the beer, Heather told us her story.

"I was married young. Right out of high school. He was *mister jock*, and I thought he was wonderful. His father had been a cop and his grandfather used to be the chief of police in New Stratley. So he followed in their footsteps. The police thing went right to his head. He got meaner and meaner. Tommy was just a baby and that's the only reason I stayed with him. I know it sounds foolish, but I could never get up the courage to leave.

"About four years ago, he picked up a side job doing security for IotaTek. He had me apply for a job there as a secretary. Said it was a great place to work. He worked for them nights and I worked days and it was great not to see him. I know I'm boring you with all this history but it's the only way I know how to tell it."

She took a sip of her beer as we all made noises and head gestures indicating we weren't bored. She went on.

"I was meeting some nice people at IotaTek, and for the first time in my married life, I was beginning to see possibilities for a change, for actually leaving the jerk. I became friendly with a guy named Kenny. He was Margot's husband's good friend. It never turned into a relationship, actually never had a chance to.

"IotaTek's main function has been to assist larger companies in testing products and setting up new or additional plants, mostly in the pharmaceutical field. Dr. Meacham came to work there about three and a half years ago and things really changed.

"He became good friends with my husband and they were always away doing something or other. I'm afraid now, that what they were doing must have been terrible.

"Anyways, one day I was having lunch with Kenny and Bruce and they were talking about the new Brazilian project Dr. Meacham had landed. They were actually whispering. The parent company, Manning Pharmaceuticals, was prepared to invest heavily in the new drug that Dr. Meacham had developed. Kenny, who worked in the lab, was concerned that some of the test results weren't valid. This was about a year ago. Both guys decided to see what they could uncover.

"Neither one of them liked Dr. Meacham. They were afraid he and Mr. Judkins would get IotaTek into trouble, costing them their jobs. Their plan was to get evidence against the good doctor and turn it over to the company's board of directors, getting the doctor fired and serving notice to Judkins to return the company to normal.

"They became little detectives and, after about a month, they enlisted me because I had access to places that they didn't. It was kinda fun at first and, like I said, I was interested in Kenny. But after a while, we began uncovering things that we didn't know how to handle."

She finished her beer. Charlie got her another and opened it. We all looked at her, as if to say "what kind of things?"

She continued.

"Things like larceny, bribery. And murder. A chemist from Manning visited IotaTek last fall. His name was Scotty Dawson and he had the cutest brogue. He had lunch with Kenny and Bruce and me one day. He told us about Manning Pharmaceuticals and what it had done for the Minneapolis area and how they hoped to soon be the world's largest pharmaceutical supplier. We told him some of the fun things to do around Boston.

"Near the end of lunch we began talking about Cali-Plus and the Brazilian deal. He didn't come right out and say it but we could tell he had some misgivings about Dr. Meacham's wonder drug. The next night on a Boston Harbor cruise with Dr. Meacham and my husband, Scotty fell overboard and drowned. Meacham said he had too much to drink and had climbed on the railing when he fell. I'm sure they pushed him or forced him to jump. I'm positive he shared his suspicions with the wrong person and they killed him. I mean *nobody* falls off those boats."

She paused her story for a bathroom break and while she was gone, Charlie called room service for a case of beer. The suds were delivered, ice cold, in under three minutes and the waiter was paid and well tipped. He left all smiles, thanking us in broken English.

Heather returned, took a long drink of beer and continued her tale.

"Scotty's death really opened our eyes to how serious these guys were. I wanted to quit my job, but Syd wouldn't hear about it. I tried to talk Bruce and Kenny into quitting, but they wanted to stick it out a little longer.

"Then Kenny was told he had to go to Brazil and assist at the IotaTek plant there for a while. We had our last lunch together the Friday before Kenny left. I again tried to talk him into quitting, but he thought he'd have a good chance to get evidence while he was down there. I had taken a post office box the week before and he was the only one who had the number. He said he would send any information he found, and I should get it to Bruce. The only thing that made it to my post office box was junk mail. We got a couple postcards—block lettered like many of the engineers used—that were signed 'Kenny' but I'm sure they weren't from him. I knew he was dead and that they'd killed him when he got to Brazil.

"Things were weirder and weirder at home. I was sure Syd had a girlfriend. I was thinking about taking the kids and heading for California. My best friend from high school lives outside San Diego and I knew she could put us up for a little while. I told Bruce about my plans and he agreed it would probably be the best thing. Bruce asked me to do one more thing before I left. He needed access to a room where some files were kept and I told him I'd find the keys.

"It was after work on a Wednesday when I met him. I had snuck a box of keys from my office and one of them got us into the file room. We'd been in the room only a couple minutes when Meacham came in. He had a gun. He said he knew what we'd been up to and he was going to bring us someplace for safekeeping until the Brazil deal was done. I told him I had to take care of my kids. He just laughed. Meacham and three of his henchmen, also carrying guns, brought us to the airport and loaded us on a private jet.

"After we were handcuffed to seats and the plane was in the air one of the goons, a real sadistic sort, told us that Dr. Meacham had ordered us to be shot and buried in Brazil. Bruce flipped out and started screaming and trying to pull the handcuff loose from the seat. The goon fired a shoot into his head. The gun was just an inch away.

"I thought he was going to shoot me next."

Heather's eyes welled up with tears. Margot was crying quietly. Charlie and I drank from our beers and reflected on the last moments of Bruce's life. After a while, Heather composed herself and finished her beer. She accepted another from Charlie and went on.

"We arrived in Brazil late at night. They took me away in a car. I had planned to scream my head off at customs, but we never went through. They must have bribed someone. I'm not sure what they did about poor Bruce's body. Armand and Rojo were supposed to kill me. I heard them talking from the backseat of the car as they brought me to the factory. My great aunt was Portuguese and I picked up a lot of it when I was a kid. I got the gist of what they were saying. Meacham wanted then to kill me and bury me in the jungle. They decided to keep me as a . . .a . . .pet. I thought about killing myself. It was horrible in that--"

She had to stop and have a large swig of beer. We all did. It was impossible to imagine what she'd been through.

"I was sure I was going crazy," she said. "Thinking about the kids was the only thing that kept me going. When you guys came in, I figured Meacham had found out that I was still alive and he was coming to finish the job." She looked at me. "I was totally amazed when you said Tommy had hired you to find me. I can't wait to see him and my daughter. Do they know you found me?"

"Not yet," Charlie said. He told her about the events that had transpired in New Stratley. She already knew that Syd had been killed. Margot had broken that news to her earlier and Margot told us she smiled when she heard it. "You, Margot and Jake are all in this country illegally. We can't just go to the airport and get tickets. I was hoping we'd get enough evidence on IotaTek to go to the

American Consulate, tell them the truth, as hard as it is to believe, and maybe they can help us."

"I have this," Heather said. She took a computer disk from her pocket and handed it to Charlie. "Bruce gave it to me just before we were caught. It's damaged but if it can be fixed it could help us."

If it can be fixed.

We all sat around the table working on how we'd present our story to the American Consulate. Margot was taking notes on a yellow pad of paper. Charlie posed my idea that we blame Dr. Dork for kidnapping Margot and me as well as Heather. We all agreed it sounded like a good idea, much more believable than the truth -- crazy Yodel and the voyage of the Gooney Bird.

Charlie was nursing a Jack Daniel's. Heather had switched to a native fruit punch that had an exotic smell. I opened two more beers for myself and Margot. There was a pleasant afternoon breeze blowing through the open window and it seemed to bring with it the city-street noises form four stories below.

I had just finished my first sip of the new bottle when I heard a bumping noise. I never saw Charlie move so fast. He overturned the table and dove to the floor. In a blur, I saw him hurl an object at the window as he yelled, "Down!"

Nobody had a chance to get down, at least not of their own volition. The object exploded just as it went through the window. I was knocked to the floor from the blast. Shards of glass and broken hunks of board and pieces of plaster flew into the room and covered us all.

I didn't lose consciousness, but for several seconds I was dizzy and disoriented. My ears hurt like hell and I didn't know if I'd lost my hearing. I saw Charlie pull himself up and brush rubble from his clothes. He had a gun drawn and he moved slowly toward the window. I could see his lips moving, but I couldn't hear him. Or hear anything. Just felt the throbbing, awful pain in my ears.

I saw Margot stagger to her feet, and I began to get up, too.

Charlie was at the hole where our window had been looking out at the street, his gun pointed downward. I couldn't tell if he was firing. Couldn't hear it if he was.

~ 178 ~

Heather sat on the floor, blood trickling from a cut on her forehead. But her eyes were open and she was moving. At least we were all alive. Margot bled from several cuts on her arms, and her hair was covered with white plaster dust. Her lips were moving but I had no idea what she was saying.

"I can't hear," I yelled and pointed at my ears. She nodded and motioned me toward Heather. Together, we helped her up. I opened the bathroom door and got a couple towels from the rack to use as bandages. Charlie joined us and motioned frantically that we had to get out. I was beginning to hear a ringing sound. At first I thought it was inside my head, but as Charlie slowly opened the hall door, I saw the flashing alarm lights in the corridor and realized their flashing corresponded with the undulating sound I was hearing. Just before we left the room, I saw Margot remove her yellow note pad from the debris.

We ran to the stairwell at the far end of the building. As we did, I saw doors opening and scared looking faces peering out. We must have been a sight running by covered with blood and plaster dust. One woman slammed her door shut when she saw us. The wavering noise was getting louder, which I hoped meant my hearing was returning. We reached the stairway and Charlie pushed the door open. I went through first, just in time for us to see a man running up to our flight. I recognized him as Armand from the IotaTek factory. His eyes grew wide when he saw me.

Apparently he figured we'd be dead or near dead from the blast and he'd just have to finish us. His mistake.

Before anyone could say or do anything, I pulled the pistol that I'd kept in my waistband since my encounter with the Lincoln and I fired point blank into the middle of the guy's chest. The blast lifted him off his feet and sent him backwards where he crashed into the landing half a flight down. We ran down the steps past the body. I was surprised when Heather turned and went back up to the landing.

She kicked at the dead guy. Fierce kicks that would have really hurt if he was still among the living. Charlie and Margot stopped below and looked back up. I went back and took Heather by the shoulder and shook her gently. Tears ran down her cheeks and she

~ 179 ~

was screaming something. Her body was trembling badly but she kept kicking. I forced her to look at me.

"It's over," I said. "He can't hurt you anymore. He's dead."

My words sunk in. She stopped kicking and started to turn to go with me. But she stopped for one last attack. She drove the heel of her shoe down onto the guy's mouth. I couldn't hear it but I imagined the sickening sound of teeth breaking against pulpy flesh. Then she turned and ran down the stairs with me. I could only imagine what he'd done to her, and deep inside I wished he'd lived long enough for her retribution to be meaningful.

As we reached them, Charlie and Margot opened the outside door that led to the back of the hotel and who knows what other dangers.

My ears were buzzing, but I was beginning to hear other sounds, like the fire alarm system and sirens approaching. People shouted somewhere, but I couldn't make out what they were saying.

Charlie went out the door first scanning the street that ran behind the hotel. He motioned us all to come out. We started walking down the street trying to look nonchalant but I bet we stuck out like four skunks walking across the queen's croquet field. And it didn't take long for us to be noticed.

A police car pulled up next to us, and two officers jumped out. They approached us warily, both had their hands on their guns. The driver, was yelling something and making motions with his free hand. I was wondering if we'd be safer letting the police take us. There had been an apparent connection between Dork and some cops, but all the boys in blue down here couldn't be on his pad. Maybe these guys would take us to the American Consulate. We'd never know because that wasn't how Charlie wanted to play it.

Chapter 21

Charlie grabbed the driver and pulled his hand away from his gun. The other guy was squawking into his portable radio. I hit him on the jaw as hard as I could. The radio flew from his hand and hit the pavement breaking into several pieces. I went to hit him again but I saw his eyes and knew he was out. He sagged to the pavement. A crowd had gathered and I could make out yelling.

I wasn't sure whose side they were on, but none of them jumped in to help the cops.

I saw that Charlie had knocked his guy out, too. He took the cop's pistol from his belt and motioned for me to do the same. I reached down and pulled but the pistol wouldn't budge. He had a safety holster like my friend Bart. I twisted the handle and the gun pulled free. The officer was starting to come around. I didn't want to hit him again. I got an ammo clip from his belt and then turned to see what the others were doing. The crowd had taken several steps back when they saw we were armed.

Charlie motioned frantically for us to get into the cruiser. The girls jumped in the back. I went to the passenger's side. I was half in when Charlie floored it, and the cruiser fishtailed and took off. I felt Margot's arm pulling me in. The door hit a guy from the crowd but I don't think it hurt him.

Fists and fingers were shaken and raised at us as we flew by, but, a minute later, we were around the corner and away from the hotel and the mob.

This was definitely not what we had wanted. Now we were outlaws in Brazil as well as the United States. I wanted my ears to get back to normal so I could talk to Charlie and the women and figure out what to do. There really wasn't much to figure out. We had to run like the four scared felons we were. Put as much distance between us and the *Belo Horizonte* Police as we could. After a few blocks, Charlie slowed to a normal speed. He was listening to the radio, trying to figure out how much time we had before we had to ditch the cop car.

That was answered quickly. Charlie grimaced at the rear view mirror. I turned and saw another cruiser after us, its lights flashing, and I could just make out its klaxon siren over the buzzing in my ears. I fumbled to buckle my seat belt as the cruiser careened through the downtown streets. Charlie was a good wheel man. I looked at him and I swear he had a smile on his face. The cruiser behind us was keeping pace and I didn't see how we could get away from it. I looked back at Margot and Heather. Their eyes were wide open in a going-down-the-roller-coaster stare.

Charlie, intent on the road, beeped at other motorists and steered around them sometimes at the last second. I was sure, several times, we were going to crash. Charlie saw something, I was pretty sure by the change in his expression. He jammed on the brakes.

"Hold on," I heard him yell through the buzz.

There wasn't much to hold onto. The car began skidding and then Charlie cut the wheel. The cruiser lurched like it was going to turn over and then in a cloud of tire smoke turned 180 degrees. Charlie mashed the gas and we were off in the opposite direction headed right at our pursuers. They didn't have time to think. They swerved to the left and crashed into a street vendor's cart in what looked like an explosion of chicken feathers and tropical fruit.

Charlie drove on several hundred feet and then took a hard left. He aimed at an alley on the right that didn't look wide enough for a car to traverse. We rocketed right for it. It was between two large buildings and there were trash cans and crates against both walls. We drove down the alley, scraping against the walls and tossing trash cans into the air. One flew up and hit the windshield sending a series of spider-web cracks through it. Both side view mirrors were torn off. One man coming out a door with a load of garbage dropped the load and got back inside, just in time. Somehow we made it through.

We stopped briefly at the end of the alley. Traffic was moderate on the street we were facing. I had no idea where we were or what direction anything was in. Not that there was any real place for us to go. Charlie picked right and pulled into traffic. Pedestrians gawked at us as we drove by in the dented cruiser with the broken windshield.

The buzzing in my ears was subsiding, replaced by a throbbing ache. I was hearing better and I preferred the pain to the buzz, as long as I could hear. I looked at the street signs as we drove past, *Avenida Afonsa Pena, Rua Cearra, Avenida Brasil,* but none of them meant anything to me. We came to a traffic circle on *Avenida Brasil* where a police officer directed traffic. He stopped cars to let us get through. The whistle fell out of his mouth when he realized we weren't *policia*. He chased after us, yelling and waving his arms. Dummy.

Buildings seemed to get smaller the further we went. We were approaching the outskirts of the city. It reminded me of the run-down places by the IotaTek plant, but I was sure we were on a different end. Charlie dove slowly, looking for a place to dump the cruiser. I spotted four youths standing on a street corner, smoking and making hand gestures at passing motorists.

"Let's give it to them," I said.

"Good idea," Charlie said. I actually heard him.

We pulled over by the boys. They looked at us warily. Charlie told us all to get out and then he spoke to the youths. He put the cruiser keys in the biggest kid's hand. I don't know what Charlie told him but the kid grinned from ear to ear. He took the keys and jumped in the driver's seat. His pals joined him and they took off in a screech of tires. They hadn't traveled a block when they figured out how to run the siren. Four dummies.

~ 183 ~

Charlie took Margot's arm and I took Heather's and we began walking. We tried to stay in the shadows as much as we could, but we needed to put distance between us and where we'd dumped the cruiser. Heather shivered, and I saw tears stream down her cheeks.

"Don't worry," I said. "We'll be out of this in no time and you'll be home with Tommy and your daughter." I tried to sound convincing, but I sure wasn't convinced myself.

We found an abandoned building after about twenty-five minutes walking. "In here," Charlie said. We all ducked quickly inside.

It was a three-story brick structure and there were signs posted by the door. "Condemned," Charlie translated. We climbed up to the second floor. The stairs going up to the third were rotted and broken and we didn't attempt them. All the glass had been smashed out of the windows and it covered the floor.

"We can hole up here until tomorrow," Charlie said. "In the morning, we'll have to find a way to get out of this city."

We swept aside some glass with our feet and sat on the floor. Somehow we'd have to get some sleep. I looked around at our sorry group. Heather and Margot huddled together shivering and whimpering quietly. Charlie stared into space, planning who knew what. My hearing was almost back to normal, but my ears still hurt. I hadn't even taken the fifty-dollar down payment on the job. *Four more dummies*, I thought.

***

In the dim light of dusk, we sat on the floor and had a meeting to assess our situation and, in a word, the outcome had been bleak. We had two Tokagypt pistols and two pistols we stole from the cops and only the rounds of ammo still left in them plus the one extra clip I'd taken. All our extra clothes and toiletries were left behind as was the sample of green glop Charlie had taken from the warehouse. Charlie still had his money and his plastic and his papers, and that was a plus. We decided we'd try to sleep on it and maybe come up with a plan in the morning. Charlie said he'd take the first watch.

I found some old cardboard boxes that we folded up to make pillows. They smelled like sour tomatoes and the floor was hard and smelled of grease and mold, but somehow I fell asleep. I dreamt all

~ 184 ~

kinds of crazy things until a shake on my shoulder woke me up. It was Charlie.

"Think you can take a watch for a few?" he whispered. "I need a little shut eye." I agreed. "It's been real quiet so far. I heard some animals roaming downstairs but they don't sound much bigger than a cat. That stairway is the only way anyone can get to us from below. If you can't stay awake, make sure you get me up."

"I'm all right, Charlie. I'll make sure you're up in time for breakfast."

With that, he settled onto the floor and closed his eyes.

I took my place at the window. From there, I could see the gray shapes, the pointed spires of *Belo Horizonte's* many skyscrapers rising through a smoggy ground cover and aiming at the heavens, like giant guns, I thought, pushed from the depths of hell to shoot stars into the night. Poetic. My hearing was back to normal and I was grateful for that. I heard traffic in the distance but nothing ventured down the street I was watching. I looked at my watch. *4:15 a.m. and all is well,* I said to myself.

***

I watched the morning light come, slowly turning the buildings across the street into recognizable shapes. At seven, Charlie woke.

"I'm gonna go see what I can rustle up for clothes and grub," he said.

"Maybe I should go," I suggested.

"You'd get lost like you did last time. Which is how I think they found us at the hotel." He smiled. "And I speak the lingo. I'll have my pistol with me. If there's trouble, I'll fire two quick rounds, you take the girls and run."

In case we got separated, we devised a system using two of the tallest skyscrapers. Facing the one with the three antennae and keeping the one with the purplish dome to it's left, we'd have a direction of travel. I was hoping we wouldn't have to use it, but it was better than no system at all. And then Charlie was gone. I looked at my watch, 7:20 a.m. Margot and Heather slept quietly and the longer they could rest the better. I looked out the window as an eerie rose-colored haze fell over the city.

~ 185 ~

Forty-five minutes later, Charlie was back. He had two paper bags, one filled with clothes and one that had lost most of its brown color to the grease seeping from inside. I didn't care if it was pure cholesterol, I was starved.

"Breakfast time, kids," he said.

"What's that smell?" Margot asked, rubbing sleep from her eyes.

"Got us a little nourishment, Magpie," Charlie said, and he helped her up. He tore open the brown paper bag and handed us each two things that reminded me of *tamales*. I ate mine greedily. It tasted like chicken hash smothered in pan drippings. I had the ominous feeling as I ate it, that it would settle and be hard as cement, but I was happy to have it. Charlie handed us bottles of fruit juice to wash everything down.

After our breakfast, we all snuck off to find bathroom corners in the abandoned building. We weren't the first. There was no running water, but we made do. Then we put on the clothes that Charlie had got at a second hand store. He said he had to bang on the door to wake the proprietor up, but the angry man was soon happy with his early morning sales.

Dressed in our native garb, we sat in a circle on the floor to plan our next moves.

"I got some bad news when I went out," Charlie told us. "I read a little story about us in the paper. The police found the rental car at the hotel and now they have all my information."

"You rented the car in your own name?" I asked.

"Yep. Well, I never said I was perfect. But that was a big *faux pas*. Now the only one who isn't wanted is Heather, and she has no papers." He finished the last of his fruit juice. "According to the newspaper, we almost caused some kind of international incident. Anyway, turning ourselves in to the consulate in this city would get us happily turned over to the police, and I fear we'd rot in a Brazilian jail cell until the food killed us."

"What are we gonna do?" Margot asked, tears streaming down her cheeks.

"Seems to me," I said, "We have to get back to the States and have Heather tell everyone what really happened, and that they are after the wrong people."

"I agree," said Charlie, "and I do have a plan." He sat back on his haunches and folded his arms on his chest.

"What is it," we said almost in unison.

"We can't get out by car, train or bus. We'd be recognized for sure. And we can't walk, so land is out. Yodel can't get back down here. That's if *he* even got home at all. And we can't take a commercial flight, so air is out. Which leaves ---"

"Sea," I cut him off. "How can we go by sea. That will be as impossible as flying."

"Not really," Charlie said. "We'll get us a small boat and sail north. Follow the coast 'til we get into Mexico and we can maybe drive from there. What-y-a think?"

"I used to think you were a little crazy, now I'm convinced you're totally, certifiably nuts."

"Thanks," he said. "I'm glad you like the plan."

Charlie laid it out for me. We'd walk out of the city, where we were a hot, sought-after commodity, and call Raul from the suburbs. Hopefully, Raul could pick us up, and drive us up the coast to one of several port cities where we would buy or rent a boat. If we stole one the Brazilian Coast Guard would get us for sure. The farther north we traveled the better, as land travel would be much easier. I suggested we lay low at Raul's house for a while but Charlie didn't agree. We had to get back to the States and Margot and Heather both nodded their support.

None of us had a lot of sailing experience. Charlie had done some in college and I'd had a sixteen foot boat for several years that Bart and I used to take up the Charles River and into Boston Harbor. And Charlie was well versed in navigation from his FBI days. We agreed the best choice would be a twin engine boat with a head. Charlie said he would get as much as he could from an ATM and we'd have to wing it when we got to a port.

We talked about a sailboat but that would have to be a last resort.

When the girls had gone out of earshot to put the finishing touches on their costumes, Charlie whispered to me, "I'd like to cool it for a while at Raul's but I don't know if you've been noticing Heather's mental state."

"We're all on the ragged edge here, Charlie."

"True," he said and smiled, "but she's been through things we can't imagine. I've been giving her Prozac and telling her it's vitamins, but wc have to get her to a real American Doctor. ASAP."

"Prozac," I said, "Where did you get that?"

"*La Pharmaceutica,*" You can get almost anything you want down here without a prescription."

"What about the boat ride? Can she make that?"

"She has to," he said.

"What if we just drop her off at the American Embassy. She hasn't done anything. Except be kidnapped. And associate with us."

"I thought about that," he said, "but in her fragile mental state, she might not tell them anything. And that won't help us."

"What are you guys talking so quietly about?" Margot asked, as she and Heather came back into the room.

Charlie whistled at them, all costumed up as Brazilian peasant women. "We were just saying what a wonderful day it is to go boating."

***

We walked away from the city keeping the skyscraper with the purple dome directly behind us. With our broad-brimmed somber-ros and the clothes Charlie had gotten us, we looked pretty much like we belonged there. I went first, followed by the girls about two hundred feet back. Charlie was another two hundred feet behind them. Since the authorities were looking for two males and one female that seemed like the best way to break us up. We planned not to scatter unless it was absolutely necessary. If that happened we would try to find each other based on our relationship to the purple dome. We had discussed secondary rendezvous spots but decided that would be too complicated.

The buildings continued to look smaller the further we got from the city proper. The air was filled with delicious cooking smells. I had lost track of days and I had to think a little to figure it was Saturday about ten in the morning. Everyone but us, it seemed, was having a late breakfast. An occasional passerby would offer a greeting. I nodded and smiled and tried to look as Brazilian as I could. My mind was running wild with thoughts about Charlie's crazy boat trip.

The ride down aboard the Gooney Bird had seemed to take forever. And that was at over two hundred miles an hour. How fast could a boat go? At least one that we could afford. Twenty, thirty, forty miles an hour? Maybe the insane old bugger was taking us out on an Ahabian suicide run. Well, I wasn't getting on any boat with him until he explained the whole trip a lot better.

On the other hand, what options did I have? No money. Didn't speak the language. Wanted by the police. How had I got myself mixed up in this? We had rescued Heather, sure, but if we couldn't get her back to New Stratley safe and sound, what good was it?

***

We'd been walking for a couple hours and were definitely in the suburbs. The streets here were mostly dirt and there was a slight upward grade to them as we neared the mountains. My feet were killing me, and I couldn't imagine how Heather was holding up a couple short days since her rescue. She could barely walk then. Soon I came upon an outside café in a small square that was dominated by shops. The café was busy but there were a couple outdoor tables left and I sat at one. Heather and Margot sat at the table with me when they arrived. We all silently hoped that Charlie wouldn't come and shoo us along and we breathed a collective sigh of relief when he sat with us.

"I hope we're far enough away to rest a little," Charlie said.

"Me, too," I said. "My dogs are killing me."

The girls nodded in agreement. None of the patrons of the café seemed to pay us any attention. Charlie went to the window and got us a pitcher of beer with plastic cups. The beer wasn't real cold, but it sure tasted good.

"I got us a platter of food," Charlie said. "The waitress will be bringing it soon. I'm going to make a phone call." He drained his cup and then got up and headed for a pay phone. I heard music start. Two men, one with a guitar and one with a ukulele-like instrument, began to entertain the diners. It would have been quite enjoyable if we weren't running for our lives.

Charlie came back just as the waitress arrived with our food. He thanked her and ordered another pitcher.

Charlie was smiling. "I got hold of Raul. He agrees with you that I'm crazy. But . . .," he emptied the first pitcher into his cup and took a long drink, "he's on his way to help us. He said he'd meet us here in about three hours."

"We're waiting here for him?" Margot asked.

"Sure," Charlie said, "We've got music, food and beer, an outhouse. What could be better?"

"I want to go home," Heather said, tears streaming down her cheeks.

Charlie got up and rubbed her back. "Easy, honey. We'll be home before you know it." He handed her a pill. "Take this with some of this great beer and you'll feel better. The hardest part for you is over. Just a little boat ride left."

I wanted to question him about the 'little boat ride,' but didn't want to get Heather more upset. We ate our tray of food. I had no idea what it was but it was good. In a while, the girls got up to find a rest room and, when they'd got out of earshot, Charlie whispered to me.

"If we can get a boat that does thirty-five miles an hour we can cover 3500 miles in just over four days. I think we can do it. We'll have to stop for gas but we'll at least get out of Brazilian waters. After Raul picks us up, we'll have to get some maps and figure our best route."

He sounded so confident and the beers were so good and the gauchos, or whatever they were, sang and played so nicely, I found myself almost happy for the first time in a long time. I pushed the bad thoughts aside and took a big gulp of beer.

"We got enough cash to buy another plate of food?" I asked.

***

We could just make out the tops of *Belo Horizonte's* tallest buildings from where we sat at the *Café Gloria* waiting for Raul to pick us up. The sun had just dropped below the purple mountains and there was a slight breeze carrying wonderful aromas our way. The spicy smell of the open barbecue where two chefs were preparing for the supper rush mixed with the sweet aroma of thousands of flowers that bloomed wild on the hillside. I have no idea what they were, but they sure did smell pretty. Luckily, we were fifty yards away upwind from the outhouse and there wasn't much wind.

"Charlie," I asked, "how can you get in touch with Raul so easily? I'd think it would take days to contact him, tucked away in his little shack in the jungle."

Charlie laughed. "Raul is kind of a complex person if you don't know him. He was the number two man in what is the equivalent of the Brazilian Secret Service. That's how I met him. In addition to his little shack, he has a very nice apartment in *Vitoria*, overlooking the Atlantic."

"Maybe he has some pull with the government, then?" Margot asked.

"He used to. He had a pretty bad falling out with the *Presidente* a few years ago and now he's retired. And not invited to any government functions, if you know what I mean. He does all right though, helping his old friends like me."

"Are we going to his house?" I asked. "The one by the sea."

"No," Charlie shook his head. "He has enemies who watch what he does and who he meets. That would be too obvious. What I'm anxious to do is see if we can get Heather's disk repaired. We're only three or four hundred miles away from *Rio de Janiero* and *Sao Paulo*. We should be able to hide out in one of those cities for a little while. Hopefully long enough to find out what's on the disk and if it will help us get home and out of this mess."

About twenty minutes later, an old blue Chevy station wagon pulled into the lot across from the café in a cloud of dust and blue smoke.

"Our chariot has arrived," Charlie said.

We were all happy to see the big smiling Brazilian. He was scuffed up and bandaged from the adventure at the IotaTek Plant, but not much the worse for wear. He insisted on a beer to celebrate before we began our journey and Charlie obliged, getting us all another round. An hour later and we were all piled in the Chevy and off to *Rio de Janiero*.

Chapter 22

I figured it would take about four hours to get to Rio. With Charlie, Raul and I sharing the wheel and driving through the night, it had been about fifteen hours when we came around a bend and Charlie pointed out the giant statue of Jesus with outstretched arms overlooking the city.

Rio reminded me somewhat of *Belo Horizonte*, except it seemed much busier. Cars flew around us on all sides with horns blaring. Charlie drove when we hit the city line and he accelerated into the madness.

"Where are we headed?" I asked.

"To the poor side of town," Charlie said and smiled. "Before we get to the real slums, the ones built along the hillsides, there's a section with some cut-rate motels. I stayed in one for a couple weeks once. It wasn't too bad. As long as you were armed."

"Sounds wonderful," Margot said. "How about a Holiday Inn or something?"

"It won't be bad, Magpie. Hopefully we can get some answers from this disk Heather has. In the morning, Jake and I are going to school."

"School?" I asked.

"Yep. The University of Brazil. I may have a contact or two there who can help us."

We found a place called *Siestra*. a cement block building, painted pink with neon signs in Portuguese decorating the office.

Charlie and Raul got us two rooms adjacent to each other in the rear of the building. The water was lukewarm, but it felt good to shower. Charlie went shopping and brought us food and beer, which we ate and drank with gusto. All of us were beat and turned in shortly after we ate.

***

Charlie woke me up early and we were on our way by seven. He said Raul would guard the women and get them breakfast. We walked for about a mile and had coffee and biscuits at an outside café.

Unlike the people in *Belo Horizonte*, who were dressed mainly in black and white, the *Cariocas*, as Charlie called them, sported colorful clothes in a myriad of hues and tints. After we ate we took a taxi to the University of Brazil's admissions office, a stately brick building on *Playa Economu*. Charlie spoke to the receptionist who motioned us to have a seat. After we had waited about fifteen minutes, a tall, skinny bald man, sporting a gray goatee and Fu-Manchu moustache strode from an elevator. He and Charlie shook hands and spoke greetings in Portuguese.

"This is Professor Karl Marquand," Charlie said, "Jake Lawless."

The professor and I shook hands. He had a powerful grip for such a thin man.

"Karl," Charlie whispered to me, "is the most dangerous man south of Mexico. At least until I get down here." Both men laughed. We took the elevator to the fifth floor and Professor Marquand led us down a long hallway to his office. The plaque on the door in English and Portuguese announced him to be a professor of political science. Bookshelves covered most of three walls. A large oak desk stood in the center of the room. Two small windows gave a nice view of the University buildings surrounding a grassy quadrangle. The fourth wall was decorated with antique weapons, knives, guns, machetes and other things I didn't know. The professor motioned us to sit, and we did.

~ 193 ~

"What can I do for you, my old friend?" Karl asked.

"Help us with this," Charlie said as he dropped the broken disk on the professor's desk. "And this." He took a small baggie from his pocket and dropped it on the disk. I made out a few small pieces inside it that looked like the vegetative stuff we had seen in the IotaTek warehouse.

The professor picked up the glassine baggie and held it under his desk lamp. He took a very large magnifying glass from his top drawer and peered at the substance through it. After several "hmms" and "hahhs" he spoke. "There's not enough here to smoke."

Charlie laughed. "I don't want to smoke it. I want to identify it," he said.

"I cannot help you there, but maybe I know who can." He picked up his phone and pushed a few buttons. After several seconds he spoke, "Vincenzo . . ." The rest in Portuguese. I was surprised at how good his English was and how he could vary languages without missing a beat. He hung up the phone. "Vincenzo, from the Biology Department will come and take a look at it."

"I thought all the stuff got left behind at the hotel," I said.

"I found those two pieces in my pocket," Charlie said. "I didn't want to get anybody's hopes up in case there isn't enough to ID."

The professor made another call and informed us that a Katrina was coming up to look at the disk. "I am not putting my people at risk with this, am I, Charlie?"

"Well Karl, there's a risk in everything, but I'm sure your folks will be fine."

"You like my collection?" The professor asked me. He had apparently seen me staring at the rows of killing implements that adorned his wall. I nodded and he got up and motioned me to follow him. He pointed out some of his most interesting pieces.

"This," he said proudly, "is an extremely rare sword—-"

He was interrupted by a knock on the door. A man came in, Vincenzo. I could tell by their greeting. The professor introduced us and then showed him the baggie. Vincenzo was short and stout and he had huge bushy eyebrows that stretched across the top of his eyes like a giant black caterpillar. He took a piece from the baggie, held it in his fingers. Then he sniffed it and touched it with his tongue. He used the big magnifying glass to study it closer. He "hmmmd" and "haahd" like the professor but with more of an accent. Finally he put the glass and the green stuff down and smiled.

"Epiphyllum," he said, then rambled on in Portuguese.

"He says this is Epiphyllum," the professor translated. "It is known as jungle cactus."

"Ask him if it's rare," I said.

"He says there are over 13,000 hybrids of this plant. This might, or might not be one that is catalogued. You have the greens, but the flower part can be very beautiful."

Professor Vincenzo took our sample and promised to analyze it properly and supply us with literature about jungle cactus.

Shortly after he left, there was another knock on the door and the woman named Katrina came in. She was a plump woman in her early thirties, I guessed, and her purple pants were way too tight.

She smiled pleasantly and shook our hands when Karl introduced us. Karl showed her the disk. She inspected it closely, nodded her head and then left with it after a few Portuguese words to the professor.

"She said she'd do the best she can," Karl told us after the door closed behind her. Then he spoke Portuguese to Charlie and they both laughed.

"What was that, a private joke?" I asked.

"Play on words about Miss Purple Pants. It wouldn't work in English," Charlie said. "Never mind her, anyways. You should be concentrating on Margot."

"Margot?" I was totally surprised by that.

"Yeah, Margot. The lady you came down here with. Every day that goes by I can sense her attraction to you. And, now that she knows about Bruce . . . .." He let the statement fade off. He and Professor Karl both grinned widely enjoying my embarrassment.

"Thanks, Dear Abby," I said. "I'll feel great knowing you're helping me with my love life."

"Jake," Charlie said, "you don't have a love life." He started laughing and the Professor joined him. When they finally stopped, I spoke.

~ 195 ~

"Okay guys, I think we should concentrate on getting us home safely, putting Dr. Dork and his pals in jail, keeping us *out* of jail and getting our lives back in order before worrying about romance. And, I don't think she's 'got a thing' for me."

"Why don't you come to my house for dinner tonight?" Karl asked. "We won't have the disk back until at least tomorrow. And my wife is a keen judge of matters of the heart. The meal will be splendid."

"Great!" said Charlie as he slapped my back. "Let's go get the women ready. We'll be at your place at six. I think I can still find it. Raul can stay at the motel and watch his TV."

***

Dinner at the professor's was splendid. His wife, Margarita, a pleasant woman who looked like she enjoyed eating as much as cooking, spoke no English, and the professor was kept busy translating. Apparently, he added to the translation as she laughed at almost everything he said. It was by far the best meal we'd had in Brazil, and everyone, even Heather, was enjoying it and the company.

Margarita served us each a stuffed bird, which I thought were pigeons but Margot said were quails. Whatever they were, they were delicious, especially washed down with the homemade wine from the professor's own grapes. For an instant, I had the image of Margarita and Karl, barefoot, stomping the grapes in a huge bucket. But it tasted too good and I drove that image from my mind quickly. We ate pastry that was out of this world, flaky, with nuts and honey, and I think the richest coffee I'd ever tasted.

After dinner, while Margot and Heather helped Margarita clean up the table, Charlie and I followed Karl into the room he called his library. There he offered Cuban cigars which I declined but Charlie accepted with a huge smile. In a minute, plumes of smoke were wending towards the ceiling. Karl poured us Cognacs and we sat at a table in the center of the room where he had two chess boards set up. Charlie spent the next half hour telling the professor our story from the beginning. I let Charlie tell it, just adding bits and pieces that he didn't know. After he'd heard the story, Karl took a deep

~ 196 ~

drag on his cigar and blew several smoke rings across the table. He sat back in his chair and smiled.

"Sounds like your kind of adventure, Old Man," the professor said. "If there's any hope for you to get out of your situation, you came to the right place.

Charlie nodded. "I was hoping you'd say that."

"Let's take our drinks outside and enjoy the night air," Karl said.

The ladies joined us on the veranda, which was dimly lit by several lanterns and by the sliver of a moon that was just rising over the dark mountains. We all had more cognac except Margarita who was enjoying her wine. Music was playing at a house several doors away and the faint sound was peaceful and haunting.

Charlie and the professor took turns telling of their adventures and kept everyone laughing. A church bell chimed in the distance, one ding for every hour. By eleven dings, we were getting pretty tipsy. The professor and Margarita both insisted we stay the night. They had plenty of room.

"I can't keep my eyes open," Margot said.

The professor spoke to Margarita and she got up and chattered in Portuguese and motioned the girls to follow her. After they left the room, the professor offered the cognac bottle. Charlie and I both held our glasses out. Margot had called them snifters. They were a lot fancier than anything I used to pour liquor in back in New Stratley. Of course this cognac tasted a lot better than the swill I used to pour back at the White Stallion.

Once the women had gone, our talk turned back to our main problem of getting back home.

"The way I see it," Karl said, "there is something mighty fishy about this IotaTek Company. Why did they have a warehouse full of worthless jungle plant?" And why do they want to kill you guys so bad? And why did they burn their own place down? It was them that started the fire and not you two?"

"Yeah," I said and took a sip of the smooth liquor, "it was them. Apparently they didn't care about the building. Or the jungle cactus."

"Maybe burning the building was in their plans all along," Charlie said. "Doing it while we were there gave them someone convenient to blame it on."

"After what Margot and Jake did to Dr. . .what is his name? Dirk?"

"No, Dork, Professor. We called him Dr Dork," I said.

"Ah, yes. I am not familiar with that colloquialism. But after what you did to him and his wife, I can't say I blame him for trying to kill you." We all chuckled at that. "Anyway," the professor went on, "it seems as though these people are up to something illegal. Maybe artificially inflate the value of the contents of the building and burn it for the insurance. What does this company do?"

"As near as I could figure from my investigating and what we learned from Heather, they are a company that helps start-up companies or helps an already going business to grow or diversify."

"So maybe they charge a company to build this business in Brazil? They charge big money for that. Then they burn the building, destroy evidence and get insurance money also."

"I've been thinking along those lines myself," Charlie said, "but how are we gonna prove it?"

"Hopefully," Karl answered, "there will be proof on that disk and we should know tomorrow." We all raised our glasses and toasted to that.

A little later, I was lying in bed in a small guest room. I could see the sliver of moon and lots of stars through the open window. All kinds of questions ran through my booze-fuzzied brain. Tomorrow we'd know. Hopefully. I didn't think I'd be able to sleep, but a few minutes later I was gone to the world.

***

I awoke to the sound of rain thrumming against the tin roof. There were no clocks in the room but, judging by the dim light coming from the window, I figured it was near dawn. I threw on my clothes and walked quietly to the bathroom. It felt like I'd been months without a toothbrush and I made a mental note to pick one up as soon as possible. There was some tooth powder in the medicine chest that I rubbed on my teeth with my finger. That would have to do.

The clock in the hall showed 5:50. I thought about going back to bed, but I knew I wouldn't be able to sleep.

I walked out to the veranda. The air was cool and damp and smelled of flowers and smoke. My eyes caught the glimmer of light in the darkest corner of the veranda; the glowing tip of a cigar. I jumped back, startled at not being alone.

"Mornin'," Charlie said. "Didn't mean to spook you."

"Guess I'm just a little jumpy," I said. "I figured you'd sleep 'til noon, what with all the booze you drank."

Charlie laughed. "I had plenty of sleep. Almost four hours worth. I find sleep to be overrated. Think of all the things people miss while they sleep. Like the sounds of this rain. There'll be plenty of time for sleepin' after your dead."

I wasn't going to get into it with him about how lack of sleep might hasten the dying process. "Any possibility we could make some coffee?" I asked.

"I think I might be able to rustle --" He put his finger to his lips. I heard it too; the squishing of tires on the rain soaked street, the hissing of brakes. The professor lived on a street where there was virtually no vehicle traffic. Charlie poked his head around the corner of the house. He turned to me. "Cops. How the hell?"

"Maybe the professor--" I began, but he cut me off.

"No. Karl wouldn't. Let's go."

We ran back into the house just as there was a loud rapping at the front door.

"Into the girls' room, quick," Charlie said. We pushed through the door. Margot and Heather were both sleeping, undisturbed by the rain or the knocking at the door, which was getting louder. We shook the women awake and motioned them to be quiet.

"What is it?" Margot asked.

"Cops," Charlie whispered, "get up quick and get dressed and be quiet."

Heather's eyes were wide and, for a few moments, I thought she'd scream. I heard the front door open against its chain and the professor's voice: "*Qui aqui munato?*"

Someone answered from the other side of the door but it was muffled and I couldn't make it out.

"There's two out back," Charlie said as he peeked out the window. Tension dripped from his voice. "Son of a bitch."

The professor was yelling at the police. It was obvious from their response that he was an important man who could possibly cause them a lot of trouble. But they persisted and finally I heard the chain undone and the front door swing open and heavy boots walk into the foyer.

"What will we do now?" Margot asked.

"Get arrested, I suppose," said Charlie.

Professor Karl screamed at the cops. I figured he'd be hand-cuffed soon and dragged away. An instant later the door was pushed open slowly. Charlie grabbed the back of a chair and I got set to fight, for what good it would do. At least we wouldn't go quietly. But it was Margarita who slipped through the door.

"Shhhh," she said and put her finger to her lips. "*Siga-me. Siga-me,*" she whispered. She opened a door which led to a closet full of multicolored dresses. She took them out and threw them on the bed. The back of the closet looked like some type of cedar. She pushed on it and a door clicked open into darkness.

Chapter 23

"*Toda à maniera*," Margarita hissed. "*Pressa. Pressa!*"

"All the way," Charlie translated. "Hurry." I hesitated for a moment and Margarita pushed my shoulder towards the opening. "Go ahead," Charlie said to me. "I'll take up the rear."

I went into the opening. Margot seemed reluctant. I offered her my hand. She took it and we were off into the tunnel. It was very dark and smelled musty like an old basement. Cobwebs clung to me and I spit them out of my mouth. It reminded me of a funhouse I used to like when I was a kid; move along by feel only. Here there were no scary heads that popped out at you. At least not yet.

I heard Professor Karl still yelling at the cops. His voice was muffled by the walls, but I knew he was giving us a chance to get away. Have to buy him a box of cigars when it was all over.

Heather was whimpering quietly and I heard Charlie trying to comfort her. "Almost over, kid," he whispered, "You'll be home with your kids before you know it."

The tunnel went on for a long way, following the contours of different rooms until finally it stopped. I felt no opening to the right, left or straight ahead. My heart was pounding against my chest and

I was beginning to feel the panicky sensation of claustrophobia. I wanted to run but there was no place to go.

"The end," I said as quietly as I could.

"Can't be," Charlie said. "Try the ceiling."

I felt the ceiling and there was nothing there but spider webs. No seams, no handles. Maybe the floor. I got down on my knees which was difficult in the confined space. At first, I felt nothing but dirt and what I was sure were dead insect bodies.

Then I found a bump. It was the knotted end of a rope. I pulled on it and it came out about ten inches. I yanked harder and a section of floor lifted up. I felt around in the hole; wet, earthen walls but I couldn't feel bottom. I slowly lowered myself in. I was about at my waist when my feet touched the ground.

I crouched down and could see a small pinpoint of light. "I see daylight," I said. I helped Margot into the hole. "We have to crawl," I said. "Grab my belt and let's go."

We began crawling towards the light. I heard Charlie closing the trap door. I was going as fast as I could, trying not to think of snakes, rats or the possibility of policemen waiting for us.

It seemed like hours but it was probably ten minutes before we came to the end. Glorious daylight was coming through a tangle of vines hiding the tunnel, and I heard rain hammering the ground. I pushed away some vines and stuck my head out. The hole opened onto the side of a small hill with a cement culvert at the bottom. I got out and helped Margot, Heather and Charlie out. We stood there, like four kids getting soaked in the rain. It felt great to let all the dust, dirt and memories of the tunnel wash away in the cool Brazilian downpour.

We were about fifty yards from the professor's house, all but the top of the roof hidden from view by a small hill. The rain was starting to let up. Charlie motioned and we followed him down a path leading into a grove of trees. We sat on the ground under a canopy of green leaves, well out of earshot of the house.

"I can't believe the professor had secret tunnels in his house," I said.

"I can't either," added Margot.

"Well," Charlie said, "old Karl has been known to be up to some pretty hairy adventures. I'm sure when he built the place, he figured he might have to make a hasty retreat some day."

"What did he do?" I asked.

"He did a few covert things for the Brazilian government and for the United States."

"Things you'd have to kill us if you told us about," I said.

"No." He laughed quietly. "Just things that had to be done that could have got him killed. Or captured. He's been out of that stuff for a while. I think."

"What are we going to do now?" Heather asked. Her voice was so quiet, I almost couldn't hear her. Tears were streaming down her cheeks. I couldn't imagine what she'd been through, or fathom how she was still holding up.

Charlie put an avuncular arm around her shoulder. "Maybe it's time we dropped you off at a hospital or maybe at the U.S. Consulate."

"No," she said. "No one will know me. They'll put me in prison and I'll die without ever seeing my babies again."

"Okay, honey," Charlie said. "I guess we're all in this together. We'll just have to hang low until Karl gets things sorted out with the police. Then . . .if there's some usable info on that disk maybe we can all go to the Consulate and try to convince them."

"Maybe we should try to contact someone back home," I said. "For all we know, the real bad guys have been caught and we're in the clear."

"Not a bad idea," Charlie said. "And I thought you were just along for the beer drinking."

"I am a private detective, you know," I said.

"You've done great at that," Charlie said. "Don't give up your bartending job."

"You don't know how happy I'd be to be back at the White Stallion, pouring drafties and making microwave pizzas."

"Speaking of that," Margot said, "I'm getting hungry." We could smell the aroma of breakfasts being cooked at the professor's neighbor's houses and they sure smelled good.

"I could eat a slab of bacon myself," Charlie said, "but I don't think we should venture too far. Karl will find us when the coast is clear and I'm sure he'll feed us."

The shower had stopped and it was getting warm. The fallen rain was now rising as a mist.

"Let's relax and enjoy our steam bath," Charlie said.

We had tucked ourselves into a small copse made up of bramble bushes and bunches of pink and yellow flowers, where we were hidden – we hoped – from any unfriendly searchers. It had been a good hour since the police visit.

Charlie had given Heather another pill and she was resting with her head on his shoulder. Something was happening between them. Maybe, I thought, the universal desire to care and be cared for. Or maybe something more. I didn't have time to ponder this as there was a rustling of underbrush about twenty yards from us.

We sat there quietly, waiting and watching. Then Margarita's portly figure appeared in the clearing. She was smiling and carrying a brown paper bag in each hand. I heard her sing-song voice. "*Vido para fora dos pássaros pequenos.*"

"What's she saying?" Margot whispered.

"I think," Charlie answered, "it's 'Come out little birdies.' Or something like that." So, like good little birds, we came out of hiding to join her in the clearing. I couldn't ever remember seeing a broader smile than Margarita's as we approached her. She handed us the paper bags.

"*Sanduíches,*" she said. "*Coma. Coma.*"

"That means 'eat.'" Charlie said.

And we did. We sat in the clearing and devoured the delicious sandwiches of bacon and cheese and thick slices of brown bread like we hadn't eaten in a month.

Margarita carried on a one-way conversation with Charlie as he ate his food. When he was done, he told us what she had said. Her husband had gotten rid of the police, for now. He was going in to the university to check on the progress with the disk and it was better for us to lay low here in the woods for a little while. He was also going to make some calls to friends of his in the government and see if he could find out how they knew we were at his house.

Margarita said she would bring more food and some wine shortly. We thanked her for the meal and she bustled off into the brush, singing.

"Let's get back into our hiding spot." Charlie nodded towards the copse. "No sense sitting out here in the open."

That seemed like a good idea, and we followed him. The sun was directly overhead and it was hot. I guessed over a hundred. Birds and insects were chirping all around us, apparently happy with the heat. I kept a wary eye on the ground. It would be a long time before I'd forget my encounter with the snake. I was just thinking how good a cold beer would taste when Margarita appeared in the clearing. She wasn't singing or smiling, but she was carrying a jug of red liquid.

"She's pretty quiet," I whispered to Charlie.

"Yeah," he said, "I'll go out and meet her. If anything Happens, you and the girls run off into the woods."

Before I could reply, he was off through the thorny brush, which didn't seem to bother his artificial legs at all. Margot, Heather and I watched as he talked quietly to the professor's wife. He took a long drink from the jug and then motioned for us to come into the clearing. Margarita smiled a little when she saw us but it wasn't the broad, happy smile of earlier.

"Wine," Charlie said quietly, and handed us the jug. We took turns drinking. It was warm but wet and tasted good. "She says Karl wants one of us to go with her. The police are still in the area. I guess we're hotter property than I thought."

"Go where?" Margot asked.

"She says he can sneak one of us off to the university but not all four."

Margarita spoke to him again. She was chattering so fast, Charlie had to motion her to slow down. After a few minutes of this, Charlie translated.

"She says it was the biology professor who turned us in. He has a relative in *Belo Horizonte* who saw us on TV. I guess he figured there'd be a reward."

"Nice guy," I said.

"I'm sure Karl will let him know how unhappy he is when all this blows over." He took a giant swig of wine. "If only one of us can go, I think it should be you, Jake."

"You mean I'm expendable."

"No." Charlie chuckled. "I mean I better stay here with Margot and Heather. If something happens, I figure I have the best chance to get them out of here."

He was right. I didn't like the idea much of sneaking off to the university with Professor Karl, but it seemed like the only way we'd ever get the mess we were in cleared up.

"Okay," I said. "Let me have one more drink of that delicious wine and tell her to lead on."

"*Está pronto. Appressar e ē seguro.*" Charlie said. "He's ready. Go. And be safe."

"Be careful, Jake," Margot said. Then she gave me a kiss on the cheek. "I'd do better if there wasn't an audience," she whispered in my ear.

"If you did better, I wouldn't leave," and with that I was off, following Margarita to who knows where or what.

She moved quickly through the underbrush and I barely kept up. About ten minutes later, we came to a clearing. She raised her arm signaling me to stop. Following her through the underbrush was tough work and the sweat was pouring off me. She pulled back a cluster of branches and pointed. About fifty feet away was a dirt road, a path actually. We watched it in silence until we heard an approaching car. The noise of the exhaust disturbed a squadron of resting birds and sent them squawking through the trees.

"*Boa sorte,*" Margarita said and waved goodbye to me. "*Goot luck.*"

"*Obrigado,*" I said, hoped that was thank you. I ran to the car, a dark green vintage Jaguar, and got in the passenger side. The car was immaculate inside and out.

"Nice car," I said.

"Thank you." The professor shifted into gear and we roared down the path. "She's a 1954 XK-140. The finest example in Brazil. Maybe even the world. I used to keep her in a barn but then I decided to get some enjoyment from her. Margarita says I love the Jag better than her." He up-shifted. "Maybe some days, she's right."

Professor Karl wheeled the Jaguar down some shabby looking back streets. He explained it was better to stay off the main roads with a fugitive aboard.

"Your wife told us the biology professor turned us in," I said. "He seemed like a nice guy to me."

"Ah, and to me also," Karl said as he downshifted and squealed the tires around a sharp bend. "Greed does funny things to some people, as does revenge."

"Revenge?" I asked.

"Yes. Right now, the good professor is trying to explain to some very mean policemen how the .25 caliber Raven pistol with filed off serial numbers got into his desk." He pulled his pipe from his jacket pocket. "And that detective who was yelling at me this morning in my own hallway," he paused for affect, "is wondering, I'm sure, why he is directing traffic at *Rue de La Sofia.*"

"Want me to light that for you?" I asked.

"Heavens no, dear boy. I never smoke when driving. I just like to bite down on something." With that he laid on the horn at two slow moving pedestrians who jumped out of the way with only inches to spare. I was wishing I had something to bite down on.

After about twenty minutes, we arrived at a parking garage next to the University. The Professor slid a plastic card into a slot and a gate raised to let us drive in.

"I have no idea what I'd do without this parking pass," he said. "It would be unthinkable to leave the Jaguar parked on the street. He said it *Jag-U-ar*, like I'd heard on TV commercials. I guess if you owned one or could afford one, it was okay to pronounce it how you wanted.

We pulled into a spot that had a placard with the Professor's name on it. I wondered what punishment would befall someone if they parked in his spot. We got out and he locked the car. "Let's go," he said, "but stay behind me." We walked through the lot and into a tunnel. He took a couple turns and I was lost. A few people passed us, but they just nodded at Professor Karl and he nodded back.

At the end of one tunnel was an elevator. The Professor used his plastic card and the elevator door opened. "Some places around here are off limits to students," he said.

We rode up three floors and exited into an older part of the building. We walked down a hallway with huge old windows on one side that looked out onto the brick rear of another building. Shortly we stopped at a door with a placard that said Katrina Blackstone-COMPUTAÇÃO.

The professor knocked and a woman's voice said, *"Entrar."*

We went in and I saw the woman sitting behind a desk who had picked up the disk at Karl's office. The professor walked over to her desk and kissed her on each cheek.

"Remember my young friend, Jake," he said, nodding at me. "He's very interested in how you made out with his damaged disk."

Katrina smiled. "I was able to save about 75% of the contents," she said. "The disc contained mostly microfilm pictures of office documents. I took the liberty of getting them developed into hard paper copies. I hope that was not a problem."

"Not at all, dear girl. Jake, here doesn't have a fiche viewer. Was there anything interesting in them?"

"Professor." Katrina blushed. "I would not read other people's documents any more than their mail." She unlocked the top drawer of her desk and handed the professor a folder. "Here," she said. "You can let me know if there is anything interesting."

"Wonderful," Karl said. "Margarita and I will have you over one night next week for octopus."

She smiled. "No one makes it like Margarita."

"And," the Professor said with a stern tone, "it is probably better that you forget about Jake and this little project."

"What project, Professor Karl?"

We thanked her and left her office. I was wondering if she knew how the Professor felt about revenge.

Professor Karl led me down a long corridor and stopped just before a stairwell. He took a ring of keys from his pocket and unlocked the door on the right side of the hall. He looked around and then opened the door. "In here, quick," he said.

I followed him into a small room that had a urinal, a toilet, and a sink. "You'll be safe in here," the professor said. "I have to leave you for about an hour. There's a manual lock on the door." He pointed at the turnbuckle just above the doorknob. "This used to be a hangout for faculty smokers until the president had those two nasty smoke detectors installed." He gazed up at the white objects with a sneer. The old bastard had them wired so that if anyone tampers with them an alarm goes off."

"A non smoker?" I asked.

"Hardly. He smokes like a fiend. It's the old do-as-I-say thing. Don't get me started on him." He walked to a small window with frosted glass and laid his hand on an oversized sill. You'll be able to use this as a desk, if you don't mind standing. I have used it many times when I was evading prying eyes." He handed me the folder. "Lock the door when I leave and I will be back as soon as I can. And good luck."

"Thanks, Professor." I took the folder from him, and as instructed, turned the knob on the door when he was gone. The room smelled of old smoky wood and disinfectant -- not the worst smell I'd ever encountered. I walked over and laid the folder on the windowsill. My fingers were trembling and I had a feeling in the pit of my stomach like I'd get waiting in a doctor's office.

Part of me wanted to dig right in, find all the info needed to end this torture and get us all home. Another part – the one that keeps me away from the doctor's office – tells me that only bad things are to be found inside the manila folder, nothing at all that will help us. And that this is the end of the line.

I bit my lip and opened the folder.

My heart beat faster as I removed the documents, about twenty pieces of paper. I laid the pile on the windowsill and began to read them. The first page had a date on it that was almost four years old. It was a copy of a formal looking letter from IotaTek to a company in Minnesota, LaPetrie, Inc. This was a biggie. Anyone who'd ever been to a drug store or watched a TV set was familiar with LaPetrie Pharmaceuticals. I read the letter:

Heloise Richter
Director of Research
LaPetrie Pharmaceuticals
404 Independence Avenue
Minneapolis, MN 87768

Heloise,

I'm pleased to let you know that the testing on the *Ploxphlora Arbovitrium* is nearly complete. So far the tests have far exceeded our expectations. This, as you well know, should be an advancement of major importance and a source of immense profit. IotaTek is proud to be on the ground floor in the development of "Cali-Plus."

We are presently looking for a site in Brazil where we can begin prototype production. I will be sending test results and a proposal for our ongoing venture by secure courier. As you know, any leaks of this information could be extremely costly. Manning wants in, also. Please advise.

Sincerely,

Bernard Meacham, Ph.D.

Bernard Meacham, AKA Doctor Dork, I thought. LaPetrie *and* Manning. Huge money. My fingers were shaking so badly that I had to lay the documents on the shelf to read them. They were out of sequence chronologically, but the more I read, the more the scheme unfolded before me.

There were several letters to Heloise outlining IotaTek's on-going involvement with the project and, except for all the talk about secrecy, seemed to be on the up and up. There were, however, internal memos that indicated all was not what it seemed. I read one of them.

B. Found a place we can get cheap in Belo Horizonte. Under 100Gs US. Should be worth 3 or 4 mil to LP with the right documents. Please advise.   K

And another:

Dr. M. Test results looked bad today. 50% DOA. Changed Documents to not reflect this. Need 1K more Mickeys with clean docs. PP

Mickeys, I thought. Mice? They needed a thousand more mice with clean paperwork. It *was* a scam. IotaTek had falsified test results to con LaPetrie into spending a bundle. All the money for the research and the bogus building in Brazil had been funneled right to Dr. Dork and his cohorts at IotaTek.

And then I came upon the most troubling memo of all:

B. Worried about BA and KO in R&D. seem very interested in Cali Project. TOO interested actually. Field trip to Brazil? Advise. K.

That was it. BA was Bruce Anderson. The proof they were on to Margot's husband and his friend. And they *had* a copy of it. That should have sent them running as fast as they could to the cops. Maybe they didn't realize it was a "final" field trip or how quickly their bosses would react.

I had been in the room almost an hour when there was a knock on the door, three quick raps. "It's in use," I mumbled. What was the Brazilian word? "*Ocupado.*" Sounded good to me.

"It is me --Karl." I recognized the professor's voice and pulled back the lock. He pushed into the room and quickly shut the door. "We have a little trouble."

"What is it?" I asked. I didn't like how he said it or the look on his face.

"Apparently your *friends* are more resourceful and determined than we had imagined."

"I can't believe they tracked us down here," I said. "And so fast."

"Not to be too surprised, son. For many Brazilian policemen, sales of information is their main job. Once my colleague turned us in to the locals, it was only a matter of time before they sold us out."

"And your friends in high places?" I asked.

"Alas," he said, "I guess even they can be bought."

"How hot on our trail are they, Professor?"

"Very hot," he answered. "I have it on good information that the police are on the way here and have notified the school security. So, my boy, I would say we have to beat feet." With that he pulled open the door slightly and peeked out into the corridor. "So far, so good."

He exited the men's room and I followed him. I rolled up the file and put it in my pant's pocket in case we had to run. It was obvious that the information gotten from the disk could put Dork and his cronies away for a long time and that they would do anything they could to get it.

"Are we headed for the garage?" I asked.

"No. I know they'll have someone watching my car. We'll have to travel on foot for a while then I will call Margarita and get her to pick us up."

We were almost at the end of the corridor when I heard a man's voice yell. "*Parada.*" I turned to look and saw two uniformed secur-ity men both holding hand guns.

"Run for it, Jake," the professor yelled. "Follow me."

We headed for the stairs at the end of the hall.

"*O batente du eu dispararemos,*" The guard yelled.

"He says they will shoot," the professor said between gulps of air. "I doubt they will."

He was wrong. A second later, two shots rang out in the corri-dor, like two cracks of evil thunder. Professor Karl crumpled up and fell against the wall at the end of the hallway. I heard the guards running toward us.

I bent to help the professor up. He looked at me and then at the guards. He pulled his wallet from his pocket and handed it to me.

"Get to Margarita," he yelled. "Hurry."

The guards were about thirty feet away and closing fast. I took his wallet and ducked into the stairwell. Another three or four shots took chunks of the door frame off behind me. I ran down the stairs, taking three and four at a time.

"Don't fall now," I said to myself. At the bottom of the stairway was a glass door and a guard was just coming in. I jumped down the last four stairs and hit him full bore, my best linebacker imitation. We both went down, but he obviously got the worst of it.

I jumped up and grabbed the professor's wallet which I'd fumbled onto the ground. I put it in my other pants pocket and walked away from the prostrate guard as nonchalantly as I could, alone again, headed for unfamiliar Brazilian streets.

Chapter 24

I heard yelling as I walked away, and distant sirens getting closer. I felt awful about leaving Professor Karl. There was nothing I could have done there except get shot along with him. I thought about his wallet in my pocket. Even though he'd taken a bullet, he kept cool. He knew that I'd need something to help me find Margarita. I could imagine the formidable team he and Charlie had made. My thoughts were jarred back to reality as a white and blue police cruiser came barreling down the street toward me. There were two officers in the car. The driver was intent on the road but the passenger was looking right at me. My first instinct was to run. I took a deep breath and tried to look casual as the cruiser slowed. I looked right at them as they approached. Anybody who isn't guilty will always gawk at a speeding police car. It seemed to work. They slid past me and skidded to a halt near the entrance to the university about one hundred yards past me. I heard a commotion behind me, but didn't turn to look.

The street I was on was lined with palm trees and had university buildings on both sides. I kept walking briskly, trying not to call attention to myself, but I knew I had to get away from the campus fast. I heard more sirens approaching. I listened for footfalls behind me but there were none. I finally got to the end of the street where it intersected with another street going right and left and two more going off at angles. I took a left and then spotted a group of pedestrians waiting to cross the main street. I joined them and we all waited until the light changed.

Across the main street I followed a group of three men dressed in business suits. They took the road to the left and that seemed as good a choice as any.

I guessed it was about noon time, and the streets were full of people. I hoped that would be in my favor. I had walked for about ten minutes when a bus pulled to the curb spouting horrible clouds of oily-smelling smoke. A man and a teenaged girl approached the rear of the bus apparently to board. I got in line behind them. They each walked up the three steps of the bus and handed a seated conductor tokens. I didn't have any tokens or any change. I was going to forget the bus when I remembered the professor's wallet. I opened it and there were several bills inside, red, orange and blue ones. I had no idea what they were but there seemed to be more red ones so I handed one of those to the man.

He looked like he was well into his eighties. He took the bill and gave me a big toothless smile. He was chattering in Portuguese and pointing at a sign behind his head.

"American," I said. This made him laugh. He handed me back three coins and motioned me into the bus. Three or four more people were behind me trying to get on and they were grumbling about the foreigner holding up the line.

I pushed through a turnstile and proceeded down the aisle. All the seats were taken and I stopped about halfway back. The bus bucked forward and I had to grab a seat back to stay standing. The old engine was straining as the driver got it going as fast as he could. Then I heard a bell ring and he jammed on the brakes.

We pulled to the corner and about a dozen people got off. They all yelled at the driver and he returned their insults. The good thing was several seats opened up and I was able to get one with a window. A thin man reeking of garlic and cigar smoke sat next to me. I ignored him and looked out through the dingy glass. I'd ride the thing as far as it went, I was determined, and, on the way, come up with a plan for getting back to Charlie and the women.

I watched for signs as the bus proceeded along its route. Even sitting, I held onto the grab rail on the seat in front of me to keep from being tossed into my neighbor. I kept looking out the window searching for some landmark, but it all looked unfamiliar. We finally pulled into a small station and everyone began to get off. I figured this was the end of the route so I got up and proceeded to the exit.

It felt good to be on the ground again even if I didn't know where I was. I began walking, looking for a quiet place to check out the professor's wallet. I'd gone about five city blocks when I came to a building that had a sign: *Biblioteca Pública*, prominently displayed over its entrance. I hoped that meant public library. It sure looked like one. It was a brick building with granite trim and granite steps. Several people were coming out as I walked up towards the entrance. Writing adorned the glass doors but nothing in English.

I went in and looked around. It looked and smelled like a library, and it was quiet. I peeked into several rooms all with shelves of books. Finally, I found a small room with four tables in it and no people, and I went in.

I took a book from the shelf and sat at a table farthest from the door. I opened the book and propped it on the table. I couldn't read a word of it but I was pretty sure I had it right side up. I took the wallet and laid it on the table where it would be hidden by the book. It held a driver's license, several university-type ID cards, a picture of the professor and Margarita seated holding two babies, grandchildren probably. He had a VISA card and some kind of key card and that was it, except for the bills. I took the money from the wallet, folded it and put it in my pocket. Then I brought the book back and put it on the shelf. I wandered around the library for a while looking for something written in English.

I finally found a section on languages and soon came up with a Portuguese/English translation book. Just what I was looking for. I brought it back to the quiet back room and sat at my table. It was nice to look at something that I could actually read. I found out that the Brazilian currency is called the real, R$. and that one real is worth about thirty-five cents American. I looked at the bills: three red ones, 10 reals, two orange ones 50 reals, and two blue ones, 100 reals. After some quick calculations I figured I had about one hundred and fifteen dollars. Not much really, but it would get me by for a little while.

I wanted to withdraw the book but I didn't have a library card. And I was pretty sure they wouldn't issue me one. I ducked behind a long bookshelf and looked around. No one. I tucked the book into my shirt. I'd mail it back from somewhere. With all the stuff pending against me, larceny of a library book wouldn't add much to my sentence.

I walked out the front door, trying to look nonchalant. No bells went off and nobody screamed at me. I walked quickly away from the library with my plunder.

***

I walked the streets in a huge city surrounded by skyscrapers. It felt even bigger than Boston, where I always got lost even though I'd been there many times. I remembered that the professor's house was near the base of some mountains but I couldn't see any mountains because of the tall buildings. I'd been wandering for about an hour since I'd left the library and I was getting nowhere. I finally came to a small park. Children were running and playing. A man was cooking something at a roadside cart and it smelled delicious.

I sat at a bench that was unoccupied and took out my book. My plan was to take a taxi to his street if I could communicate with the driver. The professor's home address was on his license, 752 *Rua Diamente*. From the book I got; *take me to* as *faça exame de me a*, and *please* as *por favor*. I practiced these phrases and the street name until I had them down pretty good. At least I hoped I did. My stomach was groaning, so I stopped at the sidewalk cart and stood in line. When it was my turn I pointed at a sandwich the man just before me had. The vendor smiled and loaded a bun with meat from his grill. I gave him one of the orange bills and he gave me change. "*Obrigado,*" he said.

"*Obrigado,*" I said. He smiled and I smiled. It was probably goat meat but I didn't care. I was proud of myself as I walked away. Goat or not, it tasted wonderful and I ate it quickly. It reminded me of something they called 'barbecue' I'd had down south on a long-ago vacation. I headed toward the street to search for a taxi.

The wonderful smells of the park disappeared as I got near the street, replaced by the odor of gasoline and hot oil fumes and of the tarmac melting under the blazing sun. I raised my hand at the first two taxis I saw, but they blasted by. The third, an old yellow Chevy Impala pulled over. I got into the back seat and smiled at the driver. Then I forgot what I was supposed to say.

"*Por favor*," I said. *Diamente Rua faka--*"

"I speaks Inglěs," he said.

Those words were like music to my ears. "Can you take me to *Diamente* Street?"

"It *costa Dez_. . .*ten reals."

"That's fine," I said. "Take me there, *por favor.*"

We sped off into the traffic. He was a lot smoother than the bus driver, only occasionally beeping the horn or shaking his fist at another driver. He asked me what number on *Diamente* Street and I told him 800. I didn't want to get off right at the professor's door. It took about twenty minutes to get there. I watched the numbers rise as we drove down the professor's street. There was a police car parked in front of number 752.

The driver craned his neck, but there was nothing to see. Two blocks later he let me off at number 800. I handed him a red bill and a couple coins. "*Obligado*," he said and sped off.

I started walking slowly back towards the professor's house. I was looking for an alley or a large yard with a lot of trees so that I could sneak into the woods that bordered the backs of the houses, and where, hopefully, Charlie and the girls were still waiting.

I stopped three houses down from the professor's and ducked behind a flowering bush that smelled like lilacs. From this point, I could see the police car parked at the curb. Two officers sat inside it. The driver was reading a newspaper, but his partner looking at the house and occasionally scanning the street with a small pair of binoculars. There was a stand of low hanging trees separating the house I was in front of from its neighbor, which I figured would hide me until I got into the woods behind the house. The problem was a twenty foot open space between me and the trees.

I knew it was only a matter of time before a passerby saw me and reported me. I watched the cops in the cruiser hoping for a break. About five minutes later it came. The driver found something in the paper he wanted to share with his partner and held it up in front of his face. As soon as I saw this, I raced for the trees. When I got to them, I just kept running until I was into the woods. I half jumped and half fell into a large leafy plant and laid flat on the ground. I looked back towards the street. If the cops had seen me, they'd be on me soon. But they never came. The only sounds I heard were the chatters and peeps of forest animals and birds.

A truck rumbled slowly down the street. It looked like milk home delivery. I stayed in my hiding spot for a good half hour.

All remained quiet. Finally, I got slowly up and began walking into the woods. I stepped on something that slithered away and scared me so bad I thought my heart would stop. All I could think of was the snake that almost killed me a few short days ago. I held onto a palm tree and took deep breaths until I felt calm enough to continue. I walked in what I thought was the area behind Karl and Margarita's house. I picked up a stick and used it to probe the underbrush in my path. The flora was getting thicker as I went along, walking slower so I wouldn't aggravate something that would bite me or stick its fangs into me.

Shortly, I came into a clearing and it felt good to be out in the open. All I could smell was the sweet aroma of flowers that reminded me of Abbott's Florist Shop back in New Stratley. I heard a rustling in the brush behind me and I began raising my stick. But I was too slow.

Someone grabbed me from behind and a giant hand clamped over my mouth. I twisted to my left and drove my elbow back into my attacker and we both fell to the ground.

I turned to look at him and was surprised to see Charlie's smiling face. "Nice greeting," I said.

"Sorry, Jake. Just wanted to make sure you were quiet."

"There's cops all over the place. Why wouldn't I be quiet?"

Charlie led me to a clearing where Margot and Heather were waiting.

"I can tell from the look on your face that all didn't go well," Charlie said.

"The professor was shot," I said.

The women gasped and Charlie winced like I'd slapped him. Then they began asking me what had happened. I sat on a log after checking under and around it for crawly things and told my story. They listened attentively until I was finished.

"So you don't know how bad he was hit?" Charlie asked.

"The shot knocked him down, but he was conscious and he flipped me his wallet, so I don't think it was too bad. I felt terrible leaving him there but there was nothing I could do."

Margot handed me a bottle and I took a drink. It was warm wine, but sweet and a little bubbly and tasted good. "Thanks, Margot. There is some good news," I said as I stood up. "I got these." I took the papers from under my shirt. "The printouts from Heather's disk. Everything they could get off it."

Charlie's eyes widened and he took the papers. He and Margot sat on the ground and began to go through them. I sat on the log and watched them and had a little more wine and some berries from a basket. Heather told me that Margarita had come with the wine and berries shortly after I left, but hadn't come since.

I asked Heather how she was doing.

"I'm okay," she said. "The medicine Charlie gives me helps a lot, but I really want to get home and see my kids. You said you saw Tommy?"

"I did." I'd told the story a few times but it probably hadn't registered with her or she just wanted to hear it again. I told her how Tommy had sought me out and convinced me to go looking for her. She smiled as I told it and I tried to remember as many details as I could. Getting her home and reunited with her family would be the best therapy.

"You done good, Jake," Charlie said. He stood up and nodded at the papers. "I think with these and Heather's testimony, we have a good shot at explaining everything to the U. S. Ambassador. I think that's our best bet."

"No boat ride?" I asked.

"No, wise guy," Charlie said. "That wasn't one of my better ideas. I think we have to go straight to the embassy or consulate, whichever we can find."

"How are we going to get there?" Margot asked.

"We have to walk through the woods for a few miles and then see if we can find a taxi." Charlie answered.

"I'd like to get his wallet to Margarita," I said.

"Maybe we can get to the house after dark," Charlie said.

It was then that we heard the first bark.

Chapter 25

The one bark was followed by others. "Dogs," Charlie said.

"No shit," I answered. "We gotta get out of here."

I've never been afraid of dogs, but these sounded like a pack of mean ones and I knew they had mean masters with them who would shoot first. No Constitutional Amendments to worry about down here.

"Scatter the food," Charlie said, "and then follow me.

We dumped the basket that Margarita had brought and poured the wine on the ground. Might stall them for a minute.

Charlie pointed towards the mountains. "There's a stream back that way about a quarter mile. It's our only chance."

Charlie led, followed by Heather, Margot and me. We were pushing through the underbrush as fast as we could. The yapping was getting louder. They were definitely gaining. I was going too fast to look down for snakes, but I was thinking about them. If one bit me, I hoped the end would come quick. Margot tripped on a branch and fell. I helped her up. Her eyes were wide in an expression of pain and fear.

"We'll get away," I said trying to reassure her, even though I didn't really think we would.

"Okay everybody," Charlie said, "we're going with the stream. Stay in the middle and go as fast as you can."

Margot bent to remove her shoes. "No," Charlie said, "leave them on. The rocks are sharp. You guys head out I'll catch up in a minute."

Heather hesitated but I urged her on and we waded into the middle of the stream. A couple minutes later, Charlie splashed up behind us. "I emptied my bladder on the other side of the stream," Charlie said. "I hope that throws them off."

"Good thinking, Charlie," I said. "Let's hope it works."

We had been following the stream for several minutes when the barks of our pursuers changed to more like yelps.

"Sounds like they're confused," Charlie said.

"My feet are freezing," Heather complained.

Charlie was holding her arm and he gave her a little tug. "We have to keep going. We'll be safe very soon."

Margot and I held on to each other as we stumbled along the slippery stream bed. "Why is the water so damn cold?" she asked.

"It's coming right down from the mountain," Charlie said.

Several minutes later, the barks and yelps were getting quieter. "I think we're gaining," I said.

Charlie nodded and put his finger to his lips. *Okay*, I thought, I'll be quiet, but I didn't think I was talking as loud as my teeth were chattering.

After another ten minutes or so we came to a small bridge. It was made from an old tree with boards nailed to it forming a rustic walkway. There was a dirt path on either side of the bridge. The hounds were still baying in the distance but didn't seem to be gaining.

"Let's take the path," Charlie said.

"Which way?" I asked.

"Left goes into the mountains and right heads back to the city. I don't think we'll find the ambassador in the mountains, so let's head for the city."

We got out of the stream and began jogging down the path towards the city. My legs were numb from the cold water and I was afraid I might lose my balance and fall. But after a while, they began to thaw and were getting painful. At least I could feel them.

We followed the path which led around the base of the mountain. After a mile or so the sound of the dogs had gone. We decided to rest for a few minutes.

"I think they lost us," Charlie said.

"Where are we?" Margot asked.

"I'm not exactly sure," Charlie said, "but we should be getting to civilization soon. Hear that?" We all listened, and over the cacophony of jungle noises heard the roar of a jet plane taking off.

"I wish I was on that thing," I said, "and I don't even care where it's going."

"Let's hope we're all on one soon," Charlie said.

After about five minutes we began trudging along the path at a much slower pace. The jungle growth was thinning and we knew we were coming out of the woods. When we'd gone maybe another mile, the sweet aroma of the jungle was overcome by another smell, definitely not as nice.

"Ugh," said Margot. "What is that?"

"Smells like a cesspool," I said.

"That's what it is," said Charlie. "I was hoping we'd come out away from this, but I guess not."

"From what?" I asked.

"From the *Favelas*. The slums of Rio. They're built on the side of the mountains. You'll see soon enough. They have no water or sewers. I had to go into them the last time I was down here and it wasn't pleasant. Some of the people who live there are more dangerous than that pack of dogs that was chasing us."

"*Favelas*," I said. "Wonderful."

The *Favelas* was like pictures I'd seen of other slums in large cities around the world, poverty at its bleakest. But even seeing those pictures hadn't prepared me for being there, for experiencing the smells and the sounds. The aroma of things cooking over wood fires mixed with the odor of excrement, musty decay and death. And the voices of people yelling, others wailing and children crying. I felt nauseous. I thought about running back into the woods and taking my chances with the dogs, but I knew I had to go on. Margot's face was white and I could tell she felt like I did. I took her arm and held it tightly, trying to reassure us both. Charlie was holding Heather's arm. I hoped he had been able to give her another pill before this.

"Any ideas which way is out?" I asked Charlie. Nothing was marked, no street signs or landmarks.

"If we head due south, we should get back into the city proper."

"Can't be too soon for me," I said.

A group of teen boys was kicking an old soccer ball around in one of the narrow lanes. They stopped to let us pass, their eyes glared at us, four raggedy white people in their land. Charlie said something to them in Portuguese and they smiled and went back to their game.

"What did you say to them?" I asked him.

"I asked them if they knew where we could get some food. Told them we had no money. I figured they wouldn't try to rob us if they knew we were broke."

We trudged along and a little while later came upon a boy, maybe three. He was wearing only a torn tee shirt and was urinating in the street.

"Look at that poor baby," Heather said. "We have to help him."

Charlie gave the boy a candy bar he had taken from his pocket. "That's all we can do for him. There are thousands of kids like that here."

Tears rolled down Heather's cheeks as she watched the boy disappear with the candy into a tin shack. Charlie gently pulled at her arm and we began walking again.

It felt like hours, but it was probably closer to forty-five minutes, before we began to see signs that we were coming out of this hell on earth.

"We're going to have to stay on our toes near the border," Charlie said. "The police patrol this area pretty heavily. They don't want the poor to infiltrate their beautiful city."

"Bad for tourism, I suppose," I said.

I felt a great relief to be out of the slums. It was hard to believe that people were born, lived and died in such extreme poverty so close to a rich city like Rio. We had been safe in the *Favelas*, safe from the authorities anyway. We talked briefly and decided that, since they would be looking for two men and two women, we should split up. Charlie and Heather would walk ahead and Margot and I would lag behind and just keep them in sight.

"If we're spotted," Charlie said, "we'll have to run for it. Don't try to follow us."

Margot's brow creased. "Where will we go then?"

"We have to get to the U.S. ambassador or consulate," Charlie answered. "If we can do it together, that will be great. If we have to divide up, then we have to do our best to get there."

"I'm not trying to be negative," I said, "but we don't have a clue where the consulate is located."

"I have this map," Charlie patted his pocket. "I also have some money left, so I'd say let's walk for an hour or so and I'll be on the lookout for a place to get food and make a few phone calls. We have to move from here."

He was right. We were in a heavy traffic area and there was a good chance that a police car would go by and recognize us. We let Charlie and Heather get ahead by about a football field. Margot took my arm as we walked along: two happy tourists soaking up the sun and taking in the scenery.

"Smile," I said to her.

"It's hard to smile when half the country is trying to kill you. And it's hotter than hell, and I'm starved."

"Don't worry. Charlie will find a good place to eat. He doesn't like to go too far without a meal."

"Well, I hope he finds it soon. And I hope they have cold beer."

We walked along for at least an hour. It wasn't too hard to keep Charlie and Heather in sight. They had to stop a few times so she could rest. We had steered clear of the main roads. Charlie occasionally looked at his map. When we stopped I was planning to look at it, too.

I saw Charlie turn Heather abruptly to look into a store window. A few seconds later, I saw a police cruiser heading towards us. I did the same to Margot.

"What --?" she seemed surprised. But then she apparently saw the cruiser, too.

The window we stopped in front of was some kind of butcher shop. Sausage hung in loops from steel hooks that looked like they were never cleaned. Carcasses of chickens and other small creatures hung there also, enticing someone with a stronger stomach than mine to put them in a pot. In the window glass I saw the reflection of the police car as it passed.

"Let's run," Margot whispered.

"No. Only if they stop." They cruised on by and disappeared around a corner.

"Nice store you picked to stop in front of," she said.

"I was looking for a sporting goods place, but this was the best I could do."

Margot smiled. It was a small smile but it was nice to see. We continued on, following Charlie's lead. True to his word, he found us a place to stop, an outdoor bistro with picnic tables set up under a canopy of trees. Half the tables were empty. We found the most secluded one and sat.

"You two stay here," Charlie said, "Heather and I will get the food." He handed me the map. I opened it and set it on the table. I was glad that he got one printed in English.

I showed it to Margot. "We have to try to memorize this as much as we can," I said. "Just in case we have to split up."

"I sure hope that doesn't happen."

Shortly Charlie and Heather were back with a big tray of pork stuff and roasted potatoes and a large pitcher of beer. "I found a phone over there," Charlie said. "You guys get started while I make a call or two."

I poured the beer into plastic cups. It was cold and tasted good. I thought for a few seconds of the poor folks in the *Favelas* and how they couldn't even enjoy a simple cold beer. I'd have to do my best to enjoy it for them. The pork stuff and potatoes really hit the spot.

Charlie came back after a few minutes. He drank half his cup of beer and then told us about the phone calls.

"Well, I've got good news and bad news." I'll start with the bad. The ambassador and most of his staff are heading to the States tomorrow. Something at the UN."

"And the good news?" I asked.

~ 226 ~

"They're throwing a big bash for him tonight, a going away thing. So the good news is -- we're going to a party!"

Chapter 26

The party was at the Malravia Hotel on *Avenida General Justo*, just around the corner from the *Santos Dumont* Airport. We had expended almost all of Charlie's money and a good portion of Professor Karl's, buying clothes at second hand stores, scattering our tattered duds in trashcans along the route. There was no way we could have gotten anywhere near the Ambassador's party dressed in our rags.

We stopped at a small café, *Casa de Santana*, across the street from the hotel and sat at a table near the back. Charlie ordered us coffee.

"Don't you think we're conspicuous here?" Margot asked.

"Maybe, Charlie said, "but we have to stay close to the hotel and we are more apt to be recognized on the street."

"How much money have we got left?" I asked.

The waitress brought us a pot and four cups.

"Not much," Charlie said as he began pouring. "I might be able to get some sent from the States, but I think this party is our last chance."

Heather looked at him and a tear formed on her cheek.

"Don't worry, kiddo," Charlie said to her. "You'll be home with your son and daughter in no time."

"I don't know if I can take much more," she said.

"If they have shrimp at that party I'm gonna eat as many as I can before they take me away," I said. That brought smiles all around, even a tiny one from Heather.

Charlie was the only one of us who had ever been at a party like this. He told us there were usually invitations and that they were checked by guards at the door.

"I think if we can get the Ambassador's ear for five minutes, we may just get him interested in our situation," Charlie said.

"Won't all the party guests be all dressed up?" I asked. "You know, tuxes and ball gowns?"

Charlie looked at me like I was asking a question he didn't want to answer. "Yes," he finally said after a long drink of coffee, "they will be. Once we get in the hotel we'll have to play it by ear, maybe steal some wait staff outfits or something."

"Maybe Heather and Margot could go without us," I said. "Say that they were both kidnapped."

"I'm not going anywhere without you guys," Margot said.

Heather nodded and I saw her dig her nails into Charlie's arm.

"It's not a bad thought," Charlie said, "but I don't know if the girls are up to it alone."

"We're not," Heather said in the loudest voice I'd heard her use.

We got another pot of coffee. It was really quite good. Customers came and went, and the place stayed about half full. Nobody seemed to want our table.

The party was scheduled to start at eight, about two hours away. We decided it would be best if one of us went into the hotel to check things out. The logical choice was Charlie because he spoke the language, but Heather was on the ragged edge and he had to stay with her.

"I'll go check it out," I said trying to sound braver than I felt.

Margot stood. "I'm in," she said. "Don't want you to have all the fun. Besides if you find the shrimp platter there won't be any left for us." She took my arm. "Honeymooning tourists will be less conspicuous than a single guy poking around."

***

~ 229 ~

The Malravia sported huge double glass doors with polished brass fittings and a pair of doormen posted there to open them. Margot and I walked up, arm in arm, like we'd been off on a sightseeing tour.

"*Olá*," he said and opened the door for us.

We nodded and smiled "*Muito obrigado*," I said, surprised that it came so easily. It was still two hours until the party and there were no signs of any dignitaries. There was a desk to the left manned by two clerks, hallways in both directions and a set of double doors straight ahead.

We went through the double door into a large hall with a chandelier that must have had a thousand shiny pieces. I had seen rooms like this the few times I'd gone to a fancy theatre to see a play. There were several closed doors leading from the hall. Artwork hung on all the walls with small gold plaques under each, noting the name of the piece and the artist.

"I don't like being out in the open like this," Margot said.

"Me neither, but I'm sure these doors lead to the ballroom. Maybe one of them will open and we can get a look inside." We pretended to look at the artwork.

About fifteen minutes later, two marines arrived. They were decked out in dress uniforms and had boots that were shined like mirrors. They also had sidearms in shiny holsters at their sides. Margot dug her fingernails into my arm almost hard enough for me to say *ouch*.

The Marines looked at us quickly, but didn't say anything. They opened one of the doors to the ballroom and went in. The door was only open for a few seconds, but I saw a lot of activity inside. Ladies in gray dresses and white aprons were setting tables. Men in tuxedo shirts were helping them. All the workers had white name badges pinned to their chests. There was a contingent of military men inside also, not as fancily dressed as the marines. They must have been the advanced guard to search for bombs and other bad stuff.

I steered Margot back into the main entrance area. "Let's try one of these hallways and see if there's an entrance to the kitchen," I said.

All the doors had signs or numbers on them but nothing in English. I tried a couple knobs. Locked. The next door had a sign, "*Mecânico.*" Its door was also locked.

"If there's anybody inside," I said, "I'm gonna pretend I'm drunk. You get back to the café and let Charlie know."

Margot nodded. The door reminded me of the one to the supply closet in high school. It was always locked but would open with a good shove providing a host of school supplies for the taking. I was hoping this door was the same. I put my shoulder to it and lifted the handle. I gave it a shove. Nothing. I tried again.

Five times I tried hitting it harder and harder and finally it opened. There were no lights inside the room. I grabbed Margot's arm, pulled her inside and closed the door plunging us into darkness.

It was actually semi darkness. Several indicator lights glowed and after a minute, my eyes began to get accustomed to the low light. The room hummed with electrical activity. I could just make out the shapes of several pieces of machinery.

"Can we turn on the lights?" Margot whispered.

"I'll see if I can find a switch," I said, "Be ready to run if someone comes in."

I felt around near the door and finally found a plate with four switches on it. I tried one. Nothing. The second turned on a bank of fluorescents that lit half the room. We were in an area about twenty feet square. There were two furnaces, four large hot water tanks and several machines that looked like water filtering devices. An electrical panel took up most of the left hand wall. Two industrial size washers and two equally large dryers were placed against the right. One of the dryers was running.

"Let's see what's in there," I said. I walked over to the dryer that was running. Just as I got to it, the thing stopped and a loud warning buzzer sounded. I fell back a few steps and I heard Margot let out a stifled scream. My heart felt like it would pound out of my chest. After a few seconds I got control of myself.

"Nothing to worry about," I said. "Just at the end of its cycle."

"Well it scared the hell out of me. And you too, tough guy, you almost fell into the furnace." She was smiling a little.

~ 231 ~

"Happy to amuse you," I said.

I went back and opened the door on the dryer. A delicious smell of warm fabric and chemical softener greeted me. The dryer was full of the gray dresses and shirts that the waiters and waitresses were wearing, mixed in with assorted tablecloths and napkins.

"Let's see if we can find some our size," I said, as I pulled out a couple tuxedo shirts. I found one that looked like it would fit and I found one that I thought would fit Charlie.

"I think this will fit me," Margot said, holding up one of the gray dresses. "Should I put it on now?"

"No," I said, "let's wait until we're ready to make our grand entrance. These just might get us into the party."

After we'd found two dresses and two shirts, I stuffed them into a cloth laundry bag that was lying on the table. "Let's go," I said.

***

Heather and Charlie grinned broadly when they saw us come into the café. Several of the patrons stopped to look at us for a few seconds, too, but then resumed their eating and talking.

"Found the laundry," I said as we sat down. I handed the bag to Charlie. "These may get us in but we need some white name tags to look authentic."

"We can't stay in here much longer," Charlie said. I think some of the locals are getting suspicious."

I wanted a beer badly to calm my jangled nerves, but Charlie was right. One call to the police and we'd be going to jail instead of the ball. We decided that Margot and I would leave first and go to the right. Charlie and Heather would then go to the left and that we'd wait until we got to the hotel to change into our uniforms. I described the nametags to Charlie as best I could and he said he'd try to improvise something.

Darkness had fallen when Margot and I emerged from the café. The streets were jammed with cars and drivers honked their horns and yelled curses into the night air.

"Wonder if they all have invitations to the ball," I said.

"The more, the merrier," Margot said. She took my arm and we headed down a side street. Our goal was to circle a few blocks and meet up with Charlie and Heather on the west side of the hotel.

We'd walked for several minutes and were on a small, particularly dark street when a man came from the shadows of an alley between two tall buildings. He was ragged and smelled like he really needed a bath, even worse than we did. He pulled a small handgun from his coat and pointed it at us. Then he mumbled something in Portuguese, words I wasn't familiar with, but I was pretty sure it was something like "Your money or your life."

"We don't have any money," I said. "We're poor Americans just trying to get home." What I said seemed to make him mad. He rattled off a few words that I'm sure were curses and then shoved the barrel of the gun hard into my chest. My heart was racing and all I could think of was that it was going to end here with a bum trying to get money that we didn't have. And that I had let Tommy, and everybody down. I couldn't let this happen.

"Give him the money," I said to Margot.

"What money?" she asked in a tone like she thought I'd gone crazy.

"The money. You know from inside your pocket." She must have got what I was trying to do. She made a motion to extract something from one of her pockets. It was enough. The ragged man took his eyes off me for a second. I took his gun hand with my left and pulled it away and past me. As he was coming forward, I caught his jaw with the heel of my right hand and drove him back as hard as I could. He crumpled to the sidewalk like a burlap sack filled with rotten potatoes.

"I think you killed him," Margot said.

I bent down and pulled the gun from his hand. I was surprised it didn't go off when I hit him. I heard footsteps coming fast down the sidewalk. I tucked the gun into my pants and bent to check his condition. I could smell his rancid breath from more than a foot away. "He's breathing," I said.

The footsteps were a man and a woman who came upon us and looked down at the ragged man. "*Vinho*," I said as I got up shaking my head. I *was* learning the language. The couple continued on their way, maybe walking a little bit faster, and Margot and I headed in the opposite direction. I was jazzed with adrenaline from the encounter. I knew I had to settle down before we got to the hotel.

~ 233 ~

"Do you think this is going to work?" Margot asked as we rounded the corner onto the main street where the hotel was.

"I sure hope so," I said. "Like Charlie says, If we can just get the ambassador's ear for a minute I think we can explain things to him. At least enough to get his interest."

"And if he's not interested?"

"He will be," I said. "After all, we are all American citizens." *And if not*, I said to myself, *we'll spend forever in a stinking Brazilian jail.*

I took her arm and stopped her. We were a block away from the hotel. There was a contingent of U.S. Marines and several local police officers standing at the main entrance. "I don't think we can go through the front now." I steered her down an alley between two buildings.

In the rear was a service road, for deliveries and trash pickup. There were no streetlights back there, but enough light came from nearby windows for us to see where we were going. We approached the rear of the Malravia Hotel. It was much larger than its neighboring buildings. There was no activity in the back. In the shadows, I made out a loading dock and several trash bins.

"It's spooky back here," Margot whispered.

"Shhh. I thought I heard something."

And I had. It sounded like air leaking from a tire. *PSSSS.*

"What is it?" Margot asked.

"A talking rat maybe," I said.

Just then a shadow appeared from behind the nearest trash bin. Margot let out a muffled yelp and I put my hand on the ragged man's gun in my pocket.

"It's us," the shadow whispered and Charlie moved into the dim light. "What took you guys so long?"

I explained briefly about our encounter with the mugger. "Any ideas how we can get in?" I asked.

"There are a couple doors up on the loading dock." Charlie said. "Let's try them." He went back into the shadows and led Heather from behind the bin. Her eyes were glazed and she looked ghostly white even in the dim light. "Won't be long now, Babe," he said softly to her. She didn't look reassured. "Hang on just a little longer."

We found three wooden steps and climbed onto the loading dock. It was slippery and smelled like decaying vegetables. Something scurried away as we approached the first door.

"Just a cat," I said. Margot dug her nails into my arm again. The door was locked but it was loose. Charlie found a slat of wood from an old packing crate and stuck it into the door jamb. He pried, and I pulled and shortly it came open. We went into a dimly lit room where trash was piled in bags and boxes and on the floor. There were two doors that led into the Hotel.

I pulled one open a crack and looked into the kitchen. It was bustling with activity; cooks yelling and hurrying about, waiters and waitresses carrying trays and pitchers. I cracked open the other door. It led into a small area where there was a time clock and a couple dozen lockers. "Must be their break room," I said.

We went in and Charlie sat Heather down at a small table. Then he took me aside and whispered. "She's ready to snap. We can't take her into the party." He was right. We wouldn't get close to the ambassador with her in such a wild-eyed condition.

"I'll go in, Charlie," I said. "You wait here with the women and I'll try to tell him our story."

"Maybe I should go, Jake," Charlie said. "I've been to plenty of functions like this."

"No. You stay here. Heather needs you. You've got to get her settled down in case she has to tell her story. I'll try to bring the ambassador here."

I began changing my shirt. Charlie handed me a name badge he'd found near the time clock. *Eduardo*. I finished buttoning and pinned it on. "Wish me luck."

Charlie shook my hand and Margot gave me a kiss that made my knees feel weaker. I gave Heather a peck on the forehead and left them there.

I opened a door and looked into the hallway leading towards the front of the building. The ballroom was on my right. I heard music, brass and drums. There were no doors leading in that way except at the front where the soldiers and police would be. It would be unlikely that a waiter would use the main entrance. I cracked open the door leading into the kitchen. That was my only way.

~ 235 ~

I pushed through the door and walked into the kitchen trying to act like I knew what I was doing. There must have been twenty people working there. I bumped into a waiter who almost dropped the tray he was carrying. He cursed and then went on his way. The smells of cooking food reminded me how long since I'd had a real meal. I had to get out of the kitchen before someone spoke to me and realized I didn't have a clue what they were saying.

I spotted a tray half full of water glasses sitting unattended on a bench and I picked it up. I had spent a couple youthful summers bussing tables at a seafood restaurant and it came right back to me as I hefted the tray and balanced it on my right hand. There were two doors leading to the ballroom and I went to the one on the right, and went through it.

Chapter 27

The orchestra was playing a Samba-type number and half a dozen couples were dancing in front of them. I moved away from the door to avoid a possible collision with another tray carrier, scanning the room as I went. A man seated at a nearby table motioned to me. "*Água, por favor,*" he said. I put a glass on the table and he smiled. I smiled back.

By a quick estimate there were twenty round tables with ten guests at each. All the tables had centerpieces that looked like ice carvings decorated with flowers. Fancy. One table near the front had a double-sized array. That had to be the ambassador's. I headed that way. I was almost at his table when a man wearing a black tuxedo stood in my way.

"It's him," he screamed, pointing at me.

And then I recognized him. It was Dr. Dork. I was as surprised to find him there as he seemed to be finding me. He began yelling for police. I dropped the tray with a loud clatter and smashing of glasses. Several women screamed and I saw police and soldiers rushing toward us. I grabbed the doctor by the back of his tux and dragged him in the direction of the ambassador's table.

I had almost left the mugger's gun with Charlie and I was glad I hadn't. I pulled it from my belt and held it against the doctor's temple. This action slowed the police and soldiers, but they kept inching forward with guns drawn aimed at me.

"I just want one minute with the ambassador," I yelled. "Then I'll give up."

"Shoot him! Shoot the bastard." A woman yelled from Dr. Dork's table. I glanced quickly. It was his wife in a pink evening gown. "Kill him."

"No," Dr. Dork cried. "You'll shoot me, too."

I heard a man's voice to my right. "Stand fast, men," he said. Then to me, "What is the meaning of this, sir?" Those ambassadors are always polite.

"This man is a criminal," I said, "and I can prove it."

"No, no, no," Dork yelled. "He's the criminal, not me."

There was a commotion behind me as a soldier was trying to pull the doctor's wife away. She was kicking at them and screaming for them to shoot.

"I'll surrender to you, Ambassador. Please just give me one minute." I edged toward him dragging the doctor with me as a shield. I heard an aide telling the ambassador he should leave and let the police handle it.

The ambassador stood his ground. "I'll give you one minute," he said. Still holding the doctor's tux, I handed the gun to the ambassador. He was several paces away but moved toward me quickly and took the gun. The soldiers and police were on me in seconds and pushed me to the floor. I could hear the doctor echoing his wife's pleas to shoot me.

"Let him up," the ambassador said in a loud voice.

"Shoot him, shoot him," the doctor yelled.

They dragged me roughly to my feet with one holding each of my arms.

"I am a man of my word, sir," the ambassador said. "You have one minute."

So it was down to one minute. Sixty seconds to convince the ambassador that I was the good guy and Dr. Dork was the bad guy. I felt like a kicker in the Super Bowl with one second left, and down by two. Kick it through and be an instant hero. Miss and be an eternal goat. Meanwhile, the doctor had pushed through the crowd and stood next to the ambassador.

"I demand he be shot," he yelled. "He burned my building and killed my people."

"Please, Dr. Meacham," the ambassador said. "Let me get to the bottom of this. I assure you no wrongdoing will go unpunished."

Meacham kept yelling and finally the ambassador had two marines lead him away. "Take him to his wife until he calms down," the ambassador looked at me. "And now you."

"Dr. Dork," I started, "I mean Meacham works for IotaTec in the United States."

"I know who he is," the ambassador said.

"But what you don't know is his whole company is crooked. They are ripping off the U.S. *and* the Brazilians. And I can prove it." *I hope.*

"What about the fire and the deaths in *Belo Horizonte*?" the ambassador asked.

"He burned his own building to destroy the evidence that there really was no magic drug. It was all a billion dollar hoax."

"And you can prove this? How?" the ambassador asked.

As if on cue, a voice came from the kitchen. "I think between the four of us we can convince you," Charlie said.

He walked toward us helping Heather. Margot followed behind. Guns were pointed at them and soldiers went to stop them.

"Let them come here," the ambassador said. "Haven't we met, sir?"

"Yes Ambassador," Charlie said. "A long time ago. We were on the same plane coming home from 'Nam. 1972."

I usually hate coincidences, but this one I loved.

"Captain," the ambassador said, "Please have these people brought to my conference room on the second floor. Guard them but no rough stuff. And make sure that Dr Meacham and his wife don't leave. Or those three gentlemen who were with them."

"Yes, sir." The captain saluted. He had four men lead us out of the ballroom and to an elevator. We were led to a conference room on the second floor. A brass plaque on the door read *The Nashua Room.*

"That doesn't sound Brazilian to me," I said.

"It's not," one of the marines said. "It's some hick town in New Hampshire where the admiral was born." *New Hampshire.* Thirty miles from home. That had a nice sound to it. There was an oval table in the conference room and a dozen soft chairs positioned around it. We took seats and waited. About fifteen minutes later, the ambassador came in and took a seat at the head of the table.

He asked an aide to have sandwiches and coffee brought up. "We don't have a lot of time. I had my flight postponed two hours, but I'm due back in Washington for a meeting with the President before I speak at the U.N." The ambassador looked at me, then at Charlie and smiled a little. "What evidence do you have?"

Charlie handed him the wrinkled printout and the broken disk. "We have the testimony of this woman, Charlie said, "Heather Baxter, who worked at IotaTek and was kidnapped and taken here to Brazil along with this woman's husband." He pointed at Margot. "This was after they discovered the fraud that the company was perpetrating. Margot's husband was killed on the trip and Heather was held captive in the warehouse that burned."

"And that's why we came to Brazil," I said. "To find them."

"Why didn't you go to the authorities in the States?" the ambassador asked.

I told him about our adventures in New Stratley and how we felt the only way to clear ourselves was by finding Heather and Bruce. Charlie told how he had been best friends with Margot's dad and when we came to him, he agreed that the best course of action would be to come here.

"Well," the ambassador said, "It seems like you've broken a lot of laws, on both continents. Even if your intentions were good."

Then Heather spoke. "They did it to help me." Her voice faltered and tears streaked down her cheeks. "Another day and I would have been . . .dead. They were going to burn that warehouse with me in it. I owe these people my life."

The ambassador looked at the printouts. Then at each of us. "I never really trusted that Meacham character," he said. "Or his trophy wife. Okay. As of right now, you are my prisoners. We will go back to D.C. and see if we can't get this straightened out. Do you all agree?"

We all nodded agreement.

"Good," the ambassador said. "Eat some sandwiches and relax. The plane leaves in four hours. Red-Eye to Washington."

Chapter 28

The flight back to the states was much smoother and quicker than the flight down. The food was excellent and there was no yodeling. The ambassador had a doctor check Heather and give her a shot before we left. She slept quietly next to Charlie. Margot and I talked a little bit, mostly about what would happen to us when we got home. And then we fell asleep under the watchful eye of two armed marines.

A light mist was falling as we deplaned at Reagan Washington National Airport. The marine guard escorted us to a waiting limo and we were brought to a secure customs location where the ambassador met us. Most of our belongings had been left behind in Brazil so customs was fairly quick. Then we were taken on a twenty minute ride to a government building in D.C. where we were separated and questioned.

My inquisitors were two forty-something agents who didn't identify themselves. One had a crew cut and the other was shaved bald.

"You and your pals are costing the taxpayers a lot of money," Baldy began.

"I am a taxpayer," I said, "and if you feel this is a waste of money just let me go."

"You are a taxpayer," Baldy mimicked. "We're not so sure about that. We haven't even confirmed you are a U.S. citizen. Maybe you'd like to sit in a federal penitentiary until we find out for sure."

Charlie had warned me briefly on the plane what to expect. He'd done the same thing many times. "Tell the truth," and "don't let them get under your skin," were his biggest warnings.

"Any place with regular meals and no snakes will be an improvement over where I've been," I said.

"You're a wise guy," Crew-cut said. "Just tell us your story and we'll decide what to do with you."

I bit my tongue on the smart comment I wanted to make and began telling the story right from the beginning. They taped it and occasionally stopped me to ask a question or clarify something. I didn't leave much out except for the plane ride down. Margot, Charlie and I had talked about that on the plane also. We agreed that if they pressed us we would say we arranged the flight with a guy we met in a bar in New Orleans and didn't know the pilot.

Baldy and Crew-cut seemed more interested in what happened in New Stratley than what we did in Brazil. And they were very interested in IotaTek. When they were done taking my statement and questioning me, they got up and left the room. No "thanks" or "goodbye," or anything.

"Don't forget my lunch," I said to the closing door.

An hour or so later another man came in. He extended his hand and I shook it. "Sam Winchell," he said, "the Ambassador's assistant. The feds are just about done with your friends, and you should be going home soon." He sat in the chair opposite me. "Turns out they've been watching this IotaTek place for a while. Kidnapping Mrs. Baxter was a bad mistake on their part, and leaving her alive to talk about it was even worse."

"Did they arrest Meacham?" I asked.

"I'm afraid that in all the confusion, he and his wife slipped away. International fugitive warrants have been issued for them. I'm sure they won't come back to America. As for your adventures in Brazil, the ambassador convinced their government you were an undercover team on a special assignment. I would avoid any travel to that country, however, if I were you.

~ 243 ~

"I have no intention of going back there," I said. "Any word on our adventures in New Stratley?"

"The Ambassador talked with the Chicf of police and most of your troubles up there have been cleared up. Two days after you left, they caught the shooters that IotaTek was using and they've been charged with the murders of a lady named Trudy James and the police officer, Baxter. Naturally, they will want statements from you and you will have to be available for court."

"I will be. There's nothing I'd like better than helping to fry those goons. Am I still under arrest?"

"The ambassador promised he would deliver you to Massachusetts. There is some paperwork to be signed. He figured you all would cooperate."

I nodded that we would. We shook hands again and he led me from the room.

***

I never thought I could be so happy to see the Boston skyline. I was staring at it as I rode alone in a taxi headed to New Stratley. Heather had been kept at the Johns Hopkins Medical Center for observation and was due to be released in a day or two. Charlie opted to stay in Washington and travel back with her. Margot was scheduled to fly back the next day. They apparently didn't want us to spend much time together until we'd been questioned by the New Stratley police and the Massachusetts District Attorney's office.

It was 10:00 a.m. on a Tuesday morning and I was scheduled to be at the New Stratley police station at 1:00. It was nice of them to give me time for lunch before they started grilling me. I had the taxi drop me off at my condo. My keys were long gone, lost probably in the Brazilian jungle, but I kept a spare in the common basement laundry area.

But I didn't need the key. Yellow crime scene tape was stuck across my door. The cops had smashed the lock and left the place unsecured. My condo looked like it had been ransacked by a horde of burglars. I didn't have much in the way of valuables. My stereo and small CD collection looked okay and the two small albums I had of family photos and pictures of my kids were lying on the floor

~ 244 ~

but were undamaged. Everything else could be replaced. I was actually more upset that the cops had done this and not burglars.

I'd have to find out which ones of the bastards did it and file it in my memory bank. You never know when you'd get a chance to get even. I knew Bart couldn't have been involved or they wouldn't have left such a mess.

It was going to take some time to get my life back in order. When I was done with the cops I'd stop at the White Stallion and see about getting my job back. All I wanted to do was work and try to forget IotaTek and Brazil and everything that had happened.

My bedroom had been tossed pretty good, clothes and hangars thrown on the floor. All my drawers had been emptied on the floor as well. They even slit open my mattress like I was gonna hide something in it and then sew it up. I don't even own a needle.

I put the drawers back in the dressers and then started to pick up the mess. I found a pair of jeans that looked clean and a Bob Marley tee shirt. I took a shower which was warmer than I was expecting and changed clothes.

They hadn't smashed the rear door lock and I had a spare key for that so I put the chain on the front door and wedged a chair up against it. I'd get a new door lock as soon as I could. I went out the back and headed toward the police station. It would be about a twenty minute walk. I stopped at a deli about half way and ordered a small sub. I wasn't very hungry, but I knew I had to eat. Chances were good the cops weren't gonna share their donuts with me.

After I ate, I walked the remaining two blocks to the police department. It was in an old building built around the turn of the century as an office for one of the towns mills. The city had appropriated it in the thirties, added a few bars to some windows and used it as their police station and jail. The chief was always in the paper saying they needed money from the taxpayers to build a new one. Not getting my vote.

***

They brought me into a small interview room with a metal table and four chairs. I took a seat in one of them. Signs on the wall in English, Spanish and a Cambodian language informed me I was being videotaped. They let me sit there for about ten minutes before two men came in. One was a tall guy in an ill-fitting suit who identified himself as Detective Simon. The other was a shorter chubby guy in uniform. I recognized him as Sergeant Pete Thompson. I'd met him a few times when I was with Bart. They didn't seem happy to see me.

Detective Simon told me to move to another chair and advised me I'd be videotaped. I guess he figured I couldn't read. I moved and they took seats opposite me. Detective Simon began by reading me my rights. I thought about telling them I wanted a lawyer which would have brought their fun to a screeching halt, but I knew that would just prolong things and I wanted to get it over with. I also knew that since I hadn't been arrested, they didn't have much on me. If it seemed like they were going someplace I wasn't comfortable with, then I'd lawyer up.

I went over the story from the beginning and answered all their questions. They seemed particularly interested in what I knew about Tommy's father. They kept me there for over three hours and finally dismissed me with the admonition that they'd be in touch if they needed more information.

A light mist was falling as I walked home. It felt refreshing after my ordeal in the stuffy police station. I stopped at a donut shop a block from my condo and bought two lemon-filled, two jelly and two chocolate-covered donuts and a large black coffee. It seemed like years since I'd had one of the little torus-shaped treats and my goal was to eat all six of them and then go to the Stallion and drink at least six beers. Maybe find out if I could get my job back.

I let myself into the kitchen and flipped on the light. I stopped just inside the door. There was something wrong but I wasn't sure what. A different smell maybe. Or perhaps I was just imagining things. I walked into the living room.

There, sitting in my favorite recliner, was a man I never thought I'd see again. Dr. Bernard Meacham.

"I was beginning to think you weren't coming," he said.

"What the hell are you doing here?"

"I came to settle a score," he said and his mouth contorted into a vicious sneer.

~ 246 ~

"I thought you'd be far away from this country by now." I said. He wasn't holding a gun. I took a step towards him.

"Luther," he said. My bathroom door opened and Luther came out, and he *was* holding a gun. Aimed right at me. "I had to come back here to retrieve some of my property and as long as I was here, I wanted to pay you a visit. You put a serious crimp into my plans."

"Get out of here, now," I said.

Meacham smiled his sinister smile and Luther seemed amused too. Hard to tell with Luther. "Tomorrow, about this time, while you're laying on a cold autopsy table, I'll be on the other side of the world counting my money."

Just then my phone rang. It wasn't much but I saw Luther's eyes look towards it. It was enough. I flicked the lid off my coffee and threw the hot liquid into Luther's face. And then I threw myself on the floor. He fired twice, wildly. I heard the glass of my slider crash. Meacham jumped from the chair and started for the door. I jumped to my feet and pushed him into Luther. They both fell backwards into the bathroom.

Luther was starting to recover. Couldn't let him get another shot off. Before he could point his gun, I kicked him in the jaw with all my might. His head flew back and thudded into the Jacuzzi. Field goal. Meacham made a move to get Luther's gun which, somehow, was still clutched in his hand. Before he could get it I gave him a kick in the side that sent him crashing into the toilet. I pulled the gun from Luther's hand and pointed it at them. Luther was out cold. I pushed Luther's feet inside the bathroom.

"Anyone opens this door, they get shot," I said and slammed the bathroom door shut. This was the second time I'd held Dr. Dork prisoner in a bathroom.

I dialed 9-1-1 and told them who I was.

"What is your emergency?" The operator asked.

"Tell Detective Simon I've got some garbage in my condo and I want it removed." I hung up. A few seconds later the police called back. This time, I explained what had happened in more detail and they said they had units responding. I took the chair away from the front door and opened it so they wouldn't have to break in again. I got my bag of donuts from the floor and sat in my recliner with

Luther's gun pointed at the bathroom door. I took a bite of a lemon-filled and waited for the police.

Scrumptious.

About an hour later, after the police had arrested Luther and Dr. Dork, and the last detective had gone, I settled into my chair to think about what had happened. I had come very close to dying.

If the phone hadn't rung when it did . . . .

My hands were shaking a little when I went and checked my caller ID. It was a number I didn't recognize. I dialed it and after four rings, a woman's voice answered.

"Margot?" I asked. "Is that you?"

"Hi, Jake. It's me. I called a little while ago. I hope it wasn't a bad time."

"It couldn't have been better," I said. "Remind me to kiss you when I see you." I told her briefly what had happened.

"I'm staying at the Hill House Motel," she said. "Room 214. I called to see if you wanted to come over for a while. Have a couple beers. Maybe take me to breakfast in the morning."

"I'll take a quick shower and be right over," I said.

"You can take a shower over here," she said.

The next day, I enjoyed the best breakfast I ever had.

Chapter 29

A week later, Margot and I went to meet Charlie at Logan Airport. He was flying back to Louisiana and Heather was going with him, along with Tommy and his sister. We met them at a fast food place just outside the airport. Heather looked great and her kids were smiling like it was Christmas morning.

"Charlie's gonna show us some alligators," Tommy said.

"And he's got two dogs," his sister added.

We all shook hands and hugged and promised to get together real soon. They would be coming back in the fall for court action but they wanted to get away for awhile.

"Better call ahead and fire your housekeeper," I whispered to Charlie. He smiled and nodded.

"Good news from Brazil," Charlie said. "Professor Karl is doing very well. He had to have surgery, but he's gonna be just fine."

"That's great," I said. "Hear anything about IotaTek?"

"One of my old friends in the bureau found out that Judkins got away with tons of money."

"Maybe he's with Dolly," I said. "Now that the good doctor will be imprisoned for many years."

"A match made in heaven. Let's go kids, Hertz is waiting for this," Charlie said and climbed into his rental. Heather and her daughter got in, but Tommy hesitated.

He came to me and reached into his pocket. He handed me a crumpled bill. "You earned it," he said. "Thanks."

I took the bill and tosseled his hair. He ran and jumped in the car.

Case closed.